GOING UNDER

JEFFE KENNEDY

Going Under was first published by Carina Press in July 2014.

Thank you for reading!

Credits
Cover: Ravven (www.ravven.com)

Game designer Emily Bartwell is in hiding. Fleeing online trolls that ruined her career, marriage, and life—pretty much in that exact order—she's made a new life on a remote island in the Pacific Northwest. Yes, it's lonely, but she has her online community for company. And she has her work: Labyrinth, a wildly popular role-playing game, one she's created under the male alias, Phoenix.

When sexy writer, Fox Mullins, rents the beach house next door, however, he entices Emily out of her isolation. Flirting, teasing, igniting desires she'd forgotten she had, Fox tempts Emily into playing games of a very different sort—ones where he makes the rules.

Fox is delighted by his luck in discovering his gorgeous, single neighbor's simmeringly passionate nature under her oh-so-private exterior. Playing with her, pushing the lovely Emily's boundaries, gives him relief from the painstaking, frustrating task of tracking the brilliant gamer, Phoenix—and discovering his elusive prey's true identity. Exposing Phoenix will be the biggest scoop of his career as an undercover tech reporter.

As Fox and Emily push the limits of intimacy, they discover that their fling is leading to something much deeper. They're both keeping secrets that could devastate the other, but which of them will win the game in the end?

DEDICATION

To Allison Pang and Marcella Burnard

My favorite gamer girls

ACKNOWLEDGEMENTS

I am indebted to a number of people who helped me understand the world of role-playing games.

- Carolyn Crane always provides amazing story insight and terrific ideas for making the story *even better*. More, she bailed me out with a particularly difficult-to-write scene. I owe her big time.
- Allison Pang keeps me up to date on female politics and gaming. She also suggested the basic structure for how Labyrinth might work.
- Marcella Burnard fact-checked all my Pacific Northwest details—any deviations are me being willful—and suggested Lopez Island as the basis for my fictional Lyra.
- C.J. Lemire graciously answered my ignorant tech questions. Again, anything I got wrong is because my fictional version just sounded more fun to me.

I'd like to acknowledge Anita Sarkeseian who, for better or worse, has become the poster girl for what happens when a woman awakens the trolls in the depths of the gaming world. She's withstood horrific pressure and attacks with her head held high—an inspiration to anyone who bucks the system. I'm proud to have backed her Kickstarter and to follow her efforts.

As always, much appreciation goes out to the Carina Press team for their continued enthusiasm and support for my books—particularly Angela James, Kerri Buckley, Stephanie

Doig, Carrie Holden, and Heather Goldberg. Very special thanks to editor Deb Nemeth, for all she does to make my books the best they can be.

Gratitude of the best kind goes out to my agent, Pam van Hylckama Vlieg, for late night DMs, being my champion and supporting my career in every way.

Much love always, of course, to David—for everything.

GOING UNDER

JEFFE KENNEDY

CHAPTER ONE

GO RUN. THIS MEANS YOU!

THE POP-UP REMINDER shook Em out of her zone, as she'd designed it to do.

Otherwise she'd forget. That was both the blessing and curse of programming. Time flew by—a good thing, because it kept her from dwelling on unpleasant thoughts. But, if she didn't have her reminders, entire days could vanish without a trace.

She glanced at her screen clock—4:03—then surveyed the mist outside the window. No actual rain, but definitely murky. Resisting the urge to snooze the reminder 15 minutes, she resolutely saved her code and changed the pop-up to 3:37 for tomorrow. She'd have to keep it earlier until after solstice, the afternoons got so soupy.

Her twice-daily runs, plus occasional walks to contemplate work-throughs, gave her pleasure she'd rarely indulged in before. She really shouldn't run the same routes every day, but the simplicity and ritual of it tempted her too much. She made up for that repetition by changing the reminder time every day, sometimes later, sometimes earlier.

Complacency killed.

And really, with all the other steps she'd taken to disguise her identity and virtual footprint, this deviation from protocol shouldn't be enough to out her. When she'd first moved to the island, she'd taken care to vary her routines, trying to never repeat the same pattern twice. But that kind of thing got amazingly exhausting over time. Vigilance required a level of alertness and interest. Even following a habit of variability grew boring and that led to dullness. After the first year, she'd allowed herself certain habits that she deemed low risk and saved the edge of paranoia for higher-risk events.

Like grocery shopping.

Reluctant to leave the work, she made herself stand. She wouldn't find her way through the latest knot in the next hour—or even the next week. Any further delay and she wouldn't be able to see. Her body creaking in protest demonstrated the other reason to get moving. Submerged in her online life, behind the various masks of her false faces, it was easy to forget to be a human being.

Living alone also did that.

Not that she minded so much. She'd never been tremendously social to begin with and she really loved that things stayed clean after she cleaned them, were never dirty unless *she* dirtied them, and everything remained in its place. But she did tend to lose track of time.

Dinah opened one baleful golden eye from her sprawl on the top tier of the cat condo with an excellent view of both the bird feeders and Lyra Sound, ignored all of it and went back to sleep. Em rubbed the Maine coon's belly anyway. Moving with more purpose, she headed to the bedroom, shucked cuddly socks and sweats, and pulled on her leggings, jog bra and zippered jacket. Yanking her hair into a ponytail took a bit of wrestling. Amazing what three years of no haircuts produced.

Her personal calendar of hermitage.

She paused in the mudroom to tie on her running shoes, still muddy from the morning's run, but it hardly seemed worth it to clean them when she'd only dirty them again, then abandoned the cloistered warmth of the house for the misty green outside.

Anansi stood with tail high at the garden gate. He made an excellent reminder, too—usually knowing the time far better than she did—but the Doberman preferred to spend his afternoons outside. Given his propensity for pacing and sighing, she preferred it too.

"Ready to go?" Her voice croaked a little, as she hadn't spoken aloud for hours save muttering at her screen.

Though Anansi could easily clear the low gate, he waited, ever polite, for her to open it, bounding through and making a wide loping circle around her while she stretched out her kinks. At her hand signal, he trotted down the cedar-planked path to the beach.

She loved many things about her house on Lyra Island—the windows, the view, the quiet of the sheltering trees and her fairy-worthy garden—but easy access to the rocky beach had sold her on it, despite the breathtaking price she'd paid in cash.

In some ways, it might have been easier to hide in a major metro area, where efficient businesses delivered food and she might have varied her running trail via an algorithm that recalculated her route over city blocks. A remote island, geographically circumscribed and populated mainly by tourist traffic in the summer and a small group of taciturn and hardy year-rounders, lacked both efficiencies and variability.

She let Anansi choose the direction. Her nod to randomness, such as it was.

However, she reflected as she found her rhythm on Lyra Sound's gravel shore, becoming part of the community had lent an unanticipated kind of disguise. People made assumptions about her—about where the money came from, her eccentric reclusiveness, even her appearance—that cloaked her better than anything she might have crafted. They figured her for a crazy trust-funder refugee from the East Coast and she, always up for a good story, played into that.

Her neighbors knew her patterns and told her things about herself that she used as they puzzled out her mystery. Kind of similar to building a game, right there. A series of clues created a story. The trick became keeping anyone from wanting to look for more, because what they thought they knew was so much prettier than the reality.

She sometimes envisioned her real self as the unsightly creature behind the curtain, working the levers. That self shouldn't ever see the light of day, so twisted and emotionally crippled, every horrible thing the trolls had ever named her.

It deserved to be locked away.

She hit her stride, the soft mist breathing easily through her, blood and muscles gratefully expanding after the day's inactivity. Anansi looped through the shallow water and out again in canine glee. Running under the draping emerald fronds, she counted the lights in the houses of her widely spaced neighbors, making a mental note that someone seemed to have moved into the Kapsucks' rental on the point.

Odd time of year for it.

Her sense of vigilance pricked. A trip into town in the morning would be in order, to suss out this unusual arrival.

You could never be too careful.

FOX STOOD OUT on the deck, watching the woman jog past on the beach with a dog he'd first mistaken for a pony. No, just a very impressive Doberman.

She ran with a ground-eating, gliding stride that spoke of years of practice. Maybe even a youth as a long-distance runner. He added the observation to his mental checklist, second nature in his line of work, to what he'd taken in about her during the thirty seconds it had taken her to cross in and out of sight—lean, glossy dark-brown hair, top-of-the-line running clothes and shoes, obvious even in the dimness. Healthy dog, not professionally groomed or docked. Probably a permanent resident, eccentric and rich with it.

The way he had it figured, his quarry made very good money, which was part of what let him avoid detection. Could the elusive game designer be married or have a girlfriend?

Fox didn't think so, but he needed to consider all possibilities. A knack for finding the unexpected clues was one of the skills that put him at the top of his profession. Noting the time and her description on one of the pocket pads he always carried, he waited for the woman's return loop. Night had nearly taken the shoreline, despite the early hour, so she'd hardly be able to stay out much longer. In L.A., sunset would be over an hour away—and you'd be able to see it, something prevented by the seemingly ever-present pea soup on Lyra. He'd only been on the island a day and already the dark was getting to him.

Not that it mattered. Sniffing out Phoenix's hiding spot and real identity would be the brass ring. He could write his own ticket after that, have his pick of assignments and live in the sunniest spot he could find. The game designer was canny and had laid more false trails than Fox had expected. Grudging respect growing, he'd followed each set of manufactured clues to their blind endings, methodically debunking each one.

In many ways, the chase had become more fun than even playing Phoenix's games—though both bore the distinctive flavor of the man's personality. His voice, Fox thought of it, though that term was more often applied to writers than video game programmers. Still, the way Phoenix had built his layers of false identities and misdirections carried that same indelible stamp of the mind-boggling clues that formed the skeleton of the man's games.

Most notably, Phoenix's masterpiece, Labyrinth, an adventure game with new modules released regularly that had taken the market by storm two years ago, showed echoes of the various false trails that formed Phoenix's obviously false identity.

Hell, the man hadn't existed before three years ago, and Fox suspected some of that history had been created. Most people in the industry speculated that Phoenix must be the retirement identity of one of the gaming community's veterans. Even among the network of anonymous hackers and basement dwellers, who lived and died by false identities, this guy eluded all efforts to decloak him. Something that spoke of long experience, the forums insisted.

In his gut, Fox knew better.

No, Phoenix had to be young. Middle-aged at most. Fox knew this, not from studying the data, but from playing the game, from knowing that voice. And he was here somewhere. Probably on Lyra, but maybe nearby. The inside tip from his NSA buddy pointed to this cluster of islands in the middle of nowhere as having the broadband signature a guy like Phoenix would need.

Intuition told him a guy who picked the name Phoenix wouldn't be able to resist the parallel of "Lyra" Island. Instinct, some would call it. Fox didn't care to name it. Call it superstitious, but he didn't question intuition.

His brand of investigative journalism required tenacity, ruthless conviction and more than a little black magic.

Always trust your gut, Sparky. The brain can lie, but your instinct knows all.

While Fox obviously had long stopped following most of his wastrel father's advice, he kept the best of it. And he always found his quarry.

So, while his competitors broke in to ISP records and plodded after the electronic breadcrumbs to nowhere, Fox had followed that instinct—luck and serendipity—to Lyra. Working on his novel, he'd told the inquisitive Gladys Kapsuck. He needed the quiet.

He'd bide his time, catch up on the backload of articles he'd been meaning to write—maybe try his hand at a few more short stories, to flesh out his cover if nothing else—and wait for

Phoenix to reveal himself. Which he would. No one could hide forever.

And there came his jogging neighbor, clocking in seventeen minutes later. He noted it down as he'd track everyone on the island. You never knew who might know the person who knew the person who knew where his target would be found. Six degrees of separation.

Luck is a lady—always treat her like one.

He went inside to enter it all in the computer.

And maybe play a little Labyrinth.

CHAPTER TWO

"GOOD MORNING, ROB!" Em called out over the tinkling bell on the coffee shop door.

The aging hippy set his week-old paper aside and came to the counter. "Look who's out and about already this fine morning."

Em stowed her drenched umbrella in the stand by the door. "Had a craving for a mocha. Regular coffee wasn't going to cut it today."

"I suppose it being Thursday and Tree's cinnamon-roll day had nothing to do with it." He'd already started steaming the almond milk he kept on hand for her and for Steve Baker, lactose intolerant and enough of a health nut to be concerned about the feminizing steroids in soy milk. Another unexpected benny of small-town life—once you picked your "favorite" thing, people remembered it.

Fortunately she liked the triple-shot almond milk mochas she'd randomly picked that first visit to the coffee shop. Not so much with other things, such as Tree's organic cinnamon rolls, which were never sweet enough. With those and a few other dishes she'd carelessly chosen those first few weeks, thinking the more random and the further from her real preferences the better, she'd gotten locked into some "usuals" she'd grown to actively despise.

But she couldn't break character now.

"Of course! You know I love Tree's rolls." And dammit—she'd thought it was Wednesday and she'd be safe. Maybe she needed a day-of-the-week reminder too.

"You haven't been in for one in a while," Rob observed, boxing up two for her. "Tree was making noises about bringing some out to you. She thought you might be sick, but then she saw you running a couple of times."

"You know how it is." She shrugged, adding a yawn for good measure. "This time of year I hibernate. And paint."

"Yup." He nodded along, then asked, politely but with a bit of reluctance Em enjoyed no end, "How is the painting coming?"

"Great!" She put some extra gushing in her response, just to see him wince. Payback for the cinnamon rolls. "I'll bring some more down."

He started to frown but managed to stop himself. Three of her "works" already hung on the coffee shop walls. Hideous abstracts she dashed out in minutes and claimed to toil over for months.

She took pity on him. "I'm doing a lot of yellow these days. Maybe we could swap the new ones out for these from my brown period."

"Oh yeah? That'll brighten things up." Rob didn't deserve her needling, but she got such a kick out of it. Small pleasures.

"I saw someone rented the Kapsuck place." She introduced her real reason for coming into town casually, plucking a copy of the local *Thrifty Nickel* from the stand.

Rob painstakingly ground a few more beans to make enough for her third shot. He believed that anything less than perfectly fresh grounds led to corporate coffee. She'd learned not to get him started on Starbucks.

"Some writer from L.A., I hear."

"Interesting. Would I know his books?"

"I don't. Tree Googled him and he writes short stories—sci fi, she said—name of Fox Mullins. Guess he's working on a novel."

"Isn't everyone?" Em quipped.

"Not me." Rob huffed a laugh and finally handed her the mocha and the box of rolls. "I'm happy with my garden and my weed. Tree keeps making noises about writing a book someday, but so far all that comes out of her is these cinnamon rolls."

"And we love 'em." Em made a show of breathing in the fragrance, unfortunately tinged with the skunky odor of Rob's beloved weed. "You forgot to charge me for two, though."

Rob waved a hand. "On the house. With visitors down for the winter, we've got 'em coming out of our ears, going stale. That writer fellow, Fox, though, came in earlier and bought a dozen. If Tree wasn't half in love with him already, she'd have swooned over him for that alone."

"In love cuz he's a writer?"

"That. Plus she's always had a thing for redheads. Something about him being 'abtastic' too." Rob rolled his eyes and patted his comfortable gut. "Scary where she gets this stuff. Too much satellite TV."

Em laughed. Tree and Rob forever tangled over the enormous dish Tree insisted she needed and he claimed sent bad vibrations into his marijuana plants. "How'd she see his abs already?"

"She didn't. Glory down at the PO claims she got an eyeful when he picked up some boxes. I worry about these women, Em."

"Well, single men are scarce on the island—can't really blame them."

"Not you too." Rob groaned. "Though better you than Tree, come to think of it. Keep him occupied, would you?"

"I'll see what I can do. Has Glory been in for her coffee yet?"

"Nope. Mail came in early."

"I'll buy hers and stop by. I probably have deliveries anyway."

Glory had the post office open, the lights gleaming cheerfully through the morning murk. Spotting Em, she disappeared in back and reemerged with a dolly stacked with three boxes. "Looks who's emerged from hiding. I hope you drove. Oh, bless you," she breathed, taking the coffee. Short and curvy, with sweet curls and a milkmaid's complexion, Glory could have been a character from *Rebecca of Sunnybrook Farm*. Until she opened her mouth.

"In this downpour? Absolutely. Though I didn't remember having this much on order." That made two unusual events in less than twenty-four hours. With a stab of anxiety, Em angled her head to read the top label for the sender information.

"Looks like more books and something from a computer place. You know, you should really get an ereader—instant gratification and no crippling up your long-suffering, increasingly decrepit postmaster." Glory glowered, though her vibrant youthfulness belied her complaints. "Or you can read on the computer too. Enter the new millennium already."

"Call me old-fashioned—I prefer print books. It's not good for us to be on computers so much. All that electricity is bad for my chakras too."

Glory toed the bottom box. "Well, whoever sent this isn't into the latest tech. Didn't even know they made this kind anymore."

"Who needs the newest thing? Amazing how some people waste their money."

"Ain't that the truth? Did you hear—this guy actually rented the Kapsuck place for the winter. Talk about a colossal waste. All that money for a view and he'll be looking at fog the next three months."

"Rob mentioned." Em leaned against the counter, sipping the mocha. "Said you thought he's cute."

"No, no, no." Glory shook her head, brown curls bouncing. "This guy is not 'cute' by any stretch. He is hot—Navy SEAL built and Tom Hiddleston charming. I know you don't date, but in case you get ideas, I totally have dibs. He's coming over for dinner tonight." She sighed dramatically and fluttered her hand over her heart. "Momma is having some Fox!"

"Somebody moved fast."

"Yes. Because once he's been socked in for a week, I figure he'll hightail it back to L.A. I fully intend to get laid before that. If you're nice, I'll let you have him when I'm done. If there's time."

Em sucked down the last of her mocha, savoring the warm buzz in her bloodstream—heat, sugar and caffeine, for the win—and chucked the cup in the bin. "Generous of you, but you can keep him."

"A girl does not live by the vibrator alone."

"Tell that to the battery companies."

ANANSI BOUNCED AT the sight of her, evidenced by the rocking of her Jeep and a slab of tongue momentarily clearing the inner fog. After awkwardly wrestling with the dolly of packages, Em had given up on the umbrella and laid it across the top. She had to shower anyway.

She did, most days. Though sometimes she skipped it. Why bother when your pets didn't care anyway?

How horrified her mother would be.

She double-checked the labels as she piled them in the passenger seat, out of Anansi's tromping range. Two used bookstores and something from her boss, this time in a Gateway computer box, complete with dappled cowhide pattern. How Jared skunked up these ancient things, she had no idea. Okay, she suspected a series of Google and eBay alerts, but seriously. All she'd asked was that the things he absolutely had to send physically not have the Jacker Games branding. This was his way of getting around that and simultaneously yanking Phoenix's chain as much as he dared. Jared didn't love that she worked remotely, that he had to ship to her via a forwarding address, which added at least a week, and the constant barrage of inquiries about her identity annoyed him. But he did enjoy having the top-selling game on the market.

Besides, the enigma of Phoenix's real identity just lent cachet to it all.

She let him have his little jokes to blow off steam. The nature of his ribbing had proved enlightening also, since he—along with everyone in the known universe—believed Phoenix to be male. Being admitted to the male-male wink-wink/nudge-nudge club gave her a subtle edge in preserving that illusion. It also salved some of those deeper wounds, to know she'd slipped inside the very barriers she'd dashed herself against.

As for the books, she'd donate most of them, keeping only the few she really wanted to read. Sometimes she amused herself by selling them back to the same used book sellers she bought them from, under another name. It helped to keep her various banking and PayPal identities active. That way, if she ever had to bail quickly, she should be able to access credit from at least one. Mixing up genres, languages and topics helped confuse the tracking algorithms.

She stayed clear of Amazon for that reason—unless she deliberately wanted to create a red herring to one of her false identities.

Back at the house, she turned Anansi loose in the garden, set the book boxes in her reading den, and carried the Gateway box to her programming desk. The multiple screens showed an echo of the view outside the big windows, a restful triplicate requiring three sets of passwords to unlock.

A sticky note tacked to a girly mag sat on top of the box's contents. Jared's latest attempt to discover Phoenix's kink. Even if she was really a guy, she didn't think *Big Black Booties* would have done it for her.

But hey, to each his own.

Prototype of the new console. If you can get it to dovetail, Alexander will kiss your pimply ass.

She snorted. "Alexander wishes he could kiss my ass." But she withdrew the sleek console that so would not make it to market for Christmas, no matter how many emails Jared sent, ran a scan and added it to her testing network. A nice, private sandbox in case anyone had tried to sneak in a location ping.

Seeing it was after nine-thirty, she turned on her phone so it could warm up and do a bit of signal bouncing. Jared should be in his office. Probably cursing her rule that she would always call him. They had a team meeting scheduled for the afternoon, but she wanted to hear for herself how things were going before that.

Enjoying the thrill of a new gadget, she put the console through its paces in her test version of Labyrinth. Very slick, indeed. Big Black Booties might not do it for her, and Glory could knock herself out banging the new guy in town.

This would always be enough.

After all, she'd given up her life for it.

CHAPTER THREE

F OX GLARED BALEFULLY at the sheeting rain and adjusted the telescope the Kapsucks thoughtfully provided. Now that he'd gotten coffee, breakfast and lens cleaner—a damn shame how badly someone had treated the device—both he and the telescope enjoyed considerably more clarity.

His neighbor had run past at 7:09, barely before sunrise, though the shimmering gray hardly showed much more brightness than the pre-dawn light. Her energy in the face of the rain prodded him enough to put on pants and go into town. It had been a mistake to buy so many of those cinnamon bricks, thinking they'd last him the week.

Maybe they'd make good clay pigeons for shooting practice.

Restlessness gnawed at him. So close to the finish line on this one. He always had to yank himself back at this point, remind himself that the stealthy predator never alerted its prey. Move too soon and he'd risk spooking Phoenix. But the combination of cabin fever from the relentless rain and the lackadaisical attitudes of the local population might just conspire to drive him out of his mind first. He'd nearly throttled Rob at the coffee shop. Seventeen minutes to make a latte had to be a world record.

What he really needed was sex. That always worked him out of his tree, the kinkier, the better. Fortunately that adorable Glory at the post office seemed ready to oblige—with the added benefit of being someone who knew everyone's business and cheerfully blabbed about it.

But that was tonight and he needed to work off this mood now.

Clearly—or not, he thought wryly—he could not wait for the rain to let up. A good, long run would take the edge off and the weather didn't stop the long-legged trophy wife down the way. Might as well learn to live the way the locals did.

He took the lane at an easy jog, letting his muscles warm and trying to be philosophical about being soaked to the bone. Damned if he'd buy one of those slickers. Get wet and dry off again—no big deal, right? By the time he reached the wooden steps that led to the beach access for the point, he'd heated up plenty, but the rain sliding down the back of his neck was about to drive him crazy.

Get used to it, Sparky. You've been through worse.

Following instinct, which usually meant chasing whatever piqued his curiosity, Fox turned down the beach in his jogging neighbor's direction. He might be able to ID the place from the dog alone. Pooches that size left their mark. Besides, not many of them looked occupied, he noted, passing the beach-front homes, most recessed into the verdant forest, verifying the information that very few people overwintered on the island.

But Phoenix stayed year round. All of Fox's research pointed to it. The guy didn't move around—although he went to a lot of trouble to make it seem like he did. Still, Fox's gut insisted that Phoenix had gone to ground somewhere around three years ago and stayed there.

All Fox needed to do was find the hiding hole behind whatever local façade the guy used.

Could be Rob. Masquerading as the perpetually stoned barista and half-assed coffee shop owner could be just misleading enough. Seemed unlikely, however. Phoenix, famous for his productivity as much as his sheer genius, needed more time to work than babysitting a coffee shop most of the day would allow. Almost certainly Phoenix faded into the many recluses living in the area, appearing in town rarely, if ever.

But everyone got mail, and obliging Glory would be most helpful.

His blood surged, contemplating the evening ahead. Would she do him on the first date? Seemed very promising. Something to be said for island boredom. He passed three more dark houses, then two with lights. The second of the two sat lower, with a boardwalk path leading up from the beach. Lots of glass and wood—five to six bedrooms at least—very nice digs.

And sure enough, great big paw prints showed in the mud at the verge, where the boardwalk ended and sand gave over to the fern-covered hillside.

Through one of the upper windows, a canvas on an easel showed. An artist? Or, more likely, a rich woman's hobby. He should wait to introduce himself, get the scoop on this woman and any other permanent neighbors from Glory, but she'd gotten his curiosity up and he'd learned to trust that sense. Sure, sometimes it led him nowhere, but it hadn't gotten him killed yet.

And many, many times he'd come away more than satisfied.

So he headed up the slick boardwalk, the silver gray a serene contrast to the ferns and dripping trees. Nicely sheltered from the worst of the rain too. "Hello the house!" he called out, as soon as he emerged from the canopy, the welcoming windows in sight.

Her pony of a dog stuck his head over a fancifully carved garden gate, leveled a long look at him and then gave full throat to a bayed warning that made his teeth rattle. Without further warning, the dog cleared the gate with boneless grace and charged straight for him.

Well, shit.

Fox braced himself, readying a forearm to deflect the dog and wishing he had a fucking slicker on after all, when a voice whipped out. "Anansi! Hold!"

She leaned out the upper window, her sleek ponytail falling over her shoulder and a decidedly unfriendly look on her face. The dog, remarkably, halted inches away, teeth bared.

"Who are you and why the hell are you on my property?" the woman snapped. Defensive. Not at all relaxed and neighborly. Who had a dog with this kind of training and reacted to the appearance of a stranger with such tension? Because she was on high alert, all right, practically vibrating with it.

Fox held up his hands, plastering on a genial, go-lucky smile. "New neighbor! I was passing by and thought I'd say hello. Didn't mean to set off the alarm system."

The woman narrowed her eyes, a very light color that showed even from this distance. "You're that writer fellow."

"Guilty as charged." He shrugged a little, working at looking harmless.

"I guess trespassing isn't a crime in Los Angeles?"

"Only if you're A-list. Otherwise, you're pretty much on your own." He resisted the urge to ask her to call off the dog. He'd taken a few classes in dealing with attack dogs—very handy skill to have if you poked around in places people didn't want you to—and he knew full well she'd only asked the dog to pause. Writer guy might not know that though, so he went with that, pretending all was well. Besides, he had a curious sensation that this woman was testing him. Interesting.

He liked interesting people.

She hadn't laughed at his joke, but she seemed to relax ever so slightly. "Stay there," she told him and disappeared inside, the window cranking shut behind her.

Reflexively, he mentally timed her, from the sealing of the window to her emergence through the sliding glass doors onto her deck. He greeted her with the same easy smile. "I'm Fox. Fox Mullins. Sorry I startled you."

Nodding slightly, she looked him over. "A bit cool for shorts."

"Took a run on the beach, but I guess I'll need better gear for this weather."

Taking her alert level down another notch, she descended the stairs, put a hand on the dog's back and held out the other. Cool, delicate hands with fingers long like her legs. "Emily Bartwell."

Fox shook her hand, resisting the urge to hold it a bit longer, to savor her personal intensity. She had an extraordinary face, finely boned with eyes such a light gray they seemed almost silver. A marked contrast to her dark brown hair and darker brows. She wore no makeup and a few glittering strands at her temples showed she didn't dye her hair. Very usual coloring. Mostly Celt, he'd bet, with a dollop of Asian in there somewhere. He couldn't get much of a feel for her figure with the shapeless sweats she wore—high end, no logos—but that restless sexual energy heated in him.

Very interested in her.

And it would be a long, boring winter.

"Some guard dog you've got there." Fox made himself look away from her to the pooch, which had sat at her touch and now beamed sheer doggie happiness, tongue lolling and tail sweeping through the bark bordering the walk. Interesting that she hadn't had his ears or tail docked. Not in it for the show then.

"Oh, Anansi is all bark and no bite. Good company, though."

And he was a horse's ass if he believed that. "Anansi, huh? From the Neil Gaiman book?"

He'd surprised her, but she smoothed it over nearly flawlessly. "I should have known a writer would pick that out." She rubbed the dog's ears with sincere affection, the mood erasing the last of her defensiveness. Fox wasn't sure which he liked better, this soft and sweet version or the impassioned, fierce one.

Both, really.

"Good company for a woman living alone?" He added some flirtation to the question. No, she wasn't some trophy wife. Everything about the place that he could see—note that she hadn't invited him inside—spoke female, from the artsy birdhouses to the pots of violet flowers to the matching cushions on the deck's Adirondack chairs.

"Sure," she replied, pretty gray eyes flicking over him, warming. "It gets lonely."

"Maybe some time when you're feeling lonely you could show me around town, introduce me to the ins and outs of the island."

She smiled at that, close lipped, but in a way that went straight to his groin, the image of that full pink mouth working him over. Maybe the interest went both ways. If so, he'd struck gold before he'd even pinned down Phoenix. He had a knack for landing in clover, as his dad used to say. Though he never forgot that his dad had also ended up in a final shitstorm instead. The great cautionary tale. Never take the luck for granted.

"Aren't you expected at Glory's tonight? I've been reliably informed that she has dibs."

Fox mentally groaned. And there was the shit, right on schedule. Screw small towns and their gossip networks. Fleetingly he considered making out as if he'd thought that was just a friendly visit, but he had a feeling Miss Emily would see right through him. Nothing to do but fess up and hope the female politics would work out.

"What can I say?" He allowed. "She invited me. I don't know anyone here. Besides, I hadn't met you yet."

She looked definitely amused, another layer of ice melting. "Are you a player, Fox Mullins, celebrity writer from L.A.?"

"What answer will get me a date with you?"

She gave him a stern glare, but that promising smile lingered on her lush lips. "None, actually. Go have dinner with Glory. I'll check in with her tomorrow. She'll let me know the answer."

Emily opened the gate and Anansi trotted through, for all the world as if he would never consider going over it like a freaking gazelle, and she went up the steps. Very nice, very tight ass. She paused, hand on the rail, and looked back at him, making sure he knew she'd caught the direction of his gaze.

Fox gave a little *mea culpa* shrug. She was some woman all right. Still testing him, only on the next level of the game. "Something tells me I'm not going to win this round, no matter how the chips fall."

"I wouldn't say that." Her voice purred a little, deliberately enticing. "Sometimes it's all about how you play it."

CHAPTER FOUR

O KAY, FOX MULLINS was hot.

Hot enough, in fact, that Em even considered asking Glory how the dibs thing worked. Not that she really needed to—the rules there seemed clear. Em didn't have so many female friends these days—or any friends, for that matter—that she'd be willing to violate the Girl Code that undoubtedly covered such things. Maybe it wouldn't come to that. Dinner conversation might not go well. *As if that mattered.*

Or, more likely, Glory might make her horrible creamed-chicken casserole and they'd be too ill to get it on.

Ha. A woman would have to be on her deathbed to bypass that opportunity.

Em would have to cross her fingers that Fox would opt out. Even if Glory had offered to share once she was done—and when would *that* happen?—it seemed...not right. Em might not have much of a moral compass, but this rule, at least, stood out in her own mind. As much as the guy appealed to her—witty, athletic, with a wicked sexy vibe that knocked her cuddly socks off and, best of all, transient—she wouldn't do him if Glory did. Too weird.

Besides, relationships of any kind had never worked out for her, even before Henry bailed. Somehow she always ended up with the low score. Amazing, really, that she'd found herself flirting with Fox. Maybe she'd finally cracked from too much time alone. It was for the best that Glory saw him first.

Didn't stop her from cooking up a little fantasy, though, inspired by the sight of those leanly muscled thighs dusted with wiry red hairs. His short hair had been sleekly dark against his skull from the rain, but she'd detected a bit of curl in it. And that bad-boy gleam in his copper-brown eyes when he'd checked her out—even if she hadn't gone without sex for over four years, that alone would have gotten to her.

A bolder, more impulsive her would have invited him in. Okay, a her who let people into her home without fretting over what clues she might have missed. But hell, this was her fantasy, which meant she could be anyone in it. Treating herself, she made an extra pot of coffee and mulled how it could have gone. They'd be standing here, while she made the coffee, only she'd have showered and would be wearing a clingy knit dress. He'd sip from his mug and comment on how hot it was.

"You think that's hot?" She'd reply with a smile, watching his speculative gaze go to her mouth. Then she'd slide those little jogging shorts down, freeing his cock. It would be very long with veins standing out and his hair would be bright as a copper penny and she wouldn't care that he was sweaty. No, she'd love it, licking him like an ice cream cone and he'd lean back against the counter, groaning her name, those muscled thighs quivering under her hands.

Shit. Maybe she should call Glory, after all. Maybe the Girl Code included some sort of emergency bat signal. Probably not, in cases of casual lust. Unless she could invoke some kind of long deprivation clause. Lord knows she'd qualify.

No, she needed to suck it up and move on, though her vibrator would feel like a very cold companion now. Finishing out the fantasy with it didn't sound all that fun, even if she didn't need to call into work and get busy. She'd thought she hadn't missed sex with a human all that much, but that little flirtation with Fox had flipped a trigger in her. If she couldn't ease the itch, she might have to consider going off island. To Seattle or Portland. Wear a disguise, use a fake identity and troll the bars. A few one-night stands could take the edge off. A different sort of fantasy to play out.

Not that the idea sounded even remotely appealing at the moment, with Fox's very sexual presence still in the air, like the scent of coffee on a cold morning. The man must have some serious pheromones or something. No wonder Glory had been so gleeful. Abtastic, indeed. Em hadn't even glimpsed that bit—though she'd briefly considered asking him to lift his T-shirt—but she had no doubt it was true, judging by the rest of him.

Shaking off the distraction, she poured the contents of the pot into her thermal carafe, returned to her sleeping computer center and reentered all her passwords. How could it only be 10:15? The interlude had felt much longer, from the heart-stopping moment when Anansi bayed his intruder alert to seriously contemplating taking the new guy to bed right then and there. Maybe that explained her reaction—attraction on top of adrenaline release.

Oh yeah, *nothing* at all to do with that Tom Hiddleston smile. Damn Glory for putting that in her head.

Resolutely, she flipped on the voice coder and called Jared. Playing the taciturn Phoenix for a while would cool her jets considerably.

"Oh, look." Jared's face popped up on her side screen, unsexily stubbled and with deep circles. "His high and mightiness finally deigns to make contact."

"Don't give me shit, J," she replied, hitting the keys to change her avatar image for him. Jurassic Park's Dennis Nedry would work nicely. None of her screens had camera function, but she kept a little arsenal of appropriate faces for virtual meetings. She liked to see her team, read their faces when they spoke, even though they couldn't see hers. It wasn't fair, but neither was life. She'd had a harsh lesson in that reality. "What's the update?"

"The update is we're fucked. The new console won't be ready for Christmas."

"Is this when I say I told you so?"

"Don't be a bitch."

She flinched a little at that, but that was only the ultimate guy insult at play, insinuating femininity. Fortunately Jared just plowed onward, not noticing she hadn't replied.

"This is when you tell me you got the prototype."

"Got it this morning."

"Are you fucking kidding me? I sent that a week ago. There has to be a faster way to get this shit to you."

"Not and meet my conditions for privacy."

"The team has a betting pool going, you know, on why you're so obsessed with privacy. Top vote at this time is disfiguring disease."

"Leprosy is a curse. Not very PC of them to joke about it."

"Nobody's laughing here. You cripple the team by not being on site. They resent that."

"I'm happy to resign anytime. I think I could find someone else to hire me."

Jared gave the screen the bird, face full of frustration. Em had worked with him in person, back in the day at Gametronix, when she'd been fresh out of school and full of ideals. Jared had been her team leader and her first real introduction to the knee-jerk misogyny in the world of gamers and game programming.

He'd been there the day they fired her.

When they called her to the meeting, she'd thought it would be another session to strategize how to deal with the trolls. They'd hacked Amazonia again overnight, though she, Jared and the rest of the team had spent the past eight hours—since 3 a.m.—getting it back up and installing the new firewall she'd designed. That she'd spent every waking hour and a bunch she should have been sleeping working on. She'd been determined to keep them from destroying her game.

She'd also thought Gametronix was on her side.

Stoned with lack of sleep and stressed to the gills from the death threats, not to mention the new "game" making the rounds where players could beat and rape an avatar with her face, it took a few minutes to realize that sleek conference room held only her, Jared, the CEO, the head of HR and a guy in a sharp suit whose face remained a blur in her memory.

"We're pulling the plug on Amazonia," Hurston, the CEO informed her without preamble. "Our parent company made the call, but the board agrees. The hacking attempts have put all of our servers at risk. The bad PR has our corporate partners uneasy."

The HR woman nodded, fiddling with her folder. "In addition, we believe you—and all our staff—will be safer with the product off the market."

"Safer, yes." The CEO frowned. "We promised our customers entertainment, not the sorts of unsavory images and stories that have been broadcast about you. It's time to restore what goodwill we can. The customers have spoken."

"Our customers—99.5% of them—love Amazonia," Em protested. "You can't let a few vicious bullies affect what we put out there. Jared, show them the numbers. We have support on every forum and the majority of gamers, male and female, are..." She trailed off because even Jared wouldn't look at her.

"This isn't a discussion," the suit said. The corporate attorney from the parent company, it turned out. He slid a folder of papers over to her. "You'll find we've given you a decent severance package. I've included the noncompete agreement you originally signed, along with a letter of resignation for you to sign."

Stunned, she fingered the letter. "You're firing me?"

"We're setting you free." Hurston pasted a fake smile on his face. "Once you're away from this, you will no longer be a target. You can move on. There's a letter of reference for you in the package."

She'd laughed, a hysterical caw fit for the banshee they'd painted her as. "Reference? Where can I go with a noncompete? No one will hire me." *Especially after this,* the unsaid words echoed in the room.

Jared's phone flashed and he glanced at the screen, then turned it over.

Nobody said anything. The lawyer handed her a pen. "It's better for you if you resign," he told her, not unkindly. "Voluntarily leaving always looks better than the alternative."

Because they will fire you. It went without saying. She could maybe get a lawyer, fight it. But, in truth, she'd lost her fight. Even her husband, Henry, who shared her bed and the next cubicle, had had no more advice to give. "Jared?"

Jared shrugged, a lift of the shoulders. "Nothing I can do," he muttered. "It's a good deal. Take it and get your life back."

So she signed. And the security guards waiting outside the door, not there to protect her after all, escorted her back to her cube. A cardboard box sat on her desk, the office weirdly empty.

"I sent everyone out," Jared explained, ducking his head. "They didn't want you talking to anyone and I thought it might be better to, you know, pack up without everyone…"

"Shunning me?" she filled in, her voice cracking. "Did they know?"

"No." Jared finally looked her in the eye. "Not even Henry. I'll call a meeting, break the news—and I'll give Henry the rest of the day off, to be with you."

"Don't bother," she snapped. Henry felt as helpless to fix the whole situation as she did. Her getting fired would be just one more thing he couldn't deal with. She picked up a few framed photos, which one guard took from her, examined, and then let her put in the box while the other watched, as if she might have rigged the place to blow.

Jared said nothing more, just waited until she'd gotten everything material. They wouldn't let her so much as touch her keyboard. Then he walked her out, both of them pretending the guards didn't follow behind. He gave a miserable wave when they shoved her out the glass doors and stood in front, barring her from returning.

As if she would. If she even could.

When Jared left Gametronix to head up his own game division in Pete Alexander's start-up, she knew why. He hadn't protected her, but he'd at least stood by her side for those last horrible moments. So, after she'd become Phoenix—fuck their noncompete agreement—and a year and a half later, she'd offered him the prototype first. No idiot, he'd snapped up the offer and agreed to Phoenix's anonymity and outrageous terms.

They worked fine together, but she didn't mind making him a little miserable here and there.

No one ever accused her of being too forgiving.

Jared didn't dignify her offer to resign with a verbal response. They both knew he needed her. The moment he didn't, she'd be gone. They both also knew that day would never come. Unless someone discovered her identity. Then the shit would well and truly hit the fan, ranging from lawsuits to devastating financial penalties to very real death threats. Though Jared obviously didn't know that.

She would never let it happen.

"Anyway," he continued, "word from Alexander is no holiday, no vacation until this fucker is live. Thanksgiving or Christmas—we're working straight through."

"Whatever." The rest of the team would be bitched out about that, but Phoenix wouldn't say anything. Complaining revealed personal details. Not as if she had anyone to spend holidays with anyway. "What's the strategy?"

"The team has an idea to float you. It would mean a new module for Christmas—a new, shiny to distract the players from the fact that their pre-ordered fancy new consoles haven't arrived. With Easter eggs that can only be unlocked later, with the console."

She didn't reply for a minute, mulling it over, idly searching for a leper gif. "We're looking at barely over seven weeks out."

"I'm aware of the date." Jared got up and poured more coffee from the pot on the windowsill. He was putting on weight. "Can you do it?"

"Is the team's concept a good one?"

"God only knows."

"Not God," she chuckled, replacing Nedry with a sore-covered leper. "*I* will know."

With a flourish, she cut the connection and set to putting the prototype through its paces. By the team meeting, she'd have a better feel for it. At least the challenge would put Fox out of her brain. If they ran with the concept, she'd be full out and too busy for a real-life lover. Especially one like that. She had a feeling Fox would not be the wham-bam, roll-over-and-fall-asleep kind of guy. Way too much intensity for that. Even a no-strings fling with him would be time-consuming, and she'd just run out of free time.

She had her priorities and her work was all of them. It had

been the reason for every decision she'd made for the past three years, seven months and twelve days. Funny that she knew that number better than the last time she'd had real-life sex. That told her something right there about what was important.

Not a hot, random stranger.

Probably for the best.

THE ENTICING EMILY did not run past that afternoon. Fox figured she'd either skipped out on a second run, had gone the other direction or was dodging him. Possibly all three, cagey as she acted. He knew he hadn't missed her because he'd moved his computer station to the windows overlooking the beach.

He'd taken the place for the view, after all, fogged in as it was.

All research about the denizens in Phoenix's realm counted as legit time spent, so Fox spent the rest of the rainy day indulging his curiosity about the woman. In this arena, his sexual and professional interests coincided. He loved the discovery a new lover brought. Now that he'd determined to seduce the elusive Emily, that restless hunger focused in and fixed on her. He wanted to learn every little thing about her, from what everyone knew to those intimate revelations only he would dig out of her.

What would make her really lose control?

The full background check on her would take until tomorrow to return, but he'd accessed everything he could immediately find on her. No remorse there. Even his novelist cover would excuse a bit of internet curiosity about the woman he intended to talk into a hot and hopefully kinky affair. After years at this game, he'd developed a deft hand at not dropping too much of what he'd learned about people.

Women, in particular, thought a man knowing their preferences meant he'd paid attention to them. It never hurt his case to remember the little details. The fact that he kept those tidbits in carefully indexed files didn't hurt them because they never knew it.

Miss Emily Bartwell turned out to be pretty much an open book. Wealthy, East Coast family, all the right schools, a very sweet newspaper photo of her as a sixteen-year-old debutante in a white dress and her dark hair in upswept ringlets so perfect they looked like they could cut glass. God, how he'd love to replicate *that* outfit with a much dirtier outcome.

One marriage, lasting two years and ending in an acrid divorce that nevertheless let her walk away with her inherited fortune intact, due to an iron-clad trust fund.

Turned out the awful paintings in the coffee shop were hers, but he wouldn't hold it against her. She had a crappy website with a few on display, an outdated Etsy shop. More fascinating, "Bartwell" was neither her maiden name nor her ex's name. She'd been born Silar Emily Stillwell and legally changed to her current name after the divorce. Sloppy to use her middle name, but typical for an amateur.

People didn't like giving up the pieces of their old identities—a sentimentality that outed the ones in hiding every time. Emily, he decided, fit the profile. The asshole ex-husband no doubt. Everything pointed to it—the dog, her nervousness.

Fox constructed her story as he showered and dressed for the ill-fated date with Glory. Too bad there, as she'd be the perfect choice for an information source. Still, the cock wanted what the cock wanted. And only Emily with her perfect mouth, long legs and fascinating depths would do for him now. He would find other ways to pump Glory.

So, Emily had found this little island, changed her name to a family one and kept to herself. No need to work, with her financial cushion, so she painted, searching for her genius, no doubt. He could give her some tips on better covering her trail. She'd done okay for an amateur, if he was right. Glory might be able to give him the scoop on her friend. Most likely enough time had passed that the asshole ex had lost interest and moved on. The last restraining order dated back over two years and seemed to have been granted mostly to set her mind at ease, since he hadn't uncovered any associated police reports.

The full check would tell him more.

So would Emily.

First, however, he needed to extract himself from the situation with Glory. Without any useful lies, either, since the odds were high of discovery. Very glad he'd snagged a bouquet of carnations from the little grocery that morning, he brought up Glory's contact info in his phone and started the mapping app. At the time he'd been irritated that the store had nothing more glamorous than the dyed-gold carnations—not exactly romantic date material—but it seemed his luck had intervened.

Nothing said "I see you as just a friend" more than flowers meant for your gran's Thanksgiving table.

Indeed, when Glory opened her door, her welcoming smile dimmed considerably at the sight of them. Perfect setup. For all that his profession required a certain amount of ruthlessness,

Fox had never been a guy to hurt a woman's feelings on purpose. He wouldn't have wanted Glory mad at him, even if she wasn't Emily's friend.

"Thanks for having me over." He slipped past her on pretext of taking off his wet jacket and took in the pretty cabin, while she hung it up for him and stuck the flowers in a vase. Family photos, all with Pacific Northwest backgrounds. Local girl for at least one generation, maybe more.

"I hope you're hungry." Glory handed him a glass of wine, her smile and voice insinuating much more. "I made my famous creamed chicken casserole."

"Starving. I still haven't figured out the Kapsucks' oven." He handed the wine back. "But I shouldn't drink—have to drive back. With your winding roads, I don't want to end up dead in a gulch."

"I thought maybe you could…stay." Glory closed the distance between them.

Dang, he'd hoped he could at least introduce the topic over dinner. "I can't." He tugged one of her curls in a friendly way. "But, as cliché as it sounds, I really hope we can be friends."

Her face went blank and he mentally winced, bracing himself for the takedown he deserved.

"Oh. My. God." Her eyes had gone calculating. "I know you were interested yesterday, so either you heard gossip about me—and that can't be it because it's all good, at least in the area you'd be interested in—or you met someone else."

He gave her his most rueful grin. "I'm an ass. I know it."

"But there is no one else to meet." She emptied his wineglass into hers, drank a healthy swallow and studied him over the rim. "Who could you have possibly... No. No fucking way!"

Liking her better all the time, and wishing the wine thing hadn't worked so well, as he could have had a glass or two, really, Fox stuck his thumbs in the loops of his jeans and waited her out.

"That witch! Emily Bartwell came over and checked you out, didn't she? I should never have tipped her off. What I get for making assumptions, dammit."

"Actually, I stopped by her house—meet the neighbors, you know."

Glory gaped at him. "Did she let you in?"

No, she hadn't. Not even a polite move toward doing so. "Not yet. We chatted outside."

Now she snorted and sipped her wine, looking smug. "And she won't either. I'm not surprised you're going for it—Lord knows every other straight male and a few not-so-straight females in a hundred-mile radius have. Not a one has turned her head. Good luck. When she turns you down, I won't harbor hard feelings."

"That's very generous of you."

"Not at all. It will be interesting to see you try. I'll start the betting pool in the morning."

"I'm not sure that's—"

"Can't stop me." She grinned, full of excellent cheer. "Come eat. I'll even give you some tips on my girl. Not that they'll do you any good."

Fox followed her with interest. This game just got better all the time.

CHAPTER FIVE

"GO AWAY," GLORY said the moment Em walked in the post office door. "I'm not speaking to you."

Stomach clutching, Em stopped in the doorway, then stepped aside for Ethyl Gillican to go out, arms laden with packages. The elderly woman winked at her. Glory glared.

Totally out of her depth, she assessed her—former?—friend, who stood in front of the counter, arms crossed. What the hell had Fox told her? She'd blown the friendship, just as she'd feared, and without really meaning to.

You know you were in the wrong. Flirting with him like that. What the hell got into you?

Miserable, knowing she deserved to be, she nodded and turned to go.

"Is that my coffee?" Glory called after her. "You can at least give me that much, to make up for stealing Fox Mullins out from under me."

Em made herself face the other woman, setting the coffee on the counter. It sang of her guilt—extra large, double cream, triple shot and with chocolate caramel. Glory surveyed it and raised her eyebrows.

"I'm sorry, Glory," Em blurted. "I didn't mean for it to happen. You called dibs and I messed up. You should have him and—"

Glory held up a hand, stopping her, then sniffed her coffee. "This is extra fancy."

"I know it doesn't change anything. I came in hoping you'd say you got it on the way you planned, but I guess you didn't and I don't know how the Girl Code covers this. Just tell me what to do. Should I call him? Yes! No—I'll go see him and I'll tell him that I'm not interested, which is the truth, and that he should…are you okay?"

Glory had turned red, apparently choking on some coffee foam and thumping her chest. Then she burst out laughing. "Dammit—you made me shoot foam up my nose! What the hell is the 'girl code'?"

Em shifted from foot to foot, wishing she hadn't come in. But you couldn't call the damn post office, with their central 800 number bullshit, and she'd been fretting, even after working all night. She'd even skipped her morning run—and yesterday afternoon's—for which Anansi had *not* forgiven her. It made her world complete to have *everyone* mad at her. This was what came of dabbling in thoughts of sexy men.

"Why are you laughing?"

"No, no, no." Glory wagged a finger. "Girl code. Explain."

"You know." Em checked her ponytail. "The rules of friendship. Not stealing each other's boyfriends. That kind of thing."

"Ohh." Glory nodded knowingly. Then made a face and shook her head. "There is no girl code."

"There isn't?"

"Well, sure, there's friends and what you do and don't do, but girls don't have some special set of rules, Em."

"I'm not sure about that." Emily had spend a fair amount of effort, in her more social days, studying the cliques of girls and how their friendships worked. The rules had never been clear and seemed very situation-specific. She'd never quite figured it out. But Glory always acted like a friend.

"Trust me—high school was a long time ago. Besides, Fox wasn't my boyfriend—only potential."

"Aha!" Em pointed at her. "So there is a rule. Potential versus actual."

Glory pursed her lips. "Okay, maybe. But it's not as if you cheated and made me screw up my routine so you got head cheerleader instead."

Em's stomach unknotted a little. Glory was joking with her, then. Em held her hand up in a vow. "I would never stand in the way of you being head cheerleader."

Glory snort-laughed. "That's better. And what the hell do you mean, you don't want him? Of course you do. He told me you said that if I cleared it, you'd go out with him, which was decent of you. Girl code points for you."

"He told you that?" The embarrassed horror crept back in. She really couldn't imagine why she'd behaved as she had. It must have been the scare. "I never said that." *In so many words.*

"Well, I teased it out of him. Guilt is a wonderful thing. But he's totally into you and you haven't wanted to go out with anyone. For that reason alone I'd step off the dance floor for you." Glory made a complicated hand gesture, a ridiculous bastardization of a gang sign. "Girl code, homie."

Em suppressed the laugh and clung to being serious. "No, you're right. I haven't wanted to date and I still don't. I'll tell him that and you can have him."

"And he's picturing your long legs wrapped around him instead? No, thank you. Besides, as I told Fox, watching him go after you and you having a bit of fun will be even more entertaining—and that's saying something."

The realization hit her. "You started a betting pool. That's why Ethyl winked at me."

Glory widened her eyes and folded her hands under her chin, imitating a manic cherub. "Me? Nooo. Gambling in a federal post office would be against the law."

Not that it had ever stopped her before. Glory ran betting pools on babies, tourist hook-ups and days without sunshine— or anything else interesting. She drew the line at predicting divorces, saying that brought bad luck. She got around the law because no one exchanged money. Bragging rights only. More than one person around town had framed certificates from their wins, including the odds they'd beaten.

And Ethyl Gillican held the grand prize.

"What did Ethyl predict?"

"I have no idea what you're talking about."

Em narrowed her eyes. "Name your price to make this go away."

Glory gasped, the picture of offense. "I cannot be bought."

"Please don't do this." Em tried making the hand sign. "Girl code?"

"You need to practice that—I think you just told me to fuck myself in Italian. Which, now that I can't have a certain hot redhead, sounds very appealing."

"Okay, seriously." Em tightened her ponytail. Too much

coffee. "I'm really not interested."

"I think you're lying. Are you protecting me or being a big weenie?"

"Really. I don't have time for him. I have—" She cut herself off, horrified that she'd nearly said something about her work. Even being tired and frazzled shouldn't have pushed her into such a careless mistake. Fortunately, Glory didn't notice the near-slip, looking over Em's shoulder with a speculative gleam in her eyes.

"Well, well, look who's headed our way."

She told herself not to look. Then called herself a coward. After all, she'd indulged in one pretty tame fantasy and spent the subsequent nearly twenty-four hours erasing the man from her mind. No matter what Glory thought, she wasn't into him. She couldn't afford to be. Here was her opportunity to make it clear to both of them. The fact that she looked about as appealing as a two-day-old microwaved dinner ought to help.

She looked. Fox crossed the street in a half jog, the breeze off the water catching his short coppery curls. If possible, he looked even better in jeans, with his narrow hips and strong thighs. He wore a deep green zippered UCLA sweatshirt and, spotting them, waved and flashed that oh-so charming grin.

That trigger inside that seemed keyed to him flipped back and forth in excitement.

"I think I get all the Girl Code points," Glory murmured, "for giving that up for you. You so owe me."

"I owe you nothing, because I'm not doing this."

"We shall *see*." Glory sing-songed the words. Em would have had to retaliate if Fox hadn't burst through the door right then, filling the stale little office with the scent of rain and his intense personality.

"Please tell me it stops raining at some point," he greeted them, nodding at Glory and turning his special smile on Em. Like chocolate under a heat lamp, she melted at the edges.

"It's not raining," she replied, taking control of the conversation. "This counts as something between mist and a drizzle."

"Are you going to tell me the Tlingit have thirty-seven words for rain or something?" His eyes sparkled with good humor and he ran his hands over his damp hair.

"You're the writer. Shouldn't you know?"

"Ah, true." His gaze traveled warmly over her. "Perhaps I need private lessons. Would you be willing to tutor me?"

Dammit, her face flushed. Glory snickered.

Fox looked back and forth between them. Stuck his hands in his sweatshirt pockets. "Cards on the table, right? Are we good here? I'd rather know now."

"Totally good," Glory chirped.

At the same instant, Em said, "I'm not interested."

Glory scowled at her and Fox grinned, not the least bothered. If anything, he seemed even more pleased.

"What would it take to make you interested?" he asked her, reminding her of a time-share salesman.

"Nothing. Glory has dibs. I'm removing myself from play."

"I forfeited dibs," Glory corrected. "And I'm getting overheated just from the vibes bouncing off you two. Go negotiate somewhere else. I have work to do. And betting odds to adjust," she added, sauntering behind the counter.

"Put me down for Sunday night," Fox told her, eyes intent

on Em's face. A shiver of heat destabilized her and she had to fight to regain her equilibrium.

"As an invested party, you can't bet. I'll be in the back. *Working.*" Glory took the innocuous folder holding the betting pool and sauntered away, humming Babyface's "Fire." Complete and total traitor to the Girl Code.

Em faced down Fox and drew on the attitude she'd learned to cultivate, back in the day. Online trolls hadn't been the only ones to try to make her life miserable. "Aren't you underselling your seductive abilities?" she taunted. "Two whole days from now?"

"Three whole dates from now," he said. "And anticipation only increases the pleasure."

"I don't date."

"Okay, we'll call it foreplay."

"I'm not going to have sex with you. I apologize if I gave any other impression." She sounded rigid, even to herself, but she felt cornered. More than a little anxious. She needed to get home. She shouldn't have skipped her run.

Fox cocked his head at her. "What changed?"

"I don't know what you mean."

"You were plenty interested yesterday. If I'm coming on too strong, I'll back off. We can take it slow. I'll be here for a while and slow has its merits too."

She wanted to reiterate that she had no time for him, but the persona she'd built wouldn't sustain it. Bad planning there. What the hell had gotten into her yesterday? She should have frozen him out then.

"You're overthinking this. I can practically smell the

smoke."

"Why won't you simply accept that I'm not interested?" A bit of desperation infused her voice. She should have stayed home. Absolutely the wrong choice to come here.

"Because you're still standing here, all sexy gorgeous and fresh-skinned, looking at me with those silvery eyes full of interest." He shook his head, as if calling a poker bluff. "You'll have to convince me, I'm afraid. One date."

"I don't date."

He rolled his eyes. "There she goes again. Date or fore-play—you decide."

"Neither."

"Okay. A run on the beach then. I'll meet you in front of my house at three-forty-five."

Tempting. She needed the run and it did get lonely going by herself. Besides, he might wear those jogging shorts again. Even if she didn't dare allow herself to indulge, she could enjoy the sights. She nearly made it a condition, but reined herself back in time. "Maybe."

He laughed, eyes alight with coppery delight. "A 'maybe' from you, Miss Emily, is worth a thousand 'yeses' from any other woman."

"I heard that!" Glory yelled from the back.

"Except for you, darling," Fox called, then made a shocked face at Glory's foul suggestion for what he could do with it.

Despite herself, Em laughed, feeling decidedly better about everything. She grabbed her now very cool latte from the counter, which let her get around Fox without having to get too close. "Okay. Um, bye."

He put a hand on her arm, staying her. Then leaned in and pressed a kiss to her cheek. "Three-forty-five," he said, his sultry tone making it sound like so much more.

She locked down on the surge of lust. "I might not be there."

Shrugging a little, he stepped back, giving her space. "I'll wait."

"You might be waiting all night."

He smiled, but not that sweet, charming one. This one looked hungry, focused. It made her think of being pushed up against a wall while he ravished her with his mouth.

"I'll wait all winter if I have to. I'm good with anticipation."

CHAPTER SIX

S HE WAS KILLING him.

He hadn't been lying about the anticipation bit. He liked a lot of foreplay. Denial and the slow build always led to the best sex. But that was always after the game was engaged. He rarely dealt with a drawn-out courtship. Though he had to laugh at himself, that this amount of time seemed extended to him.

She'd looked completely edible, however, hair pulled tight into that scalp-tugging ponytail, gray eyes huge in her delicate face, her unpainted mouth so pink and enticing. The desire to have her panting under him crawled through his veins.

Three-forty-five couldn't come soon enough.

He'd lied about waiting though. If she didn't show, he might have to go looking for her. A fine line there, chasing her enough to make her feel desired without scaring her into hiding or issuing an ultimatum she couldn't back down on. A lot went on behind her serious eyes. More than an asshole ex who hadn't put in an appearance in years.

Even Glory didn't know that much about her—and she was surely Em's closest friend on the island. He'd run hard up against the privacy ethic, though. Glory had told him what she thought he needed to know and clammed up on the rest. Lots of people on Lyra kept to themselves and that was how they liked it.

No questions asked. Ever.

He added what little Glory had spilled into his notes. Emily—Em to everyone, apparently, but she hadn't given him that permission and he planned to abide by that until she did—liked to read, but Glory didn't know what. She painted, never left the island, sometimes wouldn't come into town for weeks at a time. Glory insisted that Emily loved her creamed chicken casserole, which made him seriously question her judgment because he'd never had a worse meal—and that she never dated anyone, to Glory's knowledge.

The full background check came in, along with the one on coffee-shop Rob. Glory too. No one could accuse him of not being thorough in his search. Phoenix lurked here somewhere and Glory could have a connection to the guy.

As he'd suspected, Rob's background turned up a history of minor possession charges plus a long-ago draft dodge. He'd lived in British Columbia until the forgiveness clauses kicked in, then made his way to Lyra and stayed. If he'd developed Phoenix's skills on his own, in between marijuana harvests, Fox would be majorly surprised. Along with Glory, the local girl whose record showed her to be exactly what she seemed, Rob went onto the unlikely list.

Emily's full check, though—that set off some bells.

Not that the information itself sent up any flags, but because it didn't. No speeding tickets—unlike Glory, who'd apparently spent her years at University of Puget Sound setting new speed records—no credit bumps of any sort, no academic reprimands, which most people would be surprised to know really did show up on their permanent records. If only he could tease Glory about the streaking incident in her junior year.

No, Emily's background was too clean.

She might as well be a robot and that didn't match the passionate intelligence he suspected lurked under her prim exterior. Revising his estimates, he decided the cover she'd adopted might be far from amateurish. Someone had created this background for her, only making the mistake of crafting it too perfectly.

Most people wouldn't look at it twice. The few who did, still wouldn't find a crack.

But he would.

He liked this woman. More than wanting her body, he needed to know all about her. She'd tell him everything, in time.

In the meanwhile—hours still until three-forty-five—he'd put in some time on Phoenix. The programmer had been busy on the forums the night before. All night, by the time signatures. Dropping hints about a new Labyrinth module by Christmas. Fox left his own breadcrumbs, still trying to wrangle an invite to the private chats where Phoenix held court among a privileged few. One of his informants had provided transcripts that gave fascinating insight into Phoenix's personality—and had been key in providing clues that led Fox to Lyra—but so far he'd been unable to get in himself.

A very tight community that protected their own.

He restrained himself until three-thirty, at which point Fox couldn't contain his restlessness. Justifying his early arrival by running through some limbering exercises, he kept an eye in the direction of her house, willing her to show up. He knew he'd hit on the thing to tempt her the moment he suggested it in the squalid post office. No dinner dates with this one, but a good sweaty run. She'd done cross-country in high school and college, if that part of her paperwork jibed with reality, though without distinguishing herself with any major wins or records.

The lack of achievement in all her background niggled at him. Mediocre grades, average athletic skill, all the right social events but nothing special. And her painting—solidly crap-tastic. All of it fit how she presented herself, the schoolmarmish look, the self-effacing postures, but it didn't play for him.

An elaborate disguise, all of it.

She might have everyone else fooled, but she had too much intensity to be that dull. Somewhere under the façade, she sizzled with passion. Why she tucked it away, except for brief glimpses, was the question. Not just an uncomfortable divorce, he thought. That might have been the trigger to send her here, but the roots went deeper. Maybe she'd been sexually molested or raped at some point, which would make seducing her even trickier. Although he'd bet that wasn't it. Something, though, had scared her, way back, and she'd started hiding her real self then.

If he'd come on too strong and she'd gone to ground, he'd be kicking himself for the rest of the winter.

Three-fifty. Dammit. He'd have to develop another strate-gy to draw her out. Surely he couldn't have lost the game already.

But no.

There she was, Anansi galloping gleefully ahead, beelining for him. Emily ran easily, gracefully behind, her slim profile dark against the silvery sea. Anansi blew past him, fortunately still considering him a friend, and circled around to escort his mistress. She drew up, her cheeks flushing pink in the cool air—nothing close to the embarrassed red at the post office—and looked him over. Cool and self-possessed again. But was that a crinkle of disappointment?

"I see you wised up and ditched the shorts."

Idiot. Fox made a mental note to wear his jogging shorts as often as possible. Let his legs freeze. "I'm kind of overwarm, though. Want to come inside while I change?"

Her eyes flicked at the house—tempted?—and away again. "No, thanks. I'm for a run and then I want to get back to this painting I'm working on."

"Light won't be very good for it." He fell into pace beside her, measuring her stride. If anything her legs were longer, though he might top her by an inch overall. A good reminder he needed to stay on his toes and work at this one.

"Yeah. I didn't want to stop. I'm sure you know how it is, when the muse seizes you." She tripped ever so slightly over the word "muse." Said for his benefit. Thinking he might believe in that claptrap, even when she clearly didn't.

"I'm flattered then."

"Don't be." She gave him a sidelong look, full of that suspicion that only egged him on. "Anansi needed to get out. He was driving me crazy."

The dog, who'd looped out through the shallows, now raced toward them at top speed, water spraying from his sleek body, demonstrating his excess energy. Emily laughed, a full, sensual sound that went straight to his groin.

With an odd pang of jealousy—over a dog, no less—he wished he'd been the one to make her laugh that way. *Give it time, Sparky. Slow and steady wins this race.*

"So, is that how you spend most of your time—painting?" They rounded the point and the wind off the water hit him in the face, cold and damp.

"When the muse inspires me," she answered breezily, doing better with the word this time. "Or I read, watch TV, meditate. I'm pretty lazy, really. You'd be appalled."

"You don't work?"

"No. Money isn't an issue. Thinking to do some gold-digging?"

Ouch. The woman did not hold back. Working at driving him away, judging by the determined set to her chin. He could deal with that. And, to get her attention, he picked up the pace. "I think I can hold my own. Just interested in knowing more about you."

"Are we running or chatting?"

"We can do both. Unless you're out of breath," he added to needle her a little.

"I'm fine." She upped the pace an edge over his.

Yeah, look at that competitive spirit. "What shows do you watch?"

"The Shopping Channel, mainly. Totally addicted."

More lies. She pretended like she needed to watch the rocks, but she refused to meet his eye and pressed her lips together over the words in a telling way. Pretty much making stuff up as she went, moving her image from dull to vapid. Probably judging what she estimated attracted him to her and trying to counter it.

"What's the last thing you bought?"

Slight pause. "Oh, I never buy anything. I just look."

Yeah. He bet she'd never looked at the Shopping Channel in her life, but if he asked her again in a few hours, she'd be able to cite several items currently on sale. If he got past this conversation.

"So, what books do you read?"

"Not yours—sorry."

"You looked though."

"Tree did. Said they were all sci-fi type stories. Not my thing."

"But you read Neil Gaiman—fantasy." He called her bluff and raised.

"Gaiman based the book on an African and Caribbean god. Maybe that's where I got the name."

"Is it? You named your dog after a spider god?"

She didn't reply immediately. Something there had penetrated. "Okay, you're right. I was trying to spare your feelings. I just didn't like *your* stories."

He nearly laughed at her relentless poking at his male ego, at the way she tried to make it sound as if nothing about him was her thing. If he'd been a typical guy, he'd be feeling pretty damn deflated by now. Instead he entertained himself by cooking up a fantasy of her in dominatrix mode, making him crawl for her. He'd lay odds he could talk her into that scenario eventually. Probably more easily than getting her to kneel for him, though that image carried enough sizzle that he'd try for it.

Enjoying the fantasy, he let the silence spin out until they reached a rocky fall that extended into the water and effectively ended the beach. In mutual accord, they turned and headed back.

"I didn't mean to hurt your feelings," she said, as they approached the steps he'd climb to get to his house.

Point for you, Sparky. He kept his grin to himself. How much to play into this one? A lot depended on whether she really cared about those paintings. And if she knew how bad they were or if she'd really invested them with artistic hopefulness. Dangerous territory. Take the opening, he decided.

"It's all right. A writer's life can be tough that way. You learn to live with rejection."

If he'd been able to, he would have held his breath, but he needed it to keep the pace she'd set. One she maintained effortlessly, to all appearances.

"Okay, now I feel like crap. I apologize."

"You can make it up to me by having dinner with me."

She huffed out a breath. "You don't give up, do you?"

"No." He let a measure of his determination infuse the word, testing her.

"Look." She slowed to a walk, tightened her ponytail. Then stopped and turned to face him. "I'm flattered by the interest. Really. And I know I gave totally the wrong signals yesterday. I meant it, though, when I said I don't date. It's not you, it's me—"

She cut herself off, looking appalled at her words, and he

had to laugh. Her face flushed, bright flags of red on her cheekbones. He wanted nothing more than to yank her into his arms and kiss her breathless. Tucking his hands into his sweatshirt pockets, he reminded himself not to touch her. Not yet. No matter how much he itched to.

"I can't believe you actually said that," he teased her, enjoying the way she pressed the backs of her hands to her cheeks to check the heat there. Much closer to the real her now. Press the advantage or not? He followed instinct. "Why don't you date, Emily?"

"It's…a long story." Truth there, but no doubt one she needed time to invent properly.

"I have nothing but time. Come over, sit by the fire. I'll pour some wine and you can tell me the story."

"I don't notice you giving me your life history." She sounded irritated. Cornered.

"You haven't asked, have you? Ask me anything. Let's get to know each other."

"See!" She tightened her ponytail again. Her scalp had to be screaming from it. He wanted to see her with her hair down, all the dark silky strands flowing around her naked body.

Focus on what she's saying, Sparky.

"That's the thing. I don't want to do that. You seem like a great guy, but I don't want to get to know you. I don't want to have long chats by the fire. I'm not…built for romance."

"Okay," he answered, keeping his voice even. "How about just fucking then?"

A tactical gambit. Despite the old saw—almost certainly an urban myth—about the guy who picked up women by asking them if they wanted to fuck because eventually one would say yes, it never really worked. In rare cases, however, with the right woman, it could be the right way to cut through tangled expectations. A deliberate shock and maybe a bit of illicit thrill. If she had already been thinking about it, and Fox would bet money she had.

She stared at him, knocked out of her argument, and he returned her gaze steadily. *Come on, Emily. A hundred and eighty degrees from long chats by the fire.* Her flush returning, she looked away, but not before he noted the heat filling her eyes and her tongue flicking out to lick her lips.

Oh, he had her.

"If you don't date, then it's been a while, I'm guessing," he pointed out, very reasonably. "You have your reasons and I'm sure they're good ones. But I'm only here for a short time, so you don't have to worry about me wanting to move in with you and forcing you to have long conversations."

She smiled a little, still looking out over the water, and he knew he had her attention. *Reel her in, slow but sure.*

"I like you, Emily. Everything I know so far has me riveted. I think you feel the attraction, too. You don't want this to get personal? I'm willing to take what I can get. Let me take you to bed one time—a trial run."

Her gray eyes lighter than the darkening sky came back to him, assessing. Definitely thinking about it. "A one-night stand—no strings attached?"

"If that's what you want."

"But you think I'll want more." Her voice had a throaty quality, going whiskey dark. She was killing him, the conversation making him hotter for her by the minute. So close he could taste her on his tongue already.

He clenched his hands inside the pockets and smiled to blow off some of his raging tension. "Yes. Yes, I do."

Deliberately, a mocking tilt to her head, she stepped back and looked him over, head to toe. "You sound pretty confident."

Goddamn, she was definitely flirting with him again. Sometimes he impressed even himself. "How about a small demonstration?" He didn't have to make his voice sultry. Keeping it out of a growl was the challenge.

"I want to see your abs." She met his eyes and smiled, clearly enjoying having taken him by surprise.

"Let me guess—Glory said something."

Emily laughed, a light breath of the real one, but she looked pleased, eyes sparkling with humor and, if he didn't mistake the mark, lust.

"Right here? On a public beach?"

"You offered." She looked up and down the lonesome shore. "And I don't think you need to worry about onlookers."

"This is a first for me," he pretended to grumble, instead immeasurably excited by her gambit. She could be the hottest lover he'd ever found, with her playfully passionate nature. His cock filled and he tried to master it by acting slightly hesitant, unzipping the sweatshirt and thinking about the cold air, surreptitiously watching her. Her gaze followed his hands with definite interest. Bless Glory and thank God for all those gym hours. Peeling open the sweatshirt, making it a strip tease for her without being too obvious, he fumbled at the hem of his T-shirt, faking shyness. Then lifted it up a scant few inches. "Okay?" He asked, looking over her shoulder and taking in her delicious reaction with his peripheral vision.

Because she wound her fingers together and—holy Christ—licked her lips again.

"More," she ordered.

God help him, he went to a full cockstand, not comfortable in the tight jock strap, but hopefully it would keep her from noticing. Or, if she did, she'd take it the right way.

"Yes, ma'am," he said and raised the shirt higher.

CHAPTER SEVEN

S HE HAD NO idea what had gotten into her. Something about Fox sucked her into this morass of prurient thoughts and impulsive flirting, despite her best intentions. She'd come on the run to freeze him out and make it clear they had no future, and here she was, asking to see his abs and entertaining his salacious offer.

Seriously considering it, especially once she got a good look at him.

Her fingers itched to touch that golden skin. California tan and tight abs that begged to be nibbled. Plus a coppery treasure trail leading from his navel and disappearing under the waistband of his running pants, which bulged considerably. If she put her hand on him, he'd be hard. Her mouth actually watered with the desire to do so. When would she get another chance to do a guy with this kind of body?

"As billed?" Fox asked, eyes glittering. She had a feeling he'd pounce on her, if she gave the least sign. It alarmed her how much she wanted him to.

"Very nice," she allowed, sounding ridiculously prim, but hey, at least she hadn't pounced on *him*. "Thank you."

He lowered the shirt but left the zippered sweat open, bisecting the UC and LA. The thin cotton tee, sweat-soaked, clung to him. "Now what?"

"I don't know. I have to think."

Stepping closer, he gave her a look. Amused, aroused, impatient. "Are you sure that's what you want to do?"

"I'm not convinced this is a good idea." Was it a bad idea? Or was she just in the habit of keeping people away? He'd nearly tripped her up a few times, with the personal questions. It made her realize how sloppy she'd gotten, so accustomed to people on Lyra being used to her and not prying. Fox liked to pry. Or he thought she was like most women and wanted him to express interest in her thoughts and hobbies.

Of course she'd Googled him. And looked over his stories. She wouldn't read them, however, because she didn't want to know that much about him.

Really, the offer of "just fucking" appealed most. She could handle that. Hell, she wanted it enough she couldn't recall any of the many good reasons that had seemed so obvious when she left the house. She resisted the urge to back up, even though he'd edged even closer, crowding her. A little space to think, away from his sizzling presence, would probably bring them to the forefront again. "I need some space to think about it."

Geez, that was as bad as the "it's not you, it's me" blunder.

"That's understandable. But I'd hate to think I haven't made my best case." His voice had a musing quality, but his eyes filled with a mix of playfulness and fierce intent. "You looked. Shouldn't you at least make an informed decision, sample the merchandise?"

"What do you have in mind?" She couldn't help herself. Playing this game with him felt like sex already. By far the most fun she'd had in ages. The desire to laugh mixed with the urge to reach out those few inches separating them and touch. This close, she smelled his warm, male scent.

"Let me kiss you." He purred the words over his lips, compelling her attention.

"No."

"Why not?"

"Because, I—" *couldn't think of a reason.*

"Just take a little taste," he coaxed.

His gaze focused on her mouth and she suspected she'd be the one nibbled on. Which sounded amazing. She'd been thinking about his mouth all day—and getting absolutely nowhere with the project. If she kissed him, there would be no going back unless he sucked at it. Very doubtful he would. And if she didn't do this, she'd just keep going over it in her head. Too late to walk away and be done. Might as well purge him from her system. At least then she could work again.

Call it stress relief.

"Okay." She braced herself, expecting a kiss as ferocious as his expression.

He didn't smile. Instead, the tension between them thickened and he moved as if he felt it too. He slid an arm around her waist, almost tender, and pulled her close. His body steamed hot against her, those impressive abs hard against her belly. She pressed a hand to his chest, to hold him off if she needed to, but the crisply curling hair beneath his shirt and the flex of his pecs made her want to dig in her nails instead. With his other hand, he touched light fingers to her chin, feathering them along the sensitive skin under her jaw. Her nipples crunched hard and she felt abruptly out of breath.

"Well?" She tried to sound demanding, but her voice lacked the strength of conviction.

"Shh." His mouth pursed sensually as he blew the air across his lips. "I told you I'm into anticipation."

"I don't think I am," she breathed.

"It's an acquired taste." His lips brushed her cheekbone, the sensation zinging through her. She actually trembled from the tension of the moment, trying to hold still as his mouth made its leisurely way down her cheek to the corner of her jaw, his hand moving behind her neck. "You smell of orange blossoms."

It was in her mind to say it was her body wash, but his mouth hovered over hers, then drifted across, a bare brush of the lips. Again, a gentle sampling of her mouth, tasting her, taking her measure. Almost chaste. Except that the touch burned through her, igniting her body. She inhaled and he intensified, following her breath in, deepening the kiss. Almost lazily, he lifted his head and changed the angle to kiss her from the other side, moving back and forth, as if seeking the perfect alignment.

Relaxing into it, she slid a hand up to the back of his neck, a bit chill from the cooling sweat, the curls there damp.

Making a satisfied sound that aroused her as much as the kisses, he sank in, urging her mouth open, following with his tongue, not invading but coaxing. With an answering sound of need she responded in kind, touching his tongue with hers, feeling herself go gloriously wet, aware that she was clinging to him and not caring in the least. Pressing tight against his hard body, nearly vibrating with tensile strength, she reveled in the thrust of his erect cock against the inner curve of her hip. The wild desire to wrap her legs around him seized her and she sucked his tongue into her mouth, wanting to devour him any way possible.

"Oh, Emily," he muttered against her mouth. "You're killing me. Say you're in."

It had been a forgone conclusion. Who was she kidding? "One time."

"The whole night, with an option to continue."

"I won't want more than that." She said that with the most conviction she could muster, as much for herself as for him.

"You haven't seen anything yet. Leave that door open." The hand at the small of her back found bare skin, stroking her there.

"Fine. But, if—when I say so, you agree not to bother me anymore. No pushing."

"Can I say hello to you in the grocery store?" His fingers moved slowly over her spine, stirring and enticing.

"Yes, but no more than that." She concentrated on ignoring how the simple caress on her skin trickled arousal through her whole body. "No flirting. No asking me out on runs that are thinly veiled seduction attempts."

"I have to point out that this was more than an attempt. I'd qualify it as a raging success."

He had a point. Why his brash arrogance attracted and charmed her so much, she'd have a hard time pinning down. Maybe it was just nice knowing exactly where she stood with him. No alternate agenda or buried misogyny.

"All right then. Let's do this and get it done with." She let go of him and put distance between them, then looked about for Anansi, who was happily rooting through a nearby pile of rocks. "I'll take Anansi home and then will be over later."

"You'll be over what?" Fox asked with a teasing smile.

She didn't quite know what to say. "To your place. Not mine." No negotiating that one.

He nodded ever so slightly at that, as if confirming something he already thought. Then cast an eye at the sky. "But it's almost full dark."

"So?"

"So." He reached out a hand and she flinched a bit. Raising an eyebrow for her jumpiness, he pulled the length of her ponytail over her shoulder and ran his fingers through it. "If I maybe only get one night, I want the whole thing. We're both sweaty and you'll want to shower, if I don't miss my guess. Maybe you'll turn out to be the primping type. You wouldn't be over for two hours, at least."

Surprised at the level of her frustration, she frowned at him. "What's your point, Fox?"

"Tomorrow. Four-thirty. Don't worry, I'll feed you. And you promise to stay until daybreak."

"Are you sure you don't want to make it Saturday?" She sounded snappish, surprisingly disappointed by the delay.

"Glory wouldn't let me bet or I would."

"She would have, you know."

"I know." He grinned in that devastating way. "But I found out the prize is for bragging rights only and a gentleman never tells."

"Sorry that you're missing out on the big win."

"But I'm not." He dropped her ponytail, and trailed a finger, the bare tip of it, over her collarbone, eyes intent in the dark gray gloaming. "I suspect I've won the equivalent of the Powerball lottery."

"With that kind of buildup, I'm afraid you'll be disappointed."

He shook his head, looking thoughtful. "Not possible." The light touch went lower, finding the upper curve of her breast above the jog bra, where her own zippered sweatshirt parted. "Still, if you're concerned, I'm willing to make a concession."

"What's that?" She shouldn't ask, but he'd tucked that finger in the vee of her shirt, tugging her toward him. Damn her weakness, she let him, tipping her head slightly, anticipating the kiss that seemed forthcoming.

"Come over tonight *and* tomorrow," he suggested, then kissed her, adding a brush of his tongue against her upper lip.

"That's two nights of sex."

"No sex tonight. We can get to know each other. Build the anticipation. Talk and make out on the couch. Second base at most."

"I told you, I—"

"Not that kind of conversation," he interrupted, kissing the corner of her mouth. "No stories laden with emotional baggage. We can play a game."

"A game?" Alarm zinged through her. Was he a gamer? "What kind of game?"

He tilted his head, considering. "The foreplay kind. To

make tomorrow night even better."

"Oh." Of course.

"What did you think I meant?"

"You know—the computer kind. I'm not much of a fan."

"Role-playing games don't tempt you?"

Though she didn't want to discuss this arena at all, at the risk of tipping her hand, she needed to know if he gamed. "Which do you play?"

"I don't," he answered, without hesitation. "I prefer real life, with all the slow build it brings."

"You're really into this anticipation thing, aren't you?"

"Absolutely." Finger still hooked in her shirt, his forearm brushed her peaked nipple. She couldn't help the shiver of response and he felt it, his mouth quirking. "It ups my odds of making tomorrow night so fantastic for you that you'll want to come back, again and again."

"And when you get tired of me?" The question popped out of her mouth before she knew it was circling her mind. Not that she carried scars from that shit or anything, oh no. Henry's voice echoed in her head. *I'm just so tired of it all. It's like you can't get over this. You never talk about anything else.* "Never mind—I take that back."

He nearly challenged her on it, that inadvertent dip into revealing something personal. That danger, right there, was why she couldn't afford even sexual intimacy. Seeming to know that, he nodded and let her go. "See you in a couple of hours, Miss Emily."

SHE JOGGED THE rest of the way home, to burn off some of the steam and simmering excitement. Delighted, Anansi romped beside her. Of course she needed to shower. And maybe primp a little. Fox had seen her looking like hell and didn't seem to mind, but she could up her game a bit. The interlude would be a little holiday for her. Maybe he'd relent on the second-base thing and go for full sex tonight.

Men, in her experience, rarely refused that opportunity.

At the house, she gave Anansi a rubdown with the towels kept in the mudroom for exactly that purpose, so he could stay inside while she was gone. Hopefully he wouldn't destroy too much stuff. Like his namesake, his capacity for mischief and general troublemaking knew no bounds, particularly when left behind. Of course, she could count on one hand the number of times since coming to Lyra she'd gone out at night and left him behind.

She showered, using plenty of the orange-blossom body wash her mother had sent last Christmas, and shaved—the primary reason she couldn't have just gone for sex right then. She hadn't shaved her legs in forever and had gotten pretty lazy about the armpits too. Why bother when no one saw you?

Fox had, no doubt about it, likely been with plenty of women. California girls, with their hairless bikini bodies. Patty Kay, down at Likable Locks, offered Brazilian waxes. Em wondered if she should try to get one before tomorrow night. A guy of Fox's ilk might expect that. She'd never had one but the concept did *not* appeal. Oh well, Fox could be disappointed— she'd still get her one night of sex and get her head on straight again.

Just in case, she put on a matching bra and panties—also

courtesy of her mother, who never stopped hoping her daughter would return from Indonesia and hunt for a new husband, a more suitable one this time—and, after an intense debate with herself, jeans and low-cut sweater. Red, to match her eyes, she thought ruefully, and reached for the Visine.

It took a while to put on makeup, too, techniques that had once been second nature now rusty from long disuse. Miraculously none of it had dried up, though the mascara glopped more than it should.

An excellent argument for keeping this to a one-night stand—no need to mail-order fresh makeup. One-point-five night stand, that was.

She considered jewelry, but that sent her for a little spin. All of it pre-dated her new identity and everything seemed to shout of who she'd been before. Maybe only she would know that those pearl earrings were from her debutante ball and the diamonds a wedding gift from Henry. Both corresponded to her carefully sanitized public identity—so much easier to base lies on a framework of truth and unphotoshopped photographs, in case anyone looked too closely—but she'd never worked up the right stories to go with them.

One thing for certain, if she continued the affair with Fox, as curious as he'd proved to be so far, she'd have to tighten up her details. Probably time for that anyway. No getting comfortable. For the time being, she locked the jewelry away again.

Emily of Lyra didn't go for bling anyway.

She'd left her hair down after blowing it dry, meaning to leave it that way, but it made her feel weird. She knew it had gotten really long—she washed it regularly, after all. Still the way it hung heavy down her back, the ends brushing her behind, gave her an oddly vulnerable feeling. She looked more like the idealistic young woman she'd been and the sight bothered cynical Em more than she'd have predicted.

So she brushed it all up into the high ponytail at her crown, feeling more normal, slipped on a pair of black leather boots and headed downstairs to make a quick bite to eat. Dinah took her usual spot on the top of the silver trashcan lid, supervising the dinner prep. Which ended up being a sandwich, because she didn't want to get more elaborate than that. Buzzing with excitement, she felt more jazzed to see a guy than she remembered being since her teens, with all that silly, hopeful expectation. The long privation, no doubt.

"I have a date tonight," she confided to the cat. Between girls, they could admit it was an actual date. "Keep an eye on Anansi, would you? And no getting on the kitchen counter."

Dinah blinked agreeably, eyeing the ham. Em gave her a piece of it and some extra kibble to munch on for a few minutes before she picked it up to keep Anansi out of it. Reflecting that she should have planned better—so rusty—she went back upstairs to brush her teeth and apply a fresh coat of lipstick. She looked okay, she decided. Definitely passable.

And happy.

CHAPTER EIGHT

THE DOORBELL RANG and Fox welcomed the sound with relief. He wouldn't have been surprised if Emily had bailed. She was on the hook but by no means fully reeled in. He even braced himself for disappointment, just in case the person at his door proved to be some neighbor borrowing sugar instead.

Hallelujah, it was her.

Looking delectable too. She had the kind of natural beauty that made her gorgeous in any light, but standing on his porch in a black leather jacket and faded-to-snug jeans, she damn near took his breath away.

"Hi," he said.

"Hi," she said and hesitated.

Apparently she took his brain away too. "Come in, come in." He took her hand, drawing her inside, then, unable to resist, lifted it over her head and spun her in a dancer's twirl. The jeans looked even better from behind. She had washed her hair, but put it back up in the ponytail. He awarded himself a point for pegging that one. Time enough to get her to let it down. Meanwhile, the nape of her neck offered some very kissable spots. "You are one beautiful woman, Miss Emily."

She raised an eyebrow at him and shrugged out of the

leather jacket. "Why do you call me that? Most everyone calls me Em."

He took it from her and hung it up in the hall closet. "At first, because you hadn't said I could call you by your nickname. Some people are funny about that. And now..." He trailed off, wondering how much to reveal.

"And now?" Her red sweater clung to her breasts, not huge but enticingly full and nicely showcased by the low neckline. He allowed himself one look as he turned, before determinedly meeting her eyes.

"Now I kind of like the librarian vibe. Would you punish me if I'm naughty, Miss Emily?"

She kind of half laughed, as if not sure to take him seriously. Hell, he wasn't sure how serious he was.

"Is that what you're into?" she asked, cocking her head. Not offended. Maybe interested.

"There's not much I'm not into. You?"

"Umm." She blushed. He absolutely loved that she could blush. "I might be out of my depth here."

"Not at all." He took her hand again and guided her into the living room. Get her away from the front door, to remove the obvious temptation to run away. "Wine?"

She took in the cheerful fire, the bottle of good red wine. Then gave him that *look,* the one that was rapidly becoming his favorite. "I thought we agreed on no romance."

"This is not romance." He poured wine for both of them and handed her a glass, which she accepted readily enough. "These are basic creature comforts. Though, if you prefer, we could sit out on the deck in the cold rain and be miserable."

Her silvery eyes sparkled but she didn't laugh out loud. "It's not raining."

"Your jacket was damp."

"From the mist."

"I have so much to learn from you." He raised his glass. "To new beginnings."

She didn't love that, but didn't object, clinking her glass against his and sipping. "What's up with the index cards?"

"Those, my sweet, are for our game. Care to sit?"

Perching on the edge of the couch, she slipped a hand between her knees, keeping her fingers curled around the stem of the wineglass. Not entirely at ease. He set a stack of playing cards on the table and placed the pile of inverted sticky notes next to it. After a quick shower and shave, he'd used the rest of his time to prepare those.

"Strip poker?" she asked. "Isn't that a bit prosaic?"

"It would be," he agreed, "though it's a classic for a reason. I'm totally amenable to playing that also, or instead. But if you're thinking of getting me naked so you can take advantage of me, I have to warn you—you're not getting any until tomorrow night."

She frowned at him but relaxed a little. Definitely a good call not to let her rush this. "I do believe you're a tease, Mr. Mullins."

"One of my very favorite things." He shuffled the cards, the way his gambling father taught him. *Half the game is dazzle, son. Sparkle and they don't notice the rest.* "No, we're playing a variation of Go Fish."

"You're kidding." But she snickered and sipped her wine.

"Are we ten years old again?"

"The games of our youth live on. But okay, this will be a more interesting variation. Kind of a blend with Spin the Bottle." He gave her a very serious look. "Which means we're thirteen."

She laughed, not loudly, but with a genuine smile. Relishing the triumph, he grinned back at her. Getting a woman to laugh came second only to getting her to come. Another kind of foreplay.

"The rules are simple." He dealt them each seven cards. "We start the same way as Go Fish, but if I don't have the card you're looking for, you can fish from the deck. *But* if that card doesn't match the card either, you have to draw from the sticky note pile."

"And what's on those?"" She reached for them and he snagged her hand to stop her.

"Ah, ah, ah. They're a surprise."

She narrowed her eyes at him. "But you made them up, which means whatever is on them is slanted in your favor."

"True. Let's add this rule, if you don't like what's on the note—for either of us—then you have the option to make up your own on the spot." He turned her hand over and, watching her reaction, pressed a kiss to the center of her palm. A tremor ran through her, just as when he'd deliberately brushed her nipple on the beach. Such a sensual and responsive woman. He couldn't wait to get her naked. "Ready to play?"

She tugged her hand away, took a sip of her wine, set it on the coffee table and took up her cards. With great amusement, he watched her put them in order. People revealed their characters in ways they never thought about when playing games. "I'm first? Do you have any twos?"

"Go fish."

She drew a card from the deck, wrinkled her nose in disgust and slid it into place in her hand. Then she eyed the pile of sticky notes, sighed a little, and took the top one. "These sticky notes have no sticky."

"I cut them off. Have you ever tried shuffling a stack of sticky notes? It might be the third circle of hell."

She snorted, studying the words on the note. Reining in his impatience to know which question she'd drawn, he waited her out. She glanced up at him. "Really?"

"You can give as much or as little detail as you want to. Or, remember you have the option to make up your own question to answer. That one can go back in the pile."

But she tapped the edge of the stickyless note on her knee, her eyes thoughtful. Possibly mischievous. "I propose a rule change."

"After the game has already started? I don't know." He drank from his own wine and pretended to consider the matter. "What do you propose?"

"We both have to answer the question."

"Done."

She shook her head at him, laughing softly. "You're a terrible negotiator."

"And you're gorgeous. What's the question?"

She read off the note, eyebrows raised at him. "'What's the kinkiest thing you've ever done?'"

Though he'd added the question himself, a spark went

through him. He whistled softly. "Gold standard question, right off the bat. The perils of randomness."

"It's not truly random, though. The order is biased in a number of ways."

"How so?"

"It's not important. So, the person who draws the card answers first, I suppose." She tapped the note again, thinking and looking ever so slightly flushed. The fire, the wine or embarrassment? "I'm boring, I told you. I once had sex in a car. That's probably as kinky as it gets."

He narrowed his eyes at her. "These are supposed to be honest answers."

"Scout's honor! Your turn."

"I don't want to say now."

Her eyes lit with delight. "I think that's a forfeit."

"Make up a question for me then."

"No, no, no." She shook a finger at him. "If one person answers, the other one does too."

"That's not a rule."

"Yes, it is. I just added it." She gave him a taunting smile, clearly enjoying herself, and sipped her wine. "Spill, Fox."

He considered lying, as he suspected she had, not wanting to scare her away so early in the game. Something he hadn't planned for when he thought this up. Digging out more about her had been on his mind, not confessing the depths of his depravity. Of course, "kinkiest" could be subject to interpretation. But he also didn't want to temporize and then later have to admit to having already done something she might be interested in trying.

"I'm beginning to worry," she teased. "Is there a sordid moment with a Taiwanese underaged prostitute in your past?"

"No—never anyone underage. Solid rule with me."

She leaned in, interested. What was she hoping to hear? "But?"

"I'm realizing it's difficult to rate kinkiest with someone who thinks having sex in a car counts as wild behavior."

"Not wild at all. I was young, stupid and didn't even come." She seemed a little surprised to have confided that and sat back again.

"You would have with me."

"Promises, promises."

The way her mouth formed the words made him want to grab her, kiss her and prove it right there.

"You still haven't answered the question. At this rate, we'll be here all night before we run out of cards."

He loved watching her lose that careful guard and enjoy herself. Already the evening was an unqualified success. Now to tempt her without scaring her. "I'm going to pick a ménage."

Her mouth fell open a little. Tantalizingly. "Seriously? Two women at once?"

"One woman and one man." Hopefully it wasn't a mistake, telling her that.

"Wow." She considered it, the wheels of her mind working, visibly decided not to ask for more detail. "Is that something you're really into?"

"I'll answer that if you tell me why you didn't come in the car."

She shrugged one shoulder, reached for her wine. "I don't

always—something for you to keep in mind, with your high expectations—and it was just…meh."

More she wasn't saying there. A sadness, but not a huge one. "I liked the ménage okay, but I prefer one on one," he told her, observing her reaction. "It allows me to focus on my partner. That said, if you'd want to bring in a third, I'd be willing to accommodate you."

That flustered her. "Would be difficult to plan *that* in time for tomorrow night."

"I mean at some point down the road." He deliberately baited her with that. No way would this be a one-night-only deal.

She looked away, setting her glass down again, not replying to that. "A ménage doesn't seem kinky enough to hesitate over."

"Says the woman who insists her wildest exploit was a meh experience in a car."

"Fine, don't tell me."

"I'm not going to." He grinned when she looked surprised. "Not yet. There were other elements, but I think I answered the question."

"Then it's your turn."

"Do you have any Aces?"

"Ha! No, go fish."

He pulled a two from the pile and tucked it in his hand, then studied the sticky note pile, wishing he had not shuffled the damn things.

"Hoist by your own petard?" Emily inquired sweetly.

"Something like that," he muttered and snagged the top

note. "Ah, a nice fastball down the middle. Lost my virginity at 12. You?" He handed her the note as proof.

She made a face. "I hate this game."

"No weaseling out."

"How could you have been 12?" She burst out. "Who does that?"

"I was an early bloomer and didn't know better."

"Thus your solid rule on no underage?"

"That and other reasons. Also no animals. Total ability to consent is paramount. And now I get two more detail questions on your answer."

"Shit!" She thumped her knee. Then covered her mouth with her hand and muttered into it. Still, he heard the answer.

"Twenty-one—really? Were you waiting to be able to have a drink afterwards?"

"Shut up. I was bringing up the median for pervs like you."

"Okay. Obvious follow-up. Why did you wait so long?"

"Lack of opportunity, mostly." She retrieved her glass and tapped her nails on it. They were short and unpainted but neatly shaped. "I just wasn't one of those girls who got asked out much and I never had much reason to do the asking. And your other question? I'm magnanimously not counting the snipe about drinking age, which technically was a question."

He really wanted to ask about her date at that debutante ball. This was the payback for knowing more about people than you were supposed to. "Were you in love?" The question popped out for no clear reason and he wanted to yank it back. Why the hell had he asked her that?

"Oh! I'm sorry. That's a personal, emotional-baggage question which is against the rules." She gave him an arch look. "As your penalty, you must answer a free-form question from our panel of judges."

He held up his hands in surrender. "Fine. Do your worst. But it has to be a sexual history question. Stick to theme."

Narrowing her eyes, she leaned in. Close enough for the scent of wine and warm orange blossoms to shoot through him to tighten his balls. "Why this game, Fox?"

He leaned in, too, pulled her ponytail over her shoulder and stroked his fingers through it. "Because I didn't want this to be over too soon."

"What's with you and the anticipation thing?"

"Is that an extra question?"

"Okay, sure. And to front-load it, I thought I was in love, but I wasn't. There." But she didn't pull back.

"The anticipation thing is about discovery. About the tension and moments like this." He leaned in a bit more and, when she didn't move, indulged in kissing those alluring pink lips, a deeper, sweeter color with the lipstick she wore. This time she opened her mouth for him right away, hot and urgent. She made a little sound, a kind of moan deep in her throat and, for all his talk of anticipation, he wanted nothing more than to push her back on the couch and bury himself in her until that sound became a scream of ecstasy.

Because of that, he broke off the kiss, immeasurably pleased by the flash of frustration on her face.

"I think we should just have sex," she said.

He nearly agreed, more than over the edge at that point.

"Get it over with," she continued. "Purge this lust already."

And that was enough to change his mind. She'd asked about him growing tired of her while she plotted all the while to get away from him as fast as possible.

He kissed her again, a brush of lips, and said, "Your turn."

CHAPTER NINE

Em DIDN'T KNOW whether to laugh, smack him or make a grab for that tantalizing bulge in his jeans and force matters between them.

So, she studied her hand. "Nines."

"You have to ask if I have any," he retorted, eyes alight with desire and fun.

"This isn't Mother May I."

"Do you want to play that next? An erotic version of that game might prove very interesting."

May I suck your cock? The thought flashed into her head and she had to banish it immediately. As if she'd ever say such a thing. She was having fun, to her surprise. Too much fun, because she found herself wanting to tell him true things. Some of these arenas—her virginity, for God's sake—she did not have pre-made details for. She could make up the stories as she went, but that got tangled fast. Fox, she felt pretty sure, would remember a misstep.

"Do you have any nines, Mr. Mullins?" she asked in an arch, formal tone.

With a disgruntled frown, he handed her three and she wiggled in delight. His gaze went straight to her cleavage. Most gratifying. He had enough class to have been taking only surreptitious glances so far. Enjoying the moment, she put her elbow on her knee, pretending to study the cards while she gave him a good view. "Do you have any threes?"

"Go fish." His voice growled the words, making her wonder if he'd wanted to tell her to do something else. The idea excited her. From other hints he'd dropped, she'd thought he'd say something BDSM for the kinkiest stuff. Of course, he thought she'd been a twenty-one-year-old virgin who'd had lousy sex in the back seat of a car as her greatest excursion from vanilla. She'd bet that the "extra" aspect of that ménage had involved far more.

She drew a king, to match one other in her hand and, sitting up and preparing herself, picked another note. *How many vibrators do you own?* The prim persona would say none, but she was an adult woman, living alone, who'd already admitted to a long, dry spell. Who would believe that? She glanced at Fox through her eyelashes. As he had through the whole game, he was studying her intently, paying attention to every reaction. He noticed far too much. A dangerous guy for her to be around. But also like a plate of fresh cookies. She couldn't stop now that she'd tasted him. She'd eat the whole thing, tonight and tomorrow, and then be done.

"Two," she said and handed him the note.

He glanced at it, gave her a sly look. "Seven."

"What?" What guy owned seven vibrators?

He raised his eyebrows, daring her to open the door to more questions. When she didn't, he smiled. "Do you have any fives?"

She didn't and he ended up drawing another non-sticky

note. He shook his head at it. "This one is going to kill me." He handed it to her.

Seven minutes in heaven.

She laughed, unable to help herself. "Why did you put it in there then?"

He scowled. "I obviously wasn't thinking clearly. We can ditch it and draw another."

"No, no, no. For the full thirteen-year-old experience, I want my seven minutes in heaven. I never did that." Which was true. Her mother would never have let her attend a party with boys present. By the time she got old enough, they were all formal dates and society parties. No closets in sight. "So, the front hall closet?"

His brown eyes glittered. "Well, the walk-in closet in the bedroom is bigger."

She shook her head. "No, for verisimilitude it should be something small, cramped and full of someone else's junk."

"I thought you never played before."

"I did have friends. Girls talk." She stood up and held out a hand. "Come on. I have a condom in my pocket. You'll be perfectly safe."

He took her hand, stood and kissed her, harder this time, with more urgency. Very promising. Then he smiled. "We won't need it because I'm not having sex with you yet."

"We'll see." She might not be the player he was, but she knew turned on when she saw it. He had no real reason to hold back. Past a certain point, he wouldn't want to anymore.

The hall closet wasn't tiny, but it felt smaller when they both crowded in, pushing the jackets—and Joe Kapsuck's fishing gear—to the side. Fox pulled the door shut, plunging them in darkness and the smell of damp leather. He bumped into her and she giggled. An actual, girly giggle. His hands found her hips, sliding under her sweater and electrifying her skin. The giggly feeling evaporated instantly, a drop of water hissing on a hot stove, turning to steam. She gripped his forearms, suddenly unsure.

"Now what?" She whispered, as if there were a roomful of their friends outside the closet doors, listening. His fingers flexed on her waist, digging into her flesh and pulling her against his hips. His upthrust cock pressed into her belly through their jeans and she gasped. In the dark, he seemed different, both less familiar and more so. She smelled mostly him, his spicy aftershave, soap and his own scent.

He didn't answer her—dumb question, after all—but his lips brushed her cheek. Turning her head, she found his mouth with hers, twining her hands up and around his neck. He started with softer nibbles, gentle pulls on her lips that grew hungrier, until he was kissing her harder, their tongues tangling together while his hands slid up her back.

Her focus narrowed to the connection between their mouths, learning his taste and feel, losing herself in the moment. She could be anyone. Maybe that thirteen-year-old girl, going in the closet with that cute boy she saw in the elevator sometimes. She abandoned herself to the kiss, to being kissed. To his hands running over her skin, a profound human contact she realized she'd missed. Her thirst, drinking in the touch like a dried-up sponge, proved it.

Her bra gave way, a loosening of tension, and then his

hands were on her breasts. She cried out against his mouth at the intensity of it, rubbing her pelvis against his, her pussy wet and aching. He squeezed her breasts, tweaking her nipples and then massaging them. Shifting his hips, he moved so his thigh pressed between hers, so she opened her legs, straddling it, nearly exploding as the pressure pushed the seam of her jeans against her clit.

Mewling incoherently, she rocked herself on his hard thigh, nearly mindless with need. He turned her, pressing her against the closet wall, working his thigh between hers and rolling her nipples in a matching rhythm. Releasing her mouth, he fastened on her neck, sucking the tender skin so it became one more blazing point of driving arousal.

It hit her that she would come this way, in the dark with this man she barely knew. The thought both excited her and knocked her off balance. This wasn't how it should be. She'd never orgasmed without the guy getting off at the same time— or before. Determined not to be alone in her extremity and maybe seeking a bit of payback, she dropped her hands down his impressively cut chest, the ridges palpable through his dress shirt, and grasped his erection through his jeans.

"Oh no, you don't," he muttered and abandoned her breasts to grab her wrists in a firm grip, moving them apart and then over her head, pinning them to the wall. She resisted, reflexively, confused and aroused by the move. He kissed her, slowing his movements and rubbing sinuously against her. Her bra had ridden up and the sweater, so soft and cuddly before, chafed her taut nipples. He seemed to know it, too, deliberately pressing his chest against her, moving up his muscled thigh so she nearly rode it, the orgasm building beyond control.

She struggled a little against his grip. Impossibly, it excited her more and she whimpered.

"Are you okay?" he whispered in her ear, voice thick with desire. For some unknown reason, it catapulted her over the edge.

"Oh God!" she cried out, peripherally aware of his satisfied chuckle, while her body convulsed with the climax, the power of it wrenching through her, as if she hadn't orgasmed at all in years, instead of just with another person.

She gripped his thigh between hers, rolling with the climax, her nipples burning, her mouth seeking and finding his, anchoring herself to his body as she rode it out, helpless to do more than that.

At last the grip of it faded, though she still felt impossibly aroused. She wanted—no, absolutely needed—to have him inside her. Breaking the kiss, she turned her head, gasping, the movement driving her stimulated nipples against her sweater and his body. She twisted at her wrists, but he didn't soften his grip, so she arched her spine, pressing her pelvis against his as close as she could manage.

"Come on, Fox," she urged to the man in the dark. "Fuck me. You can't say you don't want to."

He laughed, more of a hoarse breath, as if the sound had trouble escaping him. Nibbling at her neck, he moved his thigh, making an appreciative sound when she squirmed against him. "I want nothing more at this moment. I want to strip you out of those tight jeans and feel how hot and wet you are. Then I'd bite your nipples and listen to you make those delightful sounds of pleasure. Once you were naked except for those gorgeous boots, I'd bend you over the back of the Kapsucks' couch and pound your sweet pussy until you scream."

"Oh yes." She wriggled, fought to free herself. "Please. Now."

"No." He bit her neck, the penetrating sensation on top of the rest making her sob out a sound of pure need. "Not until tomorrow night."

"You are unbelievable." She nearly screeched it, in her frustration.

"Told you." He sounded smug.

"We're not leaving this closet then."

"What an enticing thought." He shifted his grip so he held both her wrists in one hand, reaching under her sweater to cup her breast and run his thumb over her sensitized nipple. It burned like fire. He drove her crazy as nothing else. "Shall I strip you and keep you in here? I'd tie your wrists to the coat rack and let you simmer, waiting for me. Every once in a while—maybe when I needed my jacket—I'd stop by and play with you for a while."

She knocked her head against the wall, trying to snap herself out of this erotic spell he dragged over her mind. "Oh my God," she breathed, wriggling helplessly against him, "you're driving me crazy."

"Good," he purred. "Exactly where I want you. Me too. And, on that note—" His hand left her breast and the closet door opened, bathing them in startlingly bright light after the cozy darkness. She squinched up her eyes, blinking them, aware that he'd released her wrists and let her slide down his thigh so she stood on her own feet again. She swayed a little, dizzy, and he cupped the back of her neck with a warm hand, kissing her softly and drawing her into the foyer. "Sorry," he added, "a bit of an abrupt landing there. Are you okay?"

The question, the same one he'd asked that shot her straight into orgasm, went right through her. She blushed fast and furiously, her face blazing. Pressing her hands to her cheeks, she looked away from him, then at her leather jacket hanging there. Reaching behind her, she scrambled for her bra straps, tugging them down from where they'd ridden up nearly to her neck.

"Let me help you." Fox reached for her, but dropped his hands when she shook her head furiously. Strands of hair whipped her cheek—her ponytail had to be in total disarray. She tried to neaten it and gave up immediately, grabbing her jacket instead and shrugging it on.

"I should go," she said, unnecessarily, but feeling his wary silence.

"What went wrong?" he asked in a quiet tone. "Don't run, Emily. Talk to me."

"I'm just—" She risked a glance at him, full of a fury that seemed to have come from nowhere. "I can't right now. I need to go, okay?"

He held up his palms, demonstrating that he wouldn't stop her, looking a bit like a man stepping back from a bomb he'd thought was a briefcase. "But I'll see you tomorrow night still." He didn't pose it as a question, but as a certainty.

"I don't know. Maybe. Probably not."

"Emily—"

"No. We're not discussing this. I told you that from the start. If I come over tomorrow night—" she held up a hand when he opened his mouth, "—*if* I do, then it will be for sex. Just fucking, as you promised but have not delivered. No more games, understand?"

Pressing his lips together, his eyes full of unsaid words, he nodded. She turned her back on him and escaped out the door.

CHAPTER TEN

THE DOOR SHUT behind her with a gunshot click to his heart. He stared at its blank, uninteresting surface for a moment, giving the sexual haze a chance to clear so he could think again.

"Fuck me!" he shouted at it, beyond pissed, at himself, at her. Whatever. What the hell had gone wrong? For that matter, what the hell had possessed him to say all that stuff to her? She'd loved him restraining her and the way she'd struggled in his grip so sweetly, so obviously turned on by it, had made him lose his head. He'd lost himself in his own fantasy and possibly scared her off permanently. If that was what had happened. She'd been fine until he opened the closet door.

"Way to go, *Sparky,*" he growled at himself. Not so full of sparkle tonight. He stalked into the living room to glare at the detritus of their game. Seizing her half-empty glass, he downed the rest of it, his cock so hard it hurt. He'd nearly blown right then when she'd wrapped those delicate but fiercely strong fingers around it.

He wanted her insanely. No doubt because of the chase. He knew himself at least that well. It had taken massive restraint not to have her right there in the closet. But no— heady with power, bowled over by the way she'd come under his hands, so completely without reserve and with an almost naïve intensity—he'd had to have more. No, it wasn't enough for him just to have sex with her, as she'd repeatedly said she wanted. As always, he had to hold out for the brass ring, the grand fucking prize. The Powerball Lottery he never let himself play in real life.

And now maybe he'd blown it with her completely.

One thing was certain, he wouldn't have another clear thought until he rid himself of the painful hard-on, and this one would definitely not subside on its own. Unbuttoning his jeans to give himself some fucking room already, he headed for the bedroom and grabbed some lube and a washcloth from the nightstand.

"Yeah, you dipshit. Look what you brought on yourself." Too pumped to sit, he went to the sliding glass doors that led to the room's balcony. Its low wall would screen him from anyone on the beach, if anyone was out there. He entertained the fantasy that Emily was lurking out there, watching the house, looking for him. Maybe she hadn't gone home, but waited out there for him. Would she see him in the window?

He pushed his jeans midway down his thighs, blowing out an explosive breath as blood flow resumed to the compressed tissues. Greasing up his hand, he propped his forearm on the cool glass, leaning his head against it and staring out into the night, imagining Emily observing as he worked his cock with savage fury.

Within moments, his balls clenched and he came, spurting onto the glass door before he had a chance to grab the washcloth, as if he had, in fact, regressed to his thirteen-year-old self, with all the lack of finesse and control, not to mention the bumbling stupidity, that had entailed.

He leaned there a moment longer, stroking out the last of the after-climax, trying to relax and let go. The fact that his bracing arm ached with tension, his fist tightly clenched, indicated that wasn't happening any time soon. Jerking off might have momentarily relieved his cock, but he still boiled with frustration. Enough that he considered going down to Emily's house and making her talk to him. Or tearing her clothes off and burying himself in her long, lean body until neither of them could walk.

Worst idea ever.

In the morning, he'd reevaluate. Maybe things would make more sense then. Could be that Emily was one of those messed-up types who thought they wanted sex and then freaked about it. If so, he'd get over her. Lots of fish in the sea and he'd only known her for a couple of days, for chrissakes. If he never laid eyes or hands on her again, he'd live and go on to find lovers who weren't neurotic.

His breathing had leveled and he no longer felt like punching something, so he cleaned up his come from the glass and the awful powder blue plush carpet. In the morning he'd have to revisit it with some soap and cold water, to make sure he didn't leave a stain on his landlord's ugly rug. As much as he was coming to despise the place, it wasn't worth blowing the security deposit on it. *Geek Crunch* wouldn't pay that bill. He could cover it if he had to, but one come-stain from a disastrous date would not be worth it.

And he didn't care what Emily said—it had been a fucking

date.

Just without the fucking.

At least able to laugh at himself a little now, but knowing he wouldn't sleep anytime soon, he headed into the spare bedroom office and booted up the computer. He'd burn some energy stalking Phoenix through the forums. If he was in luck—unlikely, given his record so far that night—the gamer might be online. He would not, absolutely not, give in to the urge to study Emily's records any further. Whatever had spooked her so badly wouldn't be in there anyway.

No, she had that buried in the depth of her cagey brain. She was smart—a hell of a lot smarter than she liked to let on. Possibly a pathological liar? It would explain a great deal.

While the laptop revved and the obscenely slow internet connection considered giving up the goods, Fox stalked into the living room and grabbed the wine bottle and his own drained glass. Fuck Emily and her skittish ways. If he couldn't run her to ground, then he'd spend the energy on Phoenix, what he'd come here for, he reminded himself. Bag the great white whale of tech journalism and go on to fame, fortune and glory.

At least a decent payoff, a lovely zing for the portfolio and maybe a gig investigating for CNN or something. And easier lays.

Settling into his familiar routine, he began clicking through the forums, looking for traces that his quarry had passed through recently. As he did, he mused over Phoenix's access. If the guy lived on Lyra or one of the nearby private islands—a distinct possibility—then he'd need a better internet connection than the Kapsucks had. Something much more robust. He made a note to chase down the available options, though Phoenix wouldn't be using the standard residential package. His NSA buddy had clammed up on the particulars. No, Phoenix would have set up something in particular, which likely would have required someone to lay a cable or install the satellite dish or what have you.

Not Fox's area of expertise, but he'd find out.

And, oh look—Phoenix had just passed through the Labyrinth forum, leaving a blazing trail of withering remarks in his path. Fox reviewed the threads, though this wouldn't be the juicy stuff. Some gamer tried to call out the last module as lame and Phoenix had waded through the thread, laying waste to dissenters with incisive arguments. Fox found himself chuckling out loud at some of the insults—a few so veiled the recipients wouldn't know they were fatally wounded for hours.

That was the rub, really. Fox had been chasing Phoenix for years, not only because unmasking him would be the reveal of the century, particularly those the guy regularly annoyed with both his caustic attitude and gaming genius, but because the guy fascinated him. Fox had first run across Labyrinth a little over two years ago. The game had rocketed to the top in popularity, not least because of the mystery surrounding the designer. Jacker milked the hype for all it was worth, implying that anyone from an AI to aliens had created the thing.

Phoenix himself played the tease well, which became clear as soon as Fox checked out the fan forums. The guy oozed brilliance, and Fox liked to think they'd see eye to eye on a lot of stuff. Not that they'd be having a friendly beer once he'd blown Phoenix's true identity.

Unless the guy appreciated that it had all been about the game. Which was possible. Hell, Phoenix had practically set up the scavenger hunt and thrown out the dare. *Find me if you can.*

No one had.

Well, Fox could and he would. He could taste it.

He logged out and logged back in with the new alternate identity that let him into the private chat rooms. No sign of Phoenix—at least under that ID—but Fox could wait.

He was very good at anticipation.

EM WOULD HAVE run home, except that the stupid boots she'd worn had the wrong heel for it. What the hell had she been thinking, dressing up for him and playing that flirtatious game? As usual, she'd come away feeling like she'd bungled it. Loser.

Her face burned still, the cold rain chill against her skin, stinging little pelts that hinted of ice. Her slick sole skidded and she slowed her furious pace. Her body throbbed with arousal—in an unreal way. The lacy bra scratched her nipples, her breasts ached and her jeans, totally drenched, rubbed against her swollen clit as she walked. Even her heart pounded still, the blood thudding through her nerves, everything alight.

As if Fox had set her on fire with a few kisses and some heavy petting.

Inside, she churned. Humiliation? Maybe. Anger, yes, but no idea why. Oddly, she felt like she wanted to cry, as if some forlorn part of her had been carelessly injured and she'd just now noticed the blood.

None of it made any sense.

Even more bizarre, she had this impulse to call her mother, who she rarely spoke to, telling her that telephone calls from Indonesia cost too much and why bother when they could chat on the internet? It wasn't as if her perfectly cool and correct mother would have any advice, even if Emily could think how to frame the question. If she even had a question.

Hi, Mom—I went on a date with this guy, only it wasn't supposed to be a date, because he said it would be just fucking. But then it wasn't only that and then I had the best orgasm of my entire life, while he held off, and then he asked me if I was okay and I turned into a neurotic puddle.

Not the sort of letter you saw in Dear Abby.

She could maybe talk to Glory, but they'd never confided in each other that way. Em really detested women who only called up their friends when they had shit to spill anyway. Besides, it wouldn't be fair to tell Glory about how much Fox had turned her on and how she'd bolted like the frightened virgin she hadn't been since she was an adolescent.

Was that it—fear?

But of what, was the question.

With a sigh of relief, she let herself in the front door of her quiet home, her retreat, and sat on the bench to take off her boots. It seemed as if she'd been living in some kind of cocoon, working and interacting with people only virtually. She'd been, if not exactly happy, at least peaceful and content. Somehow the episode—she liked that term for it, nice and clinical-sounding—with Fox had upset that peace. With his knowing grin, intrusively sexual vibe and mind-shattering skills, he'd simply been too much for her.

Like an overloaded circuit, she'd blown. That was all it was.

Satisfied with that explanation and feeling better about it all, she hung up her jacket—*not* thinking about the Kapsucks' hall closet. Jesus she'd never be able to go to another summer barbeque there again—and headed to the kitchen to make a pot of coffee.

And stepped on dog vomit.

She'd been gone barely two hours and Anansi had managed to not only unsnap and upend the kitchen garbage, but chew up most of it and then puke it up again. The dog himself lay flat on the floor, looking repentant, miserable...and like he'd be sick again at any moment. That odd rage flared up again and, rather than risk being unreasonably mean to him, she booted Anansi outside, turned her back on the kitchen and went to her computer.

She would deal with the mess later.

Once she felt calmer.

Saturday night and the forums foamed with all the sexual repression of the home-alone gamer geek world. Not that she cast aspersions—they obviously were her tribe. Her mistake had been forgetting that for any length of time. Dates with overwhelmingly sexy men were not part of her world. Some of her favorite Neanderthals had been stinking up the place, so she let loose some of her savage frustration on their stupid complaints.

She never directly addressed the blatantly misogynistic shit, for fear of outing herself. Phoenix had a rep among the female gamers as fair-minded and one of the few programmers who built more into "his" female characters than the Fighting Fuck

Toy trope. Some of the guys played as her women, too, which she took as a compliment. As much as she itched to, however, she resisted picking up the torch against the trolls who bashed anything they perceived as impinging on their white male gamer privilege.

And she'd never tried anything as bold as Amazonia again. Not just for fear of tripping the legal system.

She'd tried fighting them head-on before and look what happened.

Instead, she worked on multiple levels within the communities. After Phoenix visited his righteous fury on the biggest lunkheads, she logged out and came back as one of her several avatars, both male and female. As those people, she lent support to the various women leading movements to make gaming more welcoming to everyone. Several of them had appealed to Phoenix to weigh in on their causes. Being the general asshole he could be, he'd turned them down, succinctly and without apology.

They never knew she circled around and did what she could, shoring them up here, defending them from attack there. Checking in on her favorite Kickstarter, led by a very smart gal who'd withstood a firestorm of shit for her project to evaluate the female tropes in video games, Em reviewed the latest reports and made some notes for the new module.

She'd always work the counter-culture angle where she could.

More settled and clear-headed now—and kind of regretting procrastinating on the kitchen mess, but oh well—she switched to an identity known only to a few trusted friends and checked out her favorite private chat rooms.

As soon as she entered one, BikerBoi flagged her down for a one-on-one. Well, he flagged Phoenix, knowing her current face was one of Phoenix's covers.

> **BikerBoi:** *Dude. Word to the wise. Heard a reporter is after U.*
>
> **X:** *They always are*
>
> **BikerBoi:** *This one got to Moondog*
>
> **X:** *Fuck 'em both*
>
> **BikerBoi:** *No lie. Word is he's been asking about access to this room*
>
> **X:** *Then we burn it down.*
>
> **BikerBoi:** *Roger that. Will ping with new deets.*
>
> **X:** *Thx*

With amusement, she watched the interface shrivel at the edges and burst into flame graphics, reminiscent of Phoenix's logo. BikerBoi had a flare for the dramatic and had clearly planned to burn the room as soon as he got Phoenix's okay. Words in crimson font, dripping drops of blood, appeared on the screen.

PIGS GO HOME

She shook her head. Brilliant with graphics but, with English as at least his second language, the slang sometimes escaped him. What did one call a journalist anyway when you wanted to piss them off?

So much for procrastinating that way. Resigned, she went to let the prodigal dog in, clean up the god-awful mess and maybe work a few hours on the new module. At least she could justify the evening with Fox that way—she felt full of energy to create. Leave a little something for her team to chew on when they showed up for work in the morning, as some of them undoubtedly would, even on a Sunday, logging in from home.

One thing about the night's debacle—she had an idea.

CHAPTER ELEVEN

F OX WOKE UP with a wicked hangover and a bad taste in his mouth. Not only from hitting the bottle of Jameson after he polished off the wine, either.

After he'd made it into the private chat room, he'd barely nosed around before they burned it. Pissed him off no end. He hadn't even said anything, but they'd seen him coming and had been tipped off, obviously. Phoenix never had returned to any of the forums, at least not as himself.

Calling the whole night a complete and utter loss, Fox proceeded to finish the whiskey, which at least suppressed the urge to jack off again, this time to the fresh fantasy of paddling Emily's ass while she wept and wriggled, with her dressed only in those fancy black boots with the suggestive gold chains.

Not thinking about her, Sparky, remember?

Nevertheless, when he decided to work out the toxins in his system with a run on the beach, he found his feet turning in the direction of her house. So what? Public beach and all. Maybe she'd be up and he'd say hi or something. Her house, however, looked dark. No welcoming lights. He couldn't see if Anansi lurked in the garden behind the trees without going up the boardwalk a ways. Which Emily would not appreciate.

Perversely, he really wanted to, just to tweak her out-of-joint nose a little.

Okay, he was still pretty pissed.

And hot as hell for her.

Besides, who was he kidding? She wouldn't be coming over that night or any night the way they'd left things. Not as if he could blow it any worse with her than he already had. So, he did what he always did when in doubt, he followed his instinct and went up the boardwalk. If nothing else, he'd please himself. God knows there was no pleasing *her.*

The garden stood empty, the gate closed. He'd thought she normally awoke early and went running, but it looked like she might be sleeping still.

Or not there.

With a strange pang, he entertained the possibility that she'd been so determined to ditch him that she'd packed up and left. No, she wouldn't do that, if only because she wouldn't want to expose herself that way.

She was in there all right.

He went up the steps to the deck and knocked on the glass door, with sharp, loud raps. That would wake her up.

Sure enough Anansi came clicking across the floor, tongue lolling in doggie delight, which he then swiped across the glass—as he'd done many times before, judging by the smears.

"Hey, buddy," Fox said, tempted to try the door handle. Restrained himself. A hundred to one she had it locked and bolted anyway. Anansi woofed and glanced over his shoulder.

Emily appeared in a bathrobe that had seen better days, her hair falling around her in a glorious dark tumble, her face soft with sleep. She blinked at him and irritation crept through, burning the drowsiness away. He was so damn gone over her that he wanted to laugh at the sight. Instead he grinned and waved.

She flipped him off and turned away. He rapped on the glass again.

With a seriously mean look, she spun around and strode to the door, unlocking the handle and at least two internal bolts. Point for him. She yanked it open, Anansi pushing past her to charge down the steps, tail high, and stepped through, closing it behind her. She was barefoot and her toenails were painted bubblegum pink, a detail that bemused him.

"What?" she snapped, folding her arms.

"Good morning to you too."

"Fuck off, Fox. I told you to leave me alone."

"I'm out for a run. It's supposed to pour later, so this might be the best window of opportunity."

"Thanks for the update. Shall I alert the media?"

She looked gorgeous, both disheveled and pissed. Was she wearing anything under the robe? He bet not. "Let me guess— you're one of those people who stay mean until they've had their morning coffee."

"And you're Mr. Bright Eyed and Bushy Tailed."

He wished. "Actually, I have a serious hangover. Drank too much whiskey after you bailed on me last night."

"I'm not talking about that."

"You don't have to. I am. Anyway, I'm hoping the run will burn off some of the haze."

"Not interested."

"I didn't ask. I thought Anansi might want to go with me." He nearly laughed at the look on her face, the beat of misstep.

"You want a play date with my dog?" Her voice had lost some of its edge and she looked past him to where Anansi sniffed around and renewed pee markings. Something about her expression seemed forlorn. Not nearly as tough as she liked to make out.

"No, Miss Emily." He waited until she looked back at him, her gray eyes the same color as the fog. "I want to play with you."

He filled the words with all desire he'd built up, picturing her in the various scenarios he'd imagined even though he wasn't supposed to be thinking about her. She flushed a little, the color pinking her cheekbones, and she looked down, a thrillingly submissive gesture that he felt sure she didn't intend. But he saved the image to add to one of the fantasies.

God knew that might be all he'd get out of her.

"If I wasn't under suspension from the game," he added, "I'd say how about you come running with me and I'll take you out for coffee and Sunday breakfast after."

She looked up at that, narrowing her eyes and unwinding one of her defensively folded arms to point at him. "That would be against the rules, regardless of all else, as it would be a date."

"Oh, come on—what do you call last night?"

"A disaster." Clearly pleased with herself for scoring the point, she unfolded more, pushing her hair over her shoulders.

"Though it was pretty awesome for a while there," he said with a smile she had to fight herself not to return. "I've been thinking," he continued, a lie, but he needed to get through to her somehow before she thought up a way to shut him down again, "that maybe our basic premise sabotaged the evening."

She tilted her head a little. Waited, curling her toes against the damp deck. Probably feeling chilly, which meant he didn't have much more time.

"See, we set it up to be just fucking. That part worked great—"

"Even though we never got to that part."

"True enough, but I think it's good we didn't or maybe you wouldn't be speaking to me at all this morning."

"I don't want to be speaking to you, in point of fact, but I can't have you standing on my deck all day, banging on the glass and scaring Dinah."

"Dinah?"

"My cat. Currently hiding under the bed."

"Alice's cat in *Alice in Wonderland*."

She yawned, deliberately. "Is this conversation going any-where? Since you rudely awakened me, I want my coffee now."

"You could invite me in and we could talk over that cof-fee—sounds wonderful."

"No. Finish your point and go away."

At least she wanted to hear it. Or would, anyway. He took a breath and wished he could risk touching her. This would be easier to say that way. "I think you ran because you don't really know me yet. After that amazing orgasm in the closet, you felt exposed and vulnerable, especially when I dragged you into the light, and you realized that you'd opened yourself to a stranger. It scared you and you shut down."

She rolled her eyes, miming contempt for the psychobab-ble, but drew the tangled mess of her hair over her shoulder and twisted it into a rope that she worked with her fingers.

"So, I think we should try being friends," he threw out

there, winging his way through this. "Starting with breakfast."

Giving him an owlish stare, she snorted. "You just want to be friends now."

"No," he contradicted her with a cheerful smile. "I still want to have you sexually in every way imaginable, but I think we should be friends first."

"And I still don't want to have the emotional-baggage conversations. I'm very uncomfortable having this one."

But she'd stayed it through and she hadn't said no to the new plan.

"You don't have to—the point is for you to get to know me. To trust me."

"I can think of about ninety-seven smart remarks to make to that one."

"And yet you didn't say any of them. How kind of you."

She made that snorting sound again, but actually smiled. "You'd be a fool to think I'm kind. I'm really not a nice person, Fox. I know that much about myself."

Ooh, a clue. That had been truth, right there. Definitely progress. "I don't need kindness, Miss Emily. I have a yen for cruel lovers too."

"Something tells me there's not much you don't have a yen for."

"An excellent observation. At this moment my yen is all about this beautiful, long-legged woman who's going to have breakfast with me."

She shook her head, sighed dramatically, but a small smile curved her pink lips. "After a run. Stay there and I'll be right out."

CHAPTER TWELVE

S HE LOCKED THE door behind her, since Fox couldn't be trusted not to come in uninvited. He'd surprised her, showing up on the deck. What really got her was that the sound of his knocking had dragged her out of such a lovely dream that she'd drifted downstairs in a lingering haze of happiness, without once giving an alarmed thought to who might have found her.

Almost as if the past four years hadn't happened. Unsettling.

Dressing quickly in her running clothes—the man knew how to tempt her, since she itched to get out there, stretch her limbs and work up a sweat—she decided to put it down to the dream's aftereffects. She'd been younger in her dream, carefree and full of hope, dancing through a field of poppies, their color an intense scarlet. Who knew what it meant.

She'd worked most of the night, so she could afford to play for a few hours. Who needed sleep?

Fox waited on the deck, sitting on the steps, scratching Anansi's ears. They both stood when they heard her, Fox giving her that easy smile of sensual appreciation that never failed to make her toes curl, even when she thought she was mad at him.

One of the good things about him—he didn't have to talk

all the time. They made their way to the beach and started in with an easy pace, in the other direction from his place, in a silence that felt nearly companionable. It gave her the head space to mull over his theory, even though she was still wading through a pool of scalding embarrassment. The way she'd reacted—both in and out of the closet, and how was that for a metaphor?—ultimately baffled her. She'd never been given to a ton of introspection, and the past few years of making up lies about even her most basic likes had created a kind of shadow over what she understood of herself.

One of the levels in Labyrinth used a magic mirror as a portal. Characters had to face themselves in it. Sometimes the mirror showed a simple reflection, sometimes it lied, other times it might offer them a truth, a clue to improving their power in a flawed area. She'd drawn that, of course, from any number of story tropes and it proved a popular feature. An entire forum had been created to track iterations of what the mirror showed and for players to debate its properties—with the ones who insisted that it worked off a random number generator and others pointing to evidence that a complex algorithm factored in.

It was some of both, but no one needed to know that.

Last night, as she'd worked up the new concept, she'd played around with the mirror, taking her test avatar through it. With her head in that creative space, the thought occurred to her that she didn't know who she'd see in the mirror, if she created a character with her personality. Because, whose personality would she use? Phoenix? Em? Emily? Silar?

Certainly not stupid, naïve Lisa White, who had ceased to

exist to most of the world. Who deserved to be dead, according to most opinions, including her own.

She also couldn't avoid the simple truth that Fox had inspired her. Working his spin-the-bottle question game into the new module—including a variation on Seven Minutes in Heaven—had brought a sense of fun she hadn't experienced in a while. Along with that special rush of creating good stuff, she'd begun kicking herself for blowing it with Fox.

And had been contemplating whether she could show up on his doorstep with her tail between her legs. He'd saved her that particular walk of shame by showing up with his sexy smiles and teasing ways.

"Something funny?" He slanted her one of those exact smiles. *Hiddleston, eat your heart out.*

"Run feels good." She let herself smile at him. "I'm glad you talked me into it."

"Damn, and me without a pen to write that on the calendar."

"Whatever."

"Isn't that the ferry dock up ahead?" He nodded his head in that direction.

"Yeah. The island is kind of deceptive. The way the beach curves around, it's a much shorter distance to town than taking the road around."

"Let's run to breakfast then?"

"And after?"

"Walk back. Work off the enormous pile of pancakes I intend to eat."

"I'll be all sweaty." No makeup. Hair in a very untidy,

hasty ponytail. Not like she didn't go to town that way all the time anyway, but—"

"So will I." He tossed an appreciative look her way. "And you'll look gorgeous across the table from me, all bright-eyed and bushy-tailed. Shit! I didn't bring money though."

"That's all right, I did."

"Really?" He glanced over with curiosity. "In case you need to indulge your shopping addiction?"

Because she always carried money. Cash, alternate ID, credit cards in two different names. In case she had to disappear fast. Not something normal people did, right?

"That's right. You never know when you'll see a sparkly you simply can't live without."

He snorted, as if he spotted the lie. "Well, this is my idea, so I'll pay you back."

FOX SNAGGED THE two-top in the window bay. They'd made it barely in time, the mist becoming a drizzle that condensed into an earnest rain by the time they reached the Sunshine Café—an ironic name, if there ever was one. Anansi curled up under the bench out front, out of the rain but where he could keep an eye on everyone coming and going. Always looking out for her safety.

"You need to invest in some Gore-Tex," she told him, as he struggled out of his soaked sweatshirt. It caught at his T-shirt beneath, raising the hem to expose his amazing abs. Her mouth nearly watered at the sight, and more than one woman in the busy café stared. A new experience for her, being seen with a guy this attractive—one interested in her, if only for the sex. In some ways, that was better. Because he had no idea who she really was, the power she wielded, albeit in her circumscribed realm, when he said he wanted her, it must be true.

Better, he seemed willing to put up with her emotional handicaps to get there.

He got the sweatshirt off, hung it on the back of his chair and tugged the shirt down, frowning at her. "Real men don't wear raincoats."

She rolled her eyes at him. "They do if they don't want hypothermia, California boy. It might be fifty degrees out, but if you get wet, that's more than enough to lower your core temperature enough to kill you. Happens all the time. To tourists."

He seized her hand and kissed it, glancing slyly up at her. "I'd rather get *you* wet."

"Don't start with me." She yanked her hand away.

"We already did start. Do you need reminding? Yesterday, on the beach, you—"

"Stop it," she hissed at him, but laughed at his outrageousness.

He looked enormously pleased. "I made you laugh."

"I laugh all the time."

Shaking his head, he perused the laminated menu. "Not true. You have that little breathy chuckle, a definite girly giggle and the snorting sound, but you only rarely laugh in that all-out way. Beautiful sound, like bells on Christmas morning."

"Oh brother. This is what I get for dating a writer."

He raised an eyebrow. "We're dating?"

"Well, since we're not doing the just…other thing." She

glanced at the elderly couple eating in companionable silence barely an arm's length away.

"I dare you to say it."

"Not in here!"

"Yes, here. Hurry, Betty White is headed our way with a coffeepot the size of China."

She laughed, then covered her mouth, self-conscious of it now.

"Coffee?" Penny Waters set down the white mugs, yellowed inside from years of use, and began pouring before they answered. "Hey there, Em. I already told Charlie to put in your usual. You know what you want?" She pinned Fox with the look she reserved for strangers. If Penny could, she'd eliminate menus altogether and serve people what they always ordered.

"Tall stack. Two—no, three eggs, over easy. Home fries. And a side of ham."

Penny sniffed with a bit of approval. She liked the hearty eaters. "Biscuits or toast?"

"You got sausage gravy for those biscuits?"

"Of course." And Penny smiled at him. A day for the calendar for sure.

"Sign me up."

Penny bustled off happily and Fox threw a mock-frightened look after her. "She's scary. What if I wanted decaf?"

"In the Pacific Northwest? You'd be shipped out on the next ferry."

"Seriously? They don't make it at all?"

"Well, Penny might serve it to you if you brought in a doctor's note for high blood pressure or something. But then she'd take away your biscuits and gravy."

"A high price to pay."

"Indeed."

A silence fell between them, awkward and not so companionable. Finished with the business of prepping her coffee, she had run out of things to do with her hands. She sipped, making herself enjoy it the way everyone thought Em liked it. Looked out at the rain, pounding in earnest now, so that the drops bounced up again from the pavement like a watery flea circus.

"This is the part where you ask me questions about myself." Fox leaned on the little table, the coppery hairs on his forearms a brighter version of his tan.

"Oh." What did people ask? More important, what would Emily want to know? Her carefully trained society self would know all the correct, socially easy conversational gambits—though not many people here knew her current identity claimed that background—but after years of keeping to herself, she might wonder different things. If she'd known she'd be put on the spot this way, she could have brainstormed some questions. She sipped from her coffee, added more sugar, even though it was so sweet already it hurt her teeth. "Let's see," she said, to stall.

Fox's lips twitched. "As fascinating as it is to watch you struggle to dredge up some curiosity about me, maybe I should offer some topics. You could choose a category, like in *Jeopardy*."

"It's not that I'm not curious about you." She made herself set the mug down. "I'm just aware of not invading your privacy."

"That's not a thing for me." He tilted his head a little. "I can always choose not to answer. You do know that goes for you, too, right? If you don't want to tell me something—or *do* something—all you have to do is say so."

She felt the blush warm her cheeks at the sensuous way he said *do*. Mrs. Lennon glanced over at her and gave her a little nod hello. Okay, a question for Fox, something to steer him away from sex, if that was even possible.

"So, tell me about your novel." There. Writers loved to talk about their work, right? Maybe he'd ramble on about it all through breakfast.

But he knocked his knuckles thoughtfully on the table and shook his head. "Uh-uh. I see what you're doing there, but that's not getting to know me. Ask something else."

Crap. Hmm. "Okay. What do you do for fun? Besides running? And, obviously, spending most of the day at the gym."

He laughed. "Cute. I don't work out all that much anymore. I got lucky with a lean build—less body fat makes you look cut with less effort—and I like to do a lot of stuff that helps me stay in shape. So, running, yes. Also rock climbing, hiking, swimming, diving, surfing."

"There's some good rock climbing around here. Hikes too. You should check them out."

"I grabbed some maps. Maybe when this storm finally clears out."

She shouldn't laugh at him, but she couldn't help giving him the local stare-down. "You mean, July fifth?"

He narrowed his eyes. "It can't rain straight through to

July."

"Nope. But it won't dry out until then, either."

"Huh." He shook his head and drank from his coffee, expectant.

"Tell me about the surfing. Do they make you learn if you live in southern California—like a requirement of residence?"

"Pretty much," he agreed. "Actually, it's great fun. Both challenging and relaxing. You'd enjoy it."

"I don't know. Trying to keep from being dragged under by huge waves doesn't sound all that peaceful."

His eyes lit up with enthusiasm. "But, see—that's just it. The challenge is to ride the wave, instead of drowning under it. It's kind of Zen."

"You don't strike me as a very Zen guy."

"Which is why I strive for it. Don't we all have our fatal flaws?"

No way would she answer that, so she tried to think up another question. Fortunately, Penny brought the food right then. Em sighed at the whipped-cream-mounded Belgian waffles and eyed Fox's ham, biscuits and gravy with more than a little envy.

"That smells good," she told him. "Looks good too."

He eyed her breakfast. "I can't say the same of yours. Is that Cool Whip from the spray can? It looks like something my five year-old niece would eat."

She mentally groaned for the truth of that but pasted on a smile. "That's me—eternally five years old."

CHAPTER THIRTEEN

THE LIES WERE starting to get under his skin. It shouldn't matter, really, and most of them were harmless enough. In truth, most people would never detect the slight hint of disgust in the turn of her mouth, the way she unconsciously licked her lip when she looked at his food.

Just as she'd done when he "accidentally" let his shirt ride up. God, he loved the way she looked at him—especially when she thought he wasn't paying attention. It had been the truth that his gym rat days were behind him, but he kept in shape pretty diligently for the investigative side of his work. You never knew when you'd need to run or defend yourself against an angry landowner. As his one ace in the hole with her, he planned to use it to maximum advantage.

Why do you order food you don't like? He burned to ask the question, but she'd never relax around him if he poked at her. All the curiosity filled his side of the table. She might appreciate his body, but she couldn't care less about him as a person. An ironic role reversal there. Not that he minded being a sex object so much, but it goaded him to try to breach her defenses even more.

When he had her in bed, their bodies meshed in the most intimate way, she'd have to pay attention to him then. He'd crawl inside her, one way or another. No, in all ways.

"Here." He cut the ham in half from his side plate and scooted it onto the pancake plate. Then dished a generous helping of biscuits and sausage gravy on top of the ham. "Potatoes too?"

"Oh, you don't have to," she protested, but her heart wasn't in it and her hungry gaze fastened on the heap of home fries with hearty chunks of browned onions. He added a big scoop of those, too, and slid the plate over to her.

"Now you won't have enough." She picked up her fork, took a bite and hummed in pleasure. Her face transformed with it, the way he imagined she'd look when caressed just the right way. Next time he touched her intimately would be in the light, he promised himself, so he could savor every nuance.

"There's plenty more where that came from. Hey, Penny!" He gave the waitress his most effective smile and moved his mug so she could refill it more easily. "Can we get more ham, biscuits and about a gallon of this amazing gravy? Emily's not feeling the Belgian waffles this morning."

The woman—who looked uncannily like Betty White—gave Emily an astonished look, then scowled at the side dish and the incriminatingly soiled fork. Absurdly, Emily squirmed with guilt and discomfort.

"But you love Charlie's waffles! It's what you always order. He even added extra strawberry syrup for you."

"I do. I don't need anything else, really. I only wanted to taste—"

Out of patience with the pretense, he picked up the waffle plate and handed it to Penny. "Let's get rid of this. She hasn't touched it—maybe someone in the kitchen wants it? Our treat. More of these excellent potatoes too. They might be best I've had in my life."

Slightly mollified, but with a last perplexed look at Emily, the woman went off.

"What's gotten into you?" Emily demanded. "What kind of person does that?"

"Aha!" He pointed his fork at her while he chewed the truly excellent potatoes, though the ones at the Green Flash on the beach in San Diego were better. "A real question. And one that speaks to my fundamental life philosophy, so I'm glad you asked. What got into me is that I believe people should always do what they most want to. As long as you're not hurting anyone else, why not have exactly what you want?"

"There might be other reasons," she retorted. Truth there.

"Such as?"

She backed away, internally, but the movement was as palpable as if she'd scooted her chair back. Shrugging, she cut her ham into smaller pieces. "Who knows? You can't know what someone else's motivations are."

"If you'd ordered the fruit plate or the steel-cut oats, I'd have thought, 'Okay, she's watching what she eats, in order to maintain that truly spectacular figure.' But no."

"Also," she continued as if he hadn't spoken. "It's rude to send back food. Penny thought she was being thoughtful and you hurt her feelings."

"You don't strike me as a person who'd be consumed with what other people thought of her." No, this came from maintaining a low profile, he figured. Except, she wasn't good at it. She didn't blend. Always she stood out from the background, vivid with her intense personality. People here remembered what she liked because they wanted her to like them.

Just as she'd sucked him in.

"You might be a temporary visitor here, but this is my home. Maybe I don't want my neighbors pissed at me."

"Pff. Penny is fine. She sold more food than she would have otherwise and I'll leave her an amazing tip—well, you will and I'll pay you back."

"We'll split the bill, plus I'll pay for the waffles."

"Nope. My idea, my treat. When you invite me out, you can pay. Or you can make me dinner."

She shook her head in dismay, forking up more of the food. "I'm not going to…"

He gave her the pause, but she didn't fill in the rest. "What? Invite me out? Make me dinner?"

Meeting his gaze with her cool silvery eyes, she looked for a moment totally without guile. "What are we doing, Fox? And don't say having breakfast."

No, he understood what she asked. The trick would be to give her the right answer. Or, at least, the one that would work for her. Maybe the raw truth.

He put down his fork and took her hand, lacing their fingers together. Her fingers felt delicate between his, like cool glass. "Can't it be that we're enjoying each other's company? Doing what we want to do. It can be that simple."

She looked out at the rain. Would she confess to not being all that simple? To having a past? No. She came to some other decision. "You're right. I'm making this more complicated than it needs to be." With a little smile, she tugged her hand away, pretending she needed to pick up her napkin. More than ever, he wanted to convince her to let him tie her up, force her to stay still while he touched her to his heart's content. The thought made him a bit hard and he smiled.

"What's that smile for?" She asked.

"Thinking about what I'm going to do to you tonight."

"Oh." Her cheeks bloomed with a hint of color. Yes, her fair skin showed every blush, but he wondered more and more just how reclusive she'd been. She flustered easily. It spoke to, not sexual inexperience, but to a certain emotional freshness. In that sense, at least, they had complete honesty. He might be lying to her about who he was and his reasons for being on Lyra, and she thought she'd fooled him with her various prevarications, but the way they felt about each other, on every level, that was absolutely real. "Are we on for tonight then?" She looked up through her thick, dark lashes, like black lace over silver, her full mouth pursed over the question.

"You tell me. Totally up to you." He congratulated himself for sounding so mellow about it. Despite the increasing erection that made him shift in his chair. "I can wait, if you need more time," he added, pretending to himself that would be fine.

"No." She smiled, that pretty curve of lips that made him wonder what images she had in her head. "I want to. And I won't freak out and leave this time."

"If you do, it's okay." He held her gaze, willing her to understand that he meant it. "I understand. Just don't bother telling me not to come after you, because I will."

She studied him. "Is this an attainability thing with you? Are you one of those guys who loves the chase? The harder to get, the more you want it?"

"Guilty, your honor." He didn't even mind that she'd seen through him because at least she'd bothered to look. "Except I always enjoy having equally as much—if not more."

"Are you sure?"

Deliberately he let his gaze fall to her sensuous mouth, then to the rise of breasts, firm and full even under the compressing jog bra. They rose and fell a little faster and, after a leisurely interval, he looked into her eyes again. "Tomorrow morning, you can give me your assessment—let me know if you think I enjoyed the having."

She responded so powerfully to those kinds of suggestions. Intelligence, imagination and a potent sexual nature. So much so that he wondered how she'd been able to stand the dry spell she'd referenced. Unless that, also, had been a lie.

Somehow though, he thought that was truth.

Possibly even at the heart of what was going on with her.

They walked back in the rain, at a fast clip, but far too full to run. The soaked sweatshirt weighed on him like a bullet-proof vest. It irked him no end, but he'd have to invest in some of the ubiquitous rain gear as Emily had taunted him he should. Might as well count it as another investment in the hunt for Phoenix.

Despite the magazine's investment, he'd paid quite a bit of his costs up front—sometimes a delicate balance to weigh against the likely bonus they'd give him, above *Geek Crunch's* miserly idea of a salary. He had additional buyers who'd pay for syndication of the final article, additional side-stories and reveal on the near mythically secretive gamer. If he played it right, breaking this story would give him the cred to get in with the serious news agencies. Not to mention pwning the ultimate gamer and all the other wannabes who thought they could out Phoenix. He was the best and they'd know it.

He walked Emily up onto her deck, after she turned Anansi loose to renew his scent marks in the fenced garden. A white cat sitting behind the glass door gave him a horrified look and disappeared.

"Seriously," she said, rummaging in her jacket pocket for her keys, "use the Kapsucks' sauna and get warmed up."

"Do you have one?"

"No, a hot tub."

"Mmm." He snagged her hand, tangling his fingers with hers and the keys, using the moment of surprise to back her against the door under the sheltering eave. He pressed against her and found the sweet spot right under her ear. She smelled of rain, salt and very faintly of orange blossoms. His cock, which had been well subdued by the chilly walk home, thickened and warmed with interest. "How about we have a nice afternoon soak?"

She didn't object immediately, to his surprise. The hot tub must be outside the house.

"Don't you have work to do—a novel to write?" But she lifted her chin, giving him access to the sweet line of her jaw and the fragile white skin there. With each press of his lips, she shivered, like the most delicate crystal singing to the lightest brush of silk. He lined up in his head all he wanted to try on her, the textures, the temperatures, levels of pleasure and maybe some pain, if she liked it.

But she'd asked him a question. "I never write on Sundays." Another rule to remember. Should be easy, since he loved a lazy Sunday.

"The Lord's day?" She asked with some amusement, her voice husky with arousal.

"If the Lord is behind big brunches, hot tubs and sexy women, then yes."

She was thinking it over, the buzz of her deliberations, inches away but still obscure to him. "All right then. It's over this way. You can give me your clothes and I'll put them in the dryer while we soak."

The door still locked, she pocketed the keys and led him to the other end of the deck, down a few steps and to a gazebo with a covered hot tub beneath, entirely screened by the emerald foliage.

"Very nice."

She smiled, a shy curve of her lips, and thumbed a switch under the rail. White lights flicked on, festive in the rainy gloom. A real insight into her here, the pretty lights and the total privacy. He helped her pull the cover off and set it to the side, then began wrestling off the sweatshirt again, beginning to hate the damn thing.

"I'll go put on a swimsuit and get us towels."

"I thought you wanted to put my clothes in the dryer?"

She'd already started up the steps and looked back, uncertain. "Don't you want to get in and then I'll come get them?"

"Then you'd have to make two trips. Besides—you want to watch, don't you?"

Her eyes darkened and she pressed her lips together.

Saving her the decision, he propped his butt against the tub and lifted his foot to untie his shoe, watching her the whole time. She moved out of the rain and leaned against the latticework post, folding her arms but body otherwise alight with interest. Protecting herself still, but as drawn to him as he was to her.

He toed off both shoes and set the socks on top of the sodden sweatshirt. Not having to fake a struggle with the equally soaked T-shirt, he pulled that over his head, then took his time easing his arms out of it, making sure he compressed his pecs for her. Judging by her rapt expression and the flush on her transparent skin, he'd done it right.

He stood to slide off his running pants. Before he'd been sorry not to be wearing the shorts she liked, but with the cold rain—no way. Using his thumbs to take the jock with them, he skimmed the fabric down his legs, keeping his eyes on her face and knowing that his cock had to be semi-erect and rapidly going for full attention under her avid gaze.

Tossing the wet pants on the pile, he let her look him over.

It gave her the power, which should help the trust issues, but he also didn't lie to himself that he got a thrill from it too. Being naked for your clothed lover created a delicious sense of being desired.

Judging by the look on her face, Emily desired him all right.

He shoots. He scores.
The crowd goes wild.

CHAPTER FOURTEEN

"WANT TO TOUCH?" he invited her in a throaty voice that matched her fogged senses.

Without coming closer, he put his hands behind his neck, the movement making his hardening cock stretch up. For a guy who came across as fairly pushy and overbearing at times, he seemed vulnerable, at her mercy in some way that filled her with a thrill of lustful power. Something she'd never before experienced in the sexual arena. Really, any arena, without being Phoenix.

"Are you—submitting to me?" She felt odd laying it out there, using a lingo that seemed to belong to an exclusive club of kinksters, but she wanted to know. Even saying the words to him made her feel in control.

His brown eyes glittered, his cock high and flushed. "Do you want me to?"

"I don't know. I've never... I don't think I've ever met a guy into that."

He laughed, a soft, sensual sound that stroked across her nerves with the same arousing enticement as his mouth created on her skin. "My theory is that all men are into it—they just can't all admit it. Women too. Everyone is, to a greater or lesser extent. Sex is about giving yourself up to your lover, after all.

Who doesn't want to be taken over by someone else's desire, even for a little while?"

"I don't know if I would want that." The idea made her nervous, even whispered of the anger she'd felt last night. She knotted her fingers together.

"Only if you want to, Miss Emily." He soothed her with his voice. "This is about you touching me. But I also enjoy having you look at me. It's just you and me, and I like it all. Don't worry about that part—what do you want to do?"

Feeling as if it could be a dream, the dim afternoon, the fog from the hot tub, the rain drumming on the tin gazebo roof, the fairy lights twinkling around this leanly muscled man who looked as if he might have stepped out of the forest, she searched herself for what she wanted. The same as looking for that image in the mirror, the true one, not the mask she'd created.

She definitely wanted him, this sexy man who looked like a satyr offering to pleasure her. Part of her tucked the image into a mental file folder of game ideas—which helped offset not actually working—even as she moved to him and wrapped her fingers around his hard length.

His breath hissed out and his lids lowered, a shiver going through him. He didn't move otherwise, but his muscles flexed—there in his chest, the twitch of biceps, his quads tightening.

"Are you cold?" she whispered and his eyes flicked open, full of a heated intensity that rocked her.

"Not at the moment. In fact, I might burst into flame."

She adjusted her grip, then gathered up his heavy balls with her other hand. Not only didn't he resist in any way, but he showed her how much he enjoyed her touch, his face open and expressive, making quiet sounds of pleasure.

"What now?" she asked.

"I believe you are in the driver's seat. Do what you wish with me, Miss Emily."

"I kind of like how you call me that."

"It does it for me too." He gave her a naughty boy grin, full of wickedness that melted into a sigh when she rolled his balls and tightened her grip.

She stroked his length, up to the tip where his semen pearled, and spread the slick liquid over the soft head. His breath came harder, and the effort to hold himself still became even more apparent as she toyed with him. Between her legs, her slickness mirrored his and she imagined telling him to kneel down and lick her there. Would he do it?

He had closed his eyes again, jaw tight and throat ridged from tension. He swallowed and his Adam's apple moved up and down. She let go of his balls and pressed her fingers to it. He groaned. Scratching him there lightly with her nails, doing the same to the tip of his cock, she teased him. A sound came out of him, part laugh, part moan of pleasure. "God, I knew you'd be good at this."

Pleased, she dragged her nails down his chest—she should make an effort to grow them longer—and circled one of his nipples. His cock flexed in her hand, moisture increasing.

"I should make you come this way," she told him, working his shaft again. "Like you did to me in the closet. Payback for that."

"Or don't let me come," he panted. "Whichever pleases you more, Miss Emily."

"What if I told you to jerk yourself off while I watch?"

"I'm yours to command."

Something she'd always wanted to see, but not something you typically ask a guy to do. At least, not the kind of guys she'd slept with. "Do that then."

She let go and stood back. Fastening his blazing eyes on hers, he wrapped one hand around his cock. The copper hairs on his forearm glinted with beads of moisture from the hot tub's steam, the tendons standing out. "How shall I do it?"

"Do it the way you like it best—so I know, for future reference."

"I like it this way." Holding her gaze, he tightened his grip and pumped, much harder and faster than she'd handled him. "But I won't last long. If you're going to withhold permission, I need to know immediately." He said the last on a rush of breath, his whole body tightening, a carved sculpture of a man, his face a rictus as he stretched his neck back, almost holding it in place with the hand behind his neck. "Ech—too late."

With an incoherent shout, he pulled his fist back tight against his groin, holding it there as his semen shot out, body arcing with the orgasm. He held there, taut as a drawn bow, then unbent slightly. His hand still worked his cock, slower now, milking himself, his face gradually relaxing from the fierce expression. As his body softened, he glanced at the puddle on the redwood floor of the gazebo and gave her a rueful look, with a strong flavor of cocky male pride beneath.

"Sorry about the mess."

She grabbed his shirt. "I'll wipe it up with this and throw the lot in the laundry."

"Let me." He took it from her and, with a sly smile, went down on his knees, slowly and carefully wiping it all up. As if he'd read her mind, he crawled over to her and pressed his forehead to the top of her running shoe. When she didn't move, he set the shirt aside and wrapped his hands around her ankles, kissing her shins through the running pants. Working his way up her legs, he caressed the shape of her, stroking her thighs, his hands stopping just below the curve of her bottom.

Then pressed a kiss right on her mound.

She gasped, her vulva clenching and moisture squeezing out of her. Far more aroused than she'd realized, she swayed and had to grab onto his naked shoulders for support. His skin was clammy and a rush of guilt hit her.

"Shit! You're freezing. What was I thinking?"

Sinking his grip into the backs of her thighs, he looked up at her. "If you were anywhere near the same headspace I was, you were more interested in how good we are together than something as boring as weather."

"Well, we can be good together without giving anyone hypothermia. Get in the tub. I'll be right back with towels after I put this stuff in the washer."

"Yes, ma'am." He grinned, then nipped her on the full part of her thigh, making her jump. "You have no idea what that imperious tone does to me."

She rolled her eyes, swept up his clothes and headed up to the house, not letting herself look back. Never mind superstitions about pillars of salt, she didn't want to get distracted by him again. Inside, Dinah gave her a betrayed look and slunk away from being petted.

"Be like that then," she called after the cat and turned on the coffeepot, feeling nearly giddy with all things Fox. Never had she met a guy so open about sex, and who treated both the intense and playful aspects with equal enthusiasm. No emotional baggage apparent at all—a good thing, since she packed around the equivalent of a steamer trunk's worth. Really she should check in for messages from her team, but when was the last time she took a full day off?

Not since becoming Phoenix, for sure. Maybe not for a while before that.

Not counting those months after they fired her, when she did nothing at all.

She put Fox's clothes in the wash. Speaking of something she hadn't done in a while. The last time she'd done a man's laundry it had been Henry's. Somehow all the domestic chores had become hers by some unspoken default after they married. She hadn't wanted to make it something to fight about—she hadn't liked confrontation back then—but she'd sometimes wondered snarkily to herself if it had been a part of the vows she'd missed. *Do you promise to love him, keep him, fix all his meals, clean up his shit and make sure he never lacks for work shirts?*

A mark of her happy mood, and maybe enough time and distance, but it didn't aggravate her so much to think of it. Henry's basic laziness had been the least of his sins. She would have forgiven him all of it if he'd only stepped up to defend her. If he hadn't been so damn happy to keep *his* job and suggest she try another field, like teaching.

In her heart of hearts, she'd always known it irked him that she'd been a better programmer, a more creative designer. They both knew it, even when they paid him more.

"Not thinking about that," she reminded herself out loud and went upstairs for a swimsuit, a robe and big bath towels. She wound her ponytail into a bun, pinning it in place. Her hair was already wet from the rain, but no sense dragging it through the hot tub water. In the kitchen, she filled a thermos with coffee and added almond milk, stevia and a dollop of Jameson whiskey. Her lean and mean version of Irish coffee.

She carried it out with her, hustling to keep the towels dryish when she had to leave the shelter of the eaves. Fox had his head tipped back against the hot tub rim, his arms out-stretched on either side, and looked like a magazine ad for spa sales. They'd no doubt go faster than hot cakes.

Setting down the towels on a bench, she put down the thermos quietly, in case he'd fallen asleep, and shrugged out of the robe.

"You've got to be kidding me," he said, startling her.

"What?" She looked behind her, wondering what put that look on his face.

"A swimsuit, really? And not even a sexy red bikini num-ber, but a something that looks like a refugee from the Olympic trials. Are you planning to swim the Channel?"

She wrinkled her nose at him and climbed in the tub, hiss-ing at the hot sting of water on her chilled skin. "You might love doing a strip tease, but I don't. I always wear a suit out here."

Scanning the dense foliage, he raised his eyebrows in question. "Am I missing the vantage point through which some nosy neighbor can see us? You were fine with hanging me out there."

So she had been. Really, she hadn't been thinking at all, once he'd started undressing. And they said men were the visual ones. "No. No one can see. I'm just…not comfortable naked."

"Ever?" He scooted closer. Not touching her, but near enough to do so easily. "Do you wear your swimsuit in the shower?"

"Don't be ridiculous. Of course I don't. Just when I'm not alone. Or might not be…private."

"What about with a lover?"

"I haven't done that recently, as I've said."

"So this is new, the not-getting-naked thing."

"It's not a thing." Irritation crawled up her spine and she handed him the thermos to have something to do. "Here— Irish coffee if you want some. Fully leaded, though."

"I plan to be awake late into the night, so great." But he set the thermos aside and lightly caressed her shoulder, toying with the swimsuit strap. "How is it not a thing?"

Sloppy of her. She should have gone with it and given him some story—anything other than the truth—that being exposed as she had made her want to keep covered all the time. As if the experience had trained her to be afraid, to forever watch for attack. She remembered the first night she'd come out to the tub. It had seemed like such a treat, to slip into it naked under the stars, all hers. But then the wind had rustled the bushes and the fear had seized her—that same chest-constricting fear from those dark weeks, triggered by footsteps in the dark, rapists in the bushes, millions of faceless men behind thousands of screens wanting her to hurt, to pay, to die.

She'd tried to stay in the tub, telling herself that they couldn't find her. It was only wind in the bushes, right? Only pixels. Only ones and zeros. But she'd lasted only minutes before she scrambled out, hiding behind her towel, and rushed into her house, locking the door with shaking hands and running to crawl under the covers and hide.

She'd been so damn cavalier when she'd first been outed as Amazonia's chief designer. Hell, she'd been amused at Jared's mood of alarm the day he'd come to her desk to inform her that the trolls had likely gotten her home address. "You should think about taking security measures," he'd said.

She'd barely looked up from her console. "That's okay, we have an alarm system."

"Maybe think about a security guy," he persisted. "An off-duty cop or something."

"To guard against *trolls?* Because what—they'll yell at me about the game?" She might have laughed, raising her eyebrows at Jared's overreaction. After all what could they really do?

That all changed when the Rape Lisa site went up. She'd known better than to look. Had resisted the urge for days. Eventually, of course, she had, sitting alone in her office, curiosity getting the best of her.

Though she'd expected something like it, the image of her face photoshopped onto a dancing naked body had stunned her. A new version of her with bouncing, water-balloon breasts, obscenely wide hips and a twig waist—the typical gamer babe done 3-D hentai style. The background was disconcertingly familiar, a jungle setting ripped directly from Amazonia. The story kicked into action right away as a massive, naked demon-man with a huge, erect penis—more like a sword, really—approached hentai-her, unseen, as she jiggled and danced like a vapid fool.

He viciously grabbed Hentai-Lisa by the breasts, like they were handles, and she laughed in hysterical delight, twisting one way and then another, her squeals like a cross between a pig and a little girl. The man shoved her facedown over a fallen tree. She landed with a gasp and another one of those squeals, kicking and flailing as he subdued her, twisting her arms behind her back at an impossible angle.

Hentai-Lisa's face was turned to the side, staring out of the screen. *Her face.*

The creator had gone to the trouble of animating her mouth to form an O as the monstrous man penetrated her from behind with that sword-like member. If the bodies had been real, his penis would've knifed clear into her lungs, killing her.

Bile-yellow sickness billowed in her gut as she watched her virtual rape, heart pounding.

He thrust again and again. With every thrust, her mouth formed that O and she emitted a squeal.

No! Not *her.*

But it had felt like her, somewhere deep down. All the horror. The shame.

She knew she should've turned it off, but she'd felt pinned

as the little girl-pig squealing modulated between distress and delight, as blood ran down her legs and flew in an exaggerated red mist. Still the man punished Hentai-Lisa with that sword of a cock, in and out. Finally he withdrew, cock shining crimson.

Her used-up, sexed-up form simply rolled off the log and onto the verdant jungle floor with an undignified plop and one last deflated squeal.

And then the ticker came up. The number 1,899,343 became 1,899,344. Her skin went clammy, her stomach roiled. The words *play again* appeared.

Play again.

Because her naked body was back up dancing.

She'd barely made it down the hall to the bathroom before she'd thrown up. It had been the number, really, that did it. All those views. All that hate.

Stupid people with too much time on their hands. They wanted everyone to see her as less than human and it worked. Even on her. They wanted to scare her and that worked too.

1,899,343.

Her mother paid for security on their apartment building, and to escort her, but everyone saw the images and looked at her differently. Sometimes she imagined glimpses of that rape in the reflection of their eyes. Every man on the street stood out to her pounding heart. Though it all stopped after they fired her—celebrated by a website that tolled the wicked witch was dead—it took months before the fear subsided. She'd thought she'd gotten over it, until she found herself naked and alone in the hot tub, the shadows flickering in unspoken menace.

The bubbling wound in her heart she never wanted Fox to see.

Stupid. She should have taken the swimsuit off when he said something. She'd be naked with him soon enough anyway. She wanted to be. She never wanted to think about that time again.

But she couldn't just take it off now. It had become a *thing*.

CHAPTER FIFTEEN

FOX WATCHED HER stall. Her tells for lying fell into the standard realm, pretty much, with a certain blandness of expression she assumed while she thought her way out of something. The happy smile she'd worn when she returned to the gazebo had faded, making him kick himself for teasing her.

By way of rescuing her—and to spare himself whatever excuse she planned to make up—he moved his hand to stroke the back of her neck. She liked light touches, responding almost involuntarily to them. Letting her chin drop, she closed her eyes and smiled, just a little.

"That feels good," she murmured.

He traced the bumps of her spine from the dip at the base of her skull down to her shoulder. She had a lovely, even elegant neck, as long and graceful as the rest of her. The tight, almost prim bun she'd put her hair in only served to reveal her more. A woman of fascinating contrasts, with her physical delicacy and iron will. She'd loved being in control over him, more than she might be admitting to herself. The way she'd worked his cock, with complete confidence and a touch of cruelty in the scratching of her nails. He'd go with that, if being in charge gave her what she needed to feel secure with him.

His cock filled at the memory and he dropped a kiss on her shoulder, her skin smooth and moist. A light breath sighed out of her, encouraging him to add another kiss, a bit higher. Then, of course, he had to move the thick swimsuit strap down slightly, so as not to miss the next inch of skin. She didn't object, angling her head away, giving implicit encouragement. He kissed his way up, enjoying the way her breasts—criminally crushed under the high neck of the suit—rose and fell as her breathing accelerated. The strap, once past the point of her shoulder, draped down her arm, forgotten by her.

He experimented with the long line of her neck, finding the spots that made her breath halt and that one sweet spot that elicited a quiet moan. Some women hated having their throats touched. Guys too. He'd had a buddy in high school who lost his shit if anyone touched his neck. But Emily loved it, moving for him as he made his way around to her throat, letting him turn her and stroke her skin under the other strap.

Maybe the pliancy came from their mutual accord for him to drop the subject of the nakedness thing, but she also seemed to have released a layer of defense between them. It had seriously turned her on to watch him jack off. If he'd managed to pull those running pants down her spectacular legs and slide his tongue between them, he would have found her hot and slick, he knew it. Too bad he had been feeling the chill.

But it had prolonged the anticipation.

And he was plenty warm now.

Tugging down the strap on the far side, he traced the fragile skin over her collarbones with his tongue, loving the way she let her head drop bonelessly, a soft hum of delight vibrating her throat. He nearly straddled her, but thought better of it and risked breaking the spell by grasping her hips, coaxing her to sit on his lap, facing him.

His cock, more than ready for more, rose between them. He kept his hips back and her hands found his shoulders as he continued to nibble and kiss his way along her collarbones and the hollow of her throat. Her hips under his hands moved in a wave, an unconscious invitation he burned to accept.

Not yet, Sparky.

Trailing his hands up her lean waist, he moved them to her arms as his mouth found the upper curves of her breasts. He tugged on the draping straps, pulling them lower. Emily opened her eyes, the gray a dreamy color like the fog. Meeting her gaze, he posed the challenge, the tight spandex of the suit giving way bit by bit. Her breasts rose as she took a deep breath and dropped her arms, giving him freedom to pull the straps all the way down.

Enjoying himself fully now that he felt certain she wouldn't stop him, he savored the moment of seeing her tits for the first time. Gradually he lowered the material, aware also of how the slow reveal affected her, the way her thighs moved restlessly where they touched his. Her nipples had hardened, upthrust against the wet suit. The band of red at the neckline caught over them in a most tantalizing way.

He left it there a moment, let her feel it bite into her, while he kissed her compressed cleavage and she made those noises of frustrated protest that sent him over the edge every damn time. Her fingers plucked at his forearms, wordlessly encouraging him, but he took his time, letting it build.

"Oh for fuck's sake, Fox," she blew out on a breath, her voice full of the whiskey sound of deep arousal. She moved to yank the top down herself, but he snagged her wrists, holding them against her thighs.

"Watch." With a whimper, she did. She might think she wouldn't enjoy being the one to submit, but it affected her powerfully when he made even small movements of domination like this. Give it time and she might be a convert.

Making sure she saw, and keeping her twitching hands pinned, he gripped the suit in his teeth, grinned around it, and yanked it down. It didn't take much, the tight spandex releasing her breasts so they popped up with gratifying fullness, her taut nipples as pink as her lips, maybe a shade deeper. Where the rest of her followed long, willowy lines, her tits were luscious globes, the kind he'd expect to see on a much more rounded woman.

Of voluptuous proportions, even, and coming to nearly perfect points with her small, tight nipples. Had he thought they weren't all that big? Maybe it was the contrast to her elegantly slim frame, but wow.

"Oh, Miss Emily, what gorgeous tits these are. How on earth did you hide these from me?"

She didn't answer because he didn't give her time. Still holding her hands against her sides, he sucked one of those tempting nipples into his mouth, not gentle. He'd moved beyond tenderness and now he really needed to fill his mouth with her.

Her heated cries of strained pleasure played like music, a soundtrack that fueled him to further consume her. Letting go of her wrists to better enjoy her, he cupped those glorious tits and squeezed them, holding them so he could move from one nipple to another, feeding his desire with the taste of her flesh. Her composure fraying, she dug her hands into his hair, pushed her pelvis against his, grinding against his erect cock.

He had plenty of experience holding off orgasm—sometimes to excruciating extremes with one particularly sadistic lover—but even with coming so recently, that friction would get to him sooner than he wanted. Emily just worked him up far too much.

So he dropped his hands to her waist and moved her back, kissing her when she objected. Such a delicious mouth. She kissed like a man, firm and strong, but with a deep softness that was all woman. Tangling her tongue with his, she made his head swim, abandoning herself with a consuming hunger that made his balls tighten. He kept it together enough to maneuver them both into a standing position, those delicate hands of hers running over his body and digging with astonishing strength into his ass, pulling his groin against her and mashing the hard points of her nipples into his chest.

If her nails were longer, he'd be done for.

Still, he managed to make enough room between them to tug her suit down her ribcage. She helped because she likely thought he'd fuck her now. He mentally braced himself to withstand the firestorm when she found out he still planned to wait until tonight. Call him stubborn, but that was the plan and he'd stick to it. Games were only as good as the rules. He fondled one breast, tweaking the nipple so she squirmed and panted, distracted enough to let him back her against the side of the tub, he considered making her wait to come until nightfall.

Probably too soon for that. Not as if she didn't have plenty of sexual energy bottled up already. In fact, that gave him an idea.

"Sit up here," he said against her mouth, then rolled her nipple between his thumb and forefinger to erase the frown line that appeared between her brows.

She edged herself up onto the lip of the tub, however, letting him help her, but looking puzzled when he pressed her thighs together. He took her in, half naked and fully aroused, her face and tits flushed with it, cream and rose against the forest backdrop. Tonight, he'd get her to let her hair down, but the look worked for him. The dark, classic upsweep of her hair, the cool silver of her eyes and the sheer carnality of her gorgeous body.

Tucking his fingers between her hot skin and the wet suit, he looked the question at her. Raising her hips, pink tongue touching her full lower lip, she complied, letting him pull the suit off. With anticipation, he took in her white belly and then the glossy, curling triangle of hair at the juncture of her thighs. She braced her hands on the tub rim and lifted one foot, then the other, for him to remove the suit completely. As she did, she pointed her toes in the way women who've taken ballet do. Her feet even had the knotted joints dancers get from being *en pointe,* which never went away, so a ballet dancer lover had told him.

There had been no ballet photos online. Even if her childhood ones had never been scanned in, there should be ones from her teenage years. He resolved to look.

He tossed the suit onto the floor of the pavilion, since she wouldn't need to wear it anymore. His bid to keep it that way, at any rate. She sat with her knees pressed together and tits high in the cool air, watching him with a wide-open, vulnerable expression.

"Cold?" He asked, trying to be considerate although it would spoil his plan if she said yes.

She shook her head slowly, as if thinking about it. Uncertain what would come next. Her, actually, and the thought made him smile.

"Would you spread your legs for me?"

She looked taken aback. Not what she'd expected, but she complied, opening her long, lovely runner's thighs, leaning back slightly for balance, which tipped her nipples up. His cock throbbed, nearly aching.

"More," he directed, his voice growling with need, but he didn't care. Neither did she, because she adjusted her bottom on the tub rim and spread herself open, her labia parting to reveal the slick pink tissues inside. A groan came out of him, a sound that apparently pleased her since her lips curved in a secretive smile, as pink and wet as her exposed pussy.

He moved to her, waist-deep in the water, and put his hands on her knees, pushing them farther apart and watching her eyes. Oh yeah, she liked that all right, her pupils dilating in the gray.

"There are condoms in my robe," she whispered.

"We don't need them." He smoothed his thumbs up her inner thighs. The skin there felt like satin. Then he kissed her when her mouth opened in an annoyed reply, taking advantage of the opportunity and nipping her argument in the bud. She softened, yielding sweetly. "Because we're not having intercourse yet."

She still wanted to argue, but the impetus got lost as his thumbs reached the deep hollows where her legs met her groin, stroking deeper. A rarely known erogenous zone for many people. He pressed in, her flesh both firm and soft, gratified when her spine arched in purely physical reaction.

"Ooh!" She moaned, the breath gasping out of her as her body convulsed and her hips rocked. Perfect. It took her a moment to recover and, while she blinked at him, fog in her gaze, he went for the surprise and slid his finger inside her to the hilt. Her eyes went wide and he curled up, pressing on her upper vaginal wall. She trembled, face pinking further. Not quite right. Keeping the pressure, he moved down a bit, curled his finger up and, at the same time, pressed the heel of his hand against her clit.

She exploded.

So much so that he had to let go of her thigh and put a hand behind her, to keep her from falling off the back of the tub. She didn't seem to notice, the orgasm ripping through her, her head thrown back to release a full cry of ecstasy. Her pussy ground against his hand, her hot liquids filling his palm. Overcome, he filled his mouth with her breast, the hard nipple satisfying against his tongue, the tremors of her climax almost a flavor, filling his head with aroused woman.

Needing more, he dropped between her spread thighs, sucking her swollen clit into his mouth in the same way, working his finger in and out of her tight passage, while the aftermath of her orgasm shuddered its way out of her. As soon as he detected returning tension to her body, her core strength repossessing her balance, he let go of her lower back—hovering a moment to make sure she had it—then took her hand and placed it on his shoulder.

"Hold on," he told her, looking up to see her face. She gazed down at him, face soft with release, her mind obviously fuzzy. But her fingers gripped his shoulder, if only in reflex. Using his elbows to lever open her knees, he used both hands to spread her labia wide. Her vulva, rimmed with sweet pink folds like a butterfly's wings, glistened with deep promise. Her clit, long as the rest of her, stood out hard, demanding attention.

Her short nails dug into his shoulder. "Fox," she breathed, throaty and delightfully uneven. Not at all her assured self now, but needy. Maybe as desperate as he felt. "I don't think I can..." She didn't finish the sentence because he blew hot breath over her sensitive tissues. Her hand convulsed, both holding him off and pulling him closer.

He loved this part. Okay, he loved it all, but this—pushing her past what she thought she could take. They'd have to discuss safewords later that night. He wanted her to be able to protest and struggle and fight against him and herself all she pleased but still be able to tell him when she truly couldn't stand any more stimulation. For the time being, however, she was far from done.

As evidenced by those throaty sounds of passion when he licked her. He settled himself on the bench between her feet—

not ideal for a long session, but decent enough—and held her open while he explored her. Going slowly now, he laved her folds, the warm ocean taste of her a sweet brine wholly her own. Every woman tasted different and he loved Emily's scent and flavor. No surprise as he rapidly discovered he liked every damn thing about her.

Even her skittishness and reflexive lies made her more interesting.

She hit every one of his buttons and he aimed to find all of hers.

Avoiding her clit, he used his lips and tongue to arouse her again, not a difficult task as she'd only come down partway from the last one. She moved under his mouth, fine trembles growing into stronger tremors until she nearly vibrated with restrained tension. Her hands—clinging to him—moved into his hair, holding his head and trying to direct him to her erect clit. He resisted, not letting her use her hip movements to direct him there either. Her thighs strained against his forearms, clamping him tighter. The little cries, the urgent pleading of her body, grew increasingly frantic until she at last emitted a high wail of frustration.

"Fox, please!"

He took his mouth away and looked up at her ferocious, demanding expression, trying to look innocent for her. "What?"

"Dammit. You know what."

"Do you want to come again, Miss Emily?"

Holding her gaze, he turned his head and placed a sweet kiss on the silky curve of her inner thigh. She groaned at him.

"You're the devil."

"Why thank you." He waited, loving the play of emotions over her face.

"Are you going to finish me or not?" she finally gritted out.

He cocked his head, then deliberately studied her pussy, which she still held spread open, despite her slickness and wriggling. Not easy, but he was dedicated.

"I thought you said you couldn't."

"Then what the hell have you been doing?"

He smiled at her, feeling wicked. Loving every minute of it. She teased so well. "Keeping you warm."

Making himself go as slow as he could, he ran his tongue along the inner rim of her vulva, enjoying even the pain of her pulling his hair as he tormented her.

"Please, Fox," she urged. "I can. Just do it. I can't stand any more of this."

She could, if he tied her down and wouldn't let her move. Filed away for the future.

"Maybe I should make you wait until tonight," he taunted, but licked slowly up to the area around her clit. "Or do what you did to me and make you finish yourself while I watch. Paybacks are hell."

She made a sobbing sound, truly unraveling now, and he took mercy on her. With one last swirl of his tongue around the thick hood over her clit, he pulled it into his mouth, and flicked the most sensitive bit with his tongue.

CHAPTER SIXTEEN

H ER BRAIN BURST, sending shrapnel through her skull.
At least that was how it felt. Like she was losing her
mind, her body out of control, with Fox's coppery head buried
between her thighs, his magical mouth clamped on her most
intimate tissues. Her vision pulsed red with a black lace overlay.
She gave up fighting it—as if she'd had a choice—not resisting
the way it clawed through her, too intense to be withstood.

Gradually the climax loosened its grip, as if an alien life
force relinquished her body, leaving behind an empty envelope.
Dimly aware of Fox helping her down in the water, she
floated—mentally, physically, emotionally—the white lights
above twinkling in the steam. The hot water prickled her
cooled skin and her pussy felt as if it pulsed with heat. If he
touched her again, she might come immediately. Or go into
some state of suspension where orgasms surged through her,
greater and smaller, until she shredded even more than she
already had.

Gradually the lights came into focus and she felt as if she
might have a nervous connection to her body again. Her
thoughts clarified, too, a less welcome transition, with niggling
worries asking her to analyze how she felt about what just
happened. Sheer, ecstatic pleasure, yes—but also a kind of

shattering that left her feeling lost, unanchored.

"Do you always come so hard?" Fox's voice asked.

She peered at him. She'd known he was there, of course, but she'd still kind of forgotten in the vast sense of losing herself. The steam formed a cloud around them, making his face a blur.

"I don't know." She wanted to sound sarcastic, but her voice came out throaty, a little anxious. "No one's ever given me head for hours before."

He chuckled, a sound of pure male satisfaction. "It wasn't *hours*. It wasn't even one."

"Tell that to the EMTs."

"I think you'll survive. Here." He nudged the thermos cup into her hand. The long-forgotten Irish coffee, no longer as hot. How long had he tormented her? Had she looked at the clock when she was inside? The rain drummed on the gazebo roof, false darkness from the heavy overcast. It couldn't be later than early afternoon. Still, she could sleep. A nap to avoid thinking and feeling for a while longer. She'd slept a lot when she first came to Lyra. Making up for months of lost sleep, she'd justified. And the rain and gloom encouraged it. She let her head fall back, that same sense of sadness welling up from some buried place.

"No you don't," Fox scolded. "I'm not done with you by a long shot. Drink your coffee like a good girl."

On one level, her hackles went up at that. Much better than that dragging depression. If she had a dollar for every time that attitude had crossed her desk, she'd have—oh wait, not nearly as much as she'd already raked in as Phoenix. Being him had saved her from the anger, fear and sorrow. Instead of sleeping all the time, she'd worked. Finally free to design exactly how she wanted to. She didn't have to wonder who she was. She'd chosen to be Phoenix, her true self, even if her body seemed to belong to someone else.

Fox didn't need to know any of that. The sex rocked her world—okay, great. Emily could have all the sex she wanted while Phoenix worked in secret. The one would fuel the other. She could be both people.

She sipped the coffee, to all appearances going along with Fox's program.

It tasted delicious. Perfect.

"What the hell is *in* this?" Fox sounded kind of horrified, which pleased her.

"Almond milk, Stevia and Jameson—why?"

"You're insane to call this Irish coffee."

"It's healthy."

"Some things should not be healthy."

"Hey—you're the one who ripped the whipped cream out of my hands this morning."

"That was chemical foam and you didn't want it anyway."

"How do you know?" This was the fly in her ointment. For the separation to work, she needed him to learn about only Emily, as he seemed so determined to do. She needed a personal, intimate firewall. "You've barely met me."

He didn't reply right away. Then offered, "It must be the writer in me. Students of human nature. Besides, you have an expressive face."

"I do?" No one had ever said something like that to her

before.

"Oh yeah. You have an expressive everything, really."

She had to ponder that, decide what that meant. Perhaps she could work it. The face in the mirror didn't have to be her own. She'd express what she wanted him to see.

"So." He stretched. "Time to take a shower and move on to Act II?"

"Just so you can tease me more?"

"You're very fun to tease, it's true. But you're always welcome to take revenge."

His words recalled that first fantasy after meeting him, of sucking him off in her kitchen. Not that it would ever happen. Keeping him out of her house would continue to be an important boundary to maintain, part of the firewall to keep him out of her head. *You have an expressive everything.* It bothered her that he somehow he might see through her. Being someone else through the lens of the internet went far more smoothly. Even the brief interactions with the people around town let her play act convincingly.

How the hell had he known she didn't want the waffles? Of course, she hadn't. She'd ordered them on her first visit to the café because she'd never ordered Belgian waffles in her life. That had been her strategy, to follow none of her recognizable patterns. Easy to do for a few weeks or months, but after years she felt like Kipling's rhinoceros, with her ill-fitting and itchy hide. And the crankiness to match.

Time to take control of this affair.

"You'll have to take a shower at your place, I'm afraid." She forced herself to move, to climb out of the tub and grab one of the huge fluffy towels. "I'll go throw your clothes in the dryer and bring them out to you."

"I'll come with you, wait inside."

"No. Not negotiable."

"Why not? What's inside that I can't see?" He sprang the question on her, the same way he'd taken her by surprise, sliding his finger inside her with no warning and finding her G-spot almost immediately. A technique of his, she suspected, to do and ask the unexpected, to catch people off guard. It worked, she could vouch, giving him the opportunity to sneak past her shields before she guessed he'd found a crack in them. The obvious solution? Seal up all cracks. She'd already accomplished far more by escaping the trolls, disappearing and reemerging like a phoenix from the ashes of her destroyed career.

It had all given her strength. The kind a guy like Fox could never hope to breach. Deliberately, she cast the towel aside and stood naked for a moment before she reached for her robe. His gazed roved over her body with desire and hunger. She let it feed her, make her feel powerful. Then she put on the robe and smiled at him, taunting.

"I'm a terrible housekeeper." She didn't care if he knew it for a lie. Which he did, apparently, because he made a wry grimace with his mouth, as if she'd cracked a bad joke. Letting it stand between them, her line in the sand, one element in her firewall, she went in the house and locked the door behind her.

Just in case.

FOX KNEW GOOD and well that she wouldn't come out until

his clothes had dried. A strategic retreat on her part—yet again. It would be helpful if he didn't find her so fascinating. Most women—even many men—after an orgasm that shattering would come back to earth softer, more open, wanting to cuddle and share affection.

Not Emily.

No, she'd almost immediately secured her personal space. Even before she consciously decided to. Oh, she'd done that as well, but she'd withdrawn behind her walls within moments of him easing her into the water, the sweet softness of post-orgasm vanishing behind a returning natural defensiveness, as if her very skin developed a static charge that discouraged him from touching her. Instinct had told him not to push, for once, to instead keep it light and her amused as he observed the way she established distance and rolled out her rules for engagement.

He didn't have to worry about her bailing on the sexual affair anymore. For the moment she liked that part too much to miss out. More, she enjoyed his hunger for her. But she'd blatantly lied about why he couldn't come inside her house and—far worse—hadn't cared that he'd known it.

She'd made it clear that she'd taken control, that he'd only know what she wanted him to know about her. And most of that would be false. Almost as if she intended to create a sexual avatar for herself. He looked forward to seeing who she decided to be for him, as much as it frustrated him that she planned to keep him from knowing her more intimately than the physical. He'd never needed an emotional connection with his lovers and nothing had changed that. It certainly shouldn't hurt his feelings that she'd determined not to let him know her and to simply use him for sex.

He'd been used plenty of times and had been fine with it. Made it much easier to use in return.

Not that he'd give up. If he'd wanted uncomplicated, he wouldn't be here. Who was he kidding? He thrived on mystery.

And at digging out and exposing the truth.

If Miss Emily wanted to up the stakes, she'd find out what kind of opponent she'd gotten. Two were playing this game.

When she emerged from the house a good twenty minutes later, she'd clearly taken a shower—likely just to rub his face in it—and had her wet hair scraped into the typical tight ponytail. She'd dressed in jeans and a sweater, both figure-hugging, and wore a smile likely meant to be sultry, though it didn't quite make it there. Not practiced enough. How much could he shape this lover she was constructing for him?

"When you come over tonight—" he took the offensive, toweling off briskly, "—I want you to wear only a coat and your highest heels. Nothing on underneath. And leave your hair down."

The almost-sultry smile faded at the edges and he dropped a quick kiss on the corner of her mouth as he took his neatly folded clothes. Orange blossoms and the lingering scent of aroused woman. Still worked up then, despite the façade she'd created. And unsettled by his request.

"Why do you get to decide?" she asked with a hint of irritation.

"Because I asked first." He grinned at her, watching her color rise. "You had your turn of having your way. Now I want mine."

She folded her arms and tapped her bare foot. Pretty pink toenails. That detail had not been crafted, he'd give good odds on that. Maybe a princess-loving girl lurked inside her armored heart. It would be interesting to dig her out.

"I'm not doing everything you tell me to do, however."

"No?" Dressed, he put the cover back on the hot tub, then circled behind her and drew her against him, sliding his hands under her sweater to her warm, satiny skin beneath. She held herself rigid, then melted slightly when he kissed *that* spot on her neck. The ponytail had its advantages, as did that sensitive point. A doorway into her, whether she realized it or not.

"No." She sounded breathier now, unlocking her arms to let him cup her breasts, encased in an underwire bra. With his thumbs, he pushed the lace down and stroked her nipples to points. "I'm not...comfortable with that."

"That's why you'll have a safeword."

"Seriously?" She might have giggled a little. Or that was the tremor working into her voice from his touch on her breasts. Her nipples were more sensitive than most. Of course, she'd probably never had them clamped or toughened in any way. She'd likely respond like a rocket to the least bit of nipple constriction. The possibilities there excited him tremendously, and he pinched them, to experiment. She squeaked and pressed her tight ass against his groin. Oh yes. Major possibilities there.

"Seriously. Pick a safeword," he coaxed.

"Are you saying we'll get into the BDSM thing?"

"Anything, really. If you don't enjoy something, you say the safeword."

"And then what happens?" She wriggled against his teasing

fingers, so he pinched her nipples a little harder. It didn't take much. She put her hands over his, gripping them through her sweater, holding them still. "Stop that."

"No." He kissed her neck and she moaned. "See how it works? I only stop if you say the safeword. If you do, then we stop and discuss."

"Why can't we discuss first?" Her voice had already gone ragged. Unable to resist, he abandoned one breast to run a hand down her body to unbutton her jeans and slip his hand inside to cup her pussy. Hot and wet, just for him. He pushed one finger between her lips and held it there.

"It's more fun this way," he murmured in her ear. "Don't you think?"

She tried to pump her hips on his hand, but he held her tight between his pelvis and hand, only the one finger steady on her clit, her nipple hard against his palm. "That's the problem. I can't think."

"Pick a safeword then and I'll stop." He moved his finger against her clit, stroking once and stopping again.

"Fuck," she gasped.

"Better to pick something else," he advised, then had to stop himself from laughing at her groan of frustration.

"Firewall. That's my safeword."

Ah, the truth that came out in extremity. A very real safeword for her there. The wall that could not be breached. They would see about that. "Firewall it is."

He let her go, stepping aside and letting her regain her composure. She fussed with adjusting her clothes—of course adjusting the damn ponytail. Did she have any idea how much of a tell that was? It would be interesting to see what she did with her hands with her hair down. If he let her use her hands. Even more enticing. "That will work for both of us."

She gave him a cool look, but her gray eyes raked him, the thoughts behind them hot. "I'm surprised you don't have one already."

"I like to change it up."

"Tailored to the lover of the hour, so you don't confuse them?"

A more accurate hit than he liked. Alas.

"Are we discussing previous love affairs? I'd love to hear about yours too."

She pressed her full lips together, glaring at him.

He laughed, if only to needle her. "I'll see you tonight. Be sure to follow my instructions."

"Is there a penalty in this game if I don't?"

He smiled at her, letting her catch a glimpse of all the wicked ways it had occurred to him to punish her. Oh, he hoped she'd give him a reason to take her there. "Absolutely. It wouldn't be a good game otherwise."

CHAPTER SEVENTEEN

S HE KICKED HERSELF for that one.

"Firewall," indeed. She'd been concentrating so much on keeping that image in place that the word slipped out through the sexual tumult. Fox drove her up the fucking wall—in every way imaginable. The time she'd taken to get her head together, the nice hot shower and a good mental talking-to, all of it had come apart as soon as he put his hands on her again.

No, sooner than that. As soon as he had issued those instructions and given her that challenging *look,* framing his bronzed-god of a body in the fluffy white towel, all her resolutions to play indifferent crumbled. Why he got to her the way he did was a mystery, but it seemed to be a law of this game she couldn't circumvent. Which meant she had to play by those rules. Build this lover-avatar with that in mind.

This Emily would go to his house dressed as he'd instruct-ed. Thinking about that, she pulled the elastic from her hair and finger-combed it down. Then went to blow it dry, so it would look decent. She took off all her clothes, studying herself in the big bathroom mirror as she used the blow-dryer, seeing what he would see. In this way, she confronted not her true self in the mirror, but someone sexier. Freer. Miss Emily, who could indulge in the wild sex Fox had brought into her life.

Fox liked her breasts, which was good. Her track coach had suggested a reduction and she'd never wanted to. Her mother had advised against it, saying all men were breast men, whether they admitted it or not. But then Henry had made fun of them, referring to her "bodacious ta-tas" even at work. Which meant the trolls picked it up and used it in some of the cartoons. Ugly old feelings there.

But Emily had no such issues. She would be a woman with gorgeous tits and many lovers. How many? She needed a number, in case Fox asked. Because that kind of woman would know, wouldn't she? She'd already established that she started late and had that self-admitted recent hiatus. Fox wouldn't know she'd been married—no one on Lyra did—and better to stay well away from that. Still, if she figured on no more than once a week, that many for about four and a half years would be over 200. An awful lot. Just call it 136 men. Fox would be number 137.

Just one of many to Miss Emily.

Instead of dressing again, she pulled on her robe and sat down at the computer. She didn't log on to any of her servers—let them wonder where Phoenix had gone—but opened a Word document and began writing Miss Emily's story.

Building that firewall.

SHE PUT ON flats to walk over to Fox's, carrying her heels. The summery, strappy things weren't great for walking far, but they were her highest. It had been a bit like rummaging through her young woman's heart, digging out her bin of shoes from before. All of them chosen because she liked them, never considering what her coworkers might whisper about her. Before she'd realized being female could be a serious liability and being girly the greatest sin of all. Ignoring the emotions they elicited, she ruthlessly chose only the ones Miss Emily would wear. Particularly the black leather thigh-high boots she'd saved up for, bought right before things got bad, and had never worn. She didn't even remember packing them up, but here they were, still in the box.

Tomorrow night she would wear them and Fox would have to do as *she* said.

It felt odd to be naked under her trench coat. Exciting. She could enjoy that, she reminded herself. Whatever Fox had in mind, Emily would go with it. She almost wanted to resolve not to use the safeword, just to see what all he'd do, but even contemplating it panicked her, deep inside.

She hated that part of herself. The terrified bit. The one who'd caved to the trolls. Who'd cried when Henry left. After the first couple of years, she'd managed to bury her pretty deep, only wrestling with her when a stranger knocked on the door. She was the one, however, who clung to the idea of the safeword and had to have it, if Emily was going to get laid. So she kept the intention of using it, like a security blanket to pacify that weak and pitiful part of her.

To shut her up and keep Fox from ever knowing about her.

Outside his door, she kicked off the flats and pulled on the heels. She smoothed her hair and any remaining nerves. Then rang the bell, feeling herself go wet with anticipation.

Pavlov's dog.

Fox opened the door wearing skin-tight black leather pants and a midnight blue silk shirt—tucked in, but unbuttoned to the low-slung waist—and carrying something by his side she couldn't quite see. He smiled, half charm and half pure sex. Her heart leaped to see him. Or, more accurately, her pussy did. Better that way too.

"I'm never quite sure you'll show until you do," he said, keeping her standing on the porch.

"I thought you preferred anticipation. Isn't uncertainty part of that?" She liked being that woman, who kept a man wondering.

"True enough." His eyes moved past her to the driveway. "You didn't drive?"

"I didn't want anyone to see my car parked here."

"People saw us together at the diner. Glory knows we're seeing each other." He seemed a bit hurt by that. Though she felt sorry for it, it helped that he cared about these things. She trusted in that honest response from him.

She shifted her weight, her feet unused to the heels. "I'm staying the night, aren't I? I didn't want to advertise that." Though Miss Emily wouldn't care about that, would she? Of course, that woman wouldn't have had to stow her kitchen trashcan in the closet to keep her dog out of it while she conducted her lurid affairs. "Are you going to let me in or should I go home?"

He looked her over. "Are you naked under the coat?"

Her face grew hot and she immediately reconsidered this particular character. Who was she kidding—she couldn't pull off that kind of sexual experience. "Yes."

"Show me."

"Here?"

"Just open the coat enough for me to see. It's not like I'm making you strip on my doorstep, though the thought has its appeal."

"I don't see why—"

"It's a test. To see if you followed my instructions, to test your willingness to continue to do so and to determine if you're into it. Now do as I say."

Stubbornly, she felt like digging in and refusing. Or showing him and going home. His lips curved as he watched her face, obviously loving this game. *You have an expressive everything.* Fine. Not as if he hadn't seen everything already. Her fingers fumbled the knotted sash and she opened the coat down the middle, holding the sides out to serve as blinds in case anyone came by.

He took his time looking, like a buyer inspecting merchandise, and her skin prickled under his gaze. At last his eyes met hers again. "You look gorgeous. No, no—I didn't say you could close the coat. Here are the rules for tonight. Once you step over the threshold, you have to do everything I tell you, without question or argument. If you fail in this, I get to punish you for it. Do you agree to my terms?"

She had a bit of trouble swallowing, the weak part of her whispering anxious warnings, the rest of her ramping up with excitement. "But I can always safeword out."

"Always." Dropping a bit of the stern attitude, he gave her a slight nod of reassurance.

Just a game. *Follow the rules and you won't be punished.* That ought to be a snap. She was nothing if not an excellent player. And, to her surprise, she trusted him to abide by the rules also. It was part of his openness. Lay the cards on the table. No hidden agenda or jealousy. "I agree."

He grinned. "Music to my ears. Do come in." He stepped aside, gesturing her in with a courtly bow. Because he hadn't told her otherwise, she continued to hold the coat open, leaving her flats and toiletry bag on the porch. She wanted to ask Fox to get them, but that might count as questioning him so she restrained herself. She didn't want to be such a n00b that she blew it immediately on a technicality.

"Hang up your coat in the closet, please. What's this—a toothbrush?"

Deciding she didn't need to reply with the obvious answer, she concentrated on hanging up her coat and not thinking about how he'd threatened to keep her naked in there, stewing and waiting for him. She'd absolutely safeword out of that scenario. Finished, she waited for the next order. It was similar to Mother May I, after all. Or Simon Says.

"Turn around and face me." Fox sounded amused. Maybe she was taking it to an extreme, but with an unspecified punishment on the line… "Stay still."

That took more effort, to hold herself without twitching while he arranged the long fall of her hair around her shoulders, his face admiring in a way she drank in. "You look almost like a different woman with your hair down," he said. "Softer, more animal. More vulnerable. Do you feel more vulnerable this way?"

She did, but she didn't answer. Hopefully that wasn't a punishable offense. The beat went on a bit long and he spoke again.

"If I could, I'd make you wear it down all the time. Of course, I'd also want you to be naked and that's hardly practical." He cupped her breast, weighing it, then traced his index finger down her midline. "So far you've passed the first two tests. Let's see about that third one."

Watching her face, he slipped the finger between her thighs. Easily done with her slick moisture. He stroked her, lightly, but she had to concentrate not to move. "Very wet," he murmured. "I'd say you're liking this just fine."

He'd set her shoes and bag on the hall bench, along with what he'd been carrying when he opened the door. Picking it up, he showed her the length of rope. "I'm going to bind your wrists now. Hold out your hands, wrists crossed."

She obeyed, though the panicky part of her whispered louder. The rope, soft, looped over her wrists. Focusing on Fox's intent face, the way his coppery lashes feathered against his cheekbones as he tightened the rope, she tried to quell the anxiety. People did this kind of thing all the time. It barely counted as kinky. What reason could she give for not wanting it? He knotted the rope.

"Firewall," she blurted, before she'd really decided to. His gaze flicked up to hers, with a bit of surprise, but he immediately undid the knot. Which also unknotted the pang in her gut. "I can't—"

He shook his head, cutting her off. "Safeword is just that. You don't have to explain. Do you want to stop altogether?"

"No." She really didn't, now that the panicky part had receded. That he'd proved he'd stick to his word. "Just…no rope."

"Is that a hard limit? No binding at all, or not rope?" He brushed her hair over her shoulder and she realized she still had her wrists crossed.

Self-consciously, she rubbed them, the sizzling sensation of the rope lingering there. "I don't know. Do I have to know this minute?"

He smiled, warmly reassuring, and leaned in to kiss her, a sweet brush of lips, his hands settling on her waist. "No. We can play it by ear. Would you rather bail on the game and keep it vanilla tonight?"

"Not necessarily." She leaned into him, enjoying the texture of his clothes against her naked skin. "I did like it up until the rope."

"Excellent. But it's harder, you know. To stay still without being tied up. You haven't practiced that at all, so it will be difficult for you. The odds of punishment for infractions goes up."

A challenge. "Try me."

His eyes gleamed. He loved it when she took up the challenge. With all his gambling references, he clearly liked to raise the stakes. "All right then. Game on."

"Wait."

All patience now, he did, listening. Such an interesting mix of dominating and ruthless determination to bend her sexually along with a similarly infinite understanding. As much as he talked as if he wanted to use her for his own pleasure, he paid more attention to what she wanted, how she felt, than any man ever had. A conundrum. Especially in light of what she was about to ask.

"I don't want answering questions to be part of it," she told him, watching the way his mouth hardened ever so slightly. He didn't like it much. "I want that off the table. I don't have to answer any questions."

"I can ask, but you don't have to answer."

She didn't love that. His questions created a certain pressure on her, whether she declined to reply or not. They continued to echo in her head. *Do you feel more vulnerable this way?*

"Fine. But asking won't do you any good."

His lips twitched in a secretive smile, the only indication he recognized the lie for what it was. "We'll see. In fact, let's do this. You may not speak. Except to say your safeword. That way I can ask all the questions I want to and you're relieved of the burden of answering—or arguing. Ready to play?"

Play, yes. Just a game. She nodded.

He brushed her cheek. "Let's get out of this damn hallway. Hands and knees. I want you to crawl into the bedroom and kneel in the center of the floor. Hands behind your neck, under your hair, thighs spread as wide as you can manage."

His words quickened her again, the heat rising back up to previous levels. She dropped to her knees, without running her hands over his body as she wanted to, just in case it wasn't allowed. Then she crawled on the Kapsucks' awful shag carpet, down the hall to the master bedroom, feeling extra wicked at the thought of the horror on their faces if they saw what she was getting up to with their newest renter.

Fox's soft footfalls followed after her, meaning that he saw everything. Her hair got in the way, snagging under her knees. It felt odd, having it sliding over her skin this way, falling into her face. Likely there was an art to this but she didn't know it. *More animal,* he'd said. *More vulnerable.*

"Hold." Fox moved beside her when she obediently paused. He gathered up her hair and held it, a leash. "Proceed."

It helped, not having the thick tendrils in the way, but the tugging at her scalp as he walked beside her became even more distracting. She felt like his pet, which shouldn't have been as arousing as it was. She recalled his excitement earlier that day when he'd kissed her foot and she understood something of it now.

It was restful, in a way, to give up thinking about who she pretended to be and just exist for a space of time. She liked that she couldn't speak. Less chance of giving something away.

In the bedroom, the curtains had been drawn and pillar candles lit around the room, making it bright. And romantic. The ambience made her nervous in a way the hallway games hadn't. She stuck to the rules, however, kneeling, saying nothing, even as he continued playing with her hair, using gentle tugs to straighten her spine and make her kneel up higher.

With her thighs spread, the position strained her muscles, neither sitting on her heels nor all the way up. "Stay right there," he told her, then arranged her hair down her back. "How does that feel? Oh, sorry—you can't answer."

He walked around her, the smug look on his face showing

he knew full well that her muscles were already vibrating with the effort to stay that way. Crouching in front of her, he toyed with her nipples, smiling when her breathing quickened. "So," he said in a conversational tone, "here's how this works. I want you to hold that position. Don't move."

For how long? Damn him, he read the question in her eyes and declined to answer. Messing with her head.

As if reading her mind, in fact, he dipped his chin in cheerful agreement. "If you move up or down, there will be a penalty."

CHAPTER EIGHTEEN

EMILY STARED AT him, defiance and determination darkening her silvery eyes.

He almost regretted that she'd wanted to continue the game. For that everlasting moment in the hallway, when she'd panicked over the rope, he'd glimpsed something of the real her. Soft and frightened. Wounded. He'd wanted nothing more than to sweep her into bed and make love to her, melt that tension away. Why had the binding gotten to her when so little else had?

Not rape or assault, though she sometimes read that way. No, something else triggered her there. Not that she'd ever explain, with her determination to keep him out.

She thought she could avoid answering his questions, as if she didn't know how much she revealed with her small tells— the flick of her gaze away when she hid something, the way she looked up slightly when making up a story or referencing a previous lie. Even now she thought to disguise how much it affected her for him to touch her hair. She'd taken his breath away, looking like a woman out of a storybook. A sexual Snow White, her hair that much darker and her skin that much whiter for the contrast.

A flush rose from her breasts as he worked her nipples, the

strenuous position and arousal eating at her from both sides. Even her iron will couldn't withstand this kind of physical strain.

Soon she couldn't help but fail, and then he'd get to punish her.

While he waited, he contemplated what kind of penalty would be most effective to get through to her. There was more than one way to a woman's heart. If she wouldn't let him romance her, wouldn't trust him with her secrets, then he'd break the lock on the back door and prowl around, look for himself.

The realization dawned on her that he meant for her to fail, the knowledge transforming her face. She hated losing, but he'd stacked the deck so he'd win. The loss—and a bit of punishment—would chisel at those walls. How best to get to her? An edge of desperation made her firm her lips.

"When you fail, as I can see you've figured out is inevitable, how shall I punish you?" He let go of her nipples, running his hands over her narrow ribcage to her waist, then palmed her thighs. Runner's legs, but she hadn't trained for this. They trembled. It wouldn't be long. "Have you ever been spanked, Miss Emily?" He watched her face, looking for real fear, like she'd shown with the rope. It helped to know she would safeword out. A lot wouldn't, especially stubborn newbies. "No? Not as an adult, I think. Maybe not even as a child. Were you a spoiled little girl? I bet you were Mommy and Daddy's little princess."

Careful, Sparky, don't think about her in that white debutante's dress. Turned over your knee and no panties beneath. She reacted, though, her flesh electric under his touch.

He moved his hands up her thighs. "Too bad you can't tell me how you feel about it, the idea of me punishing you. Let's see what your body says." He cupped her mound, the silky dark hair tickling his palm, her pussy lips hot and swollen. She dripped with moisture. More, she shuddered at the light touch, closing her eyes, her whole body seeming to moan, though she repressed the sound itself.

His balls tightened with the need to have her, the power of holding her in the palm of his hand. He wanted her like this, focused on him, responding to him, seeing *him.*

"Look at me," he demanded, and ran his fingers over her folds, savoring the way her eyes flew open, startled by the order, unguarded, without guile, and how she vibrated as his touch, close to orgasm just from this much. He established the rhythm, finding the one that affected her most, driving her up. Amazing, really, that she'd managed to hold the position this long. "Did I mention the rule that you can only come with permission? Of course, you have to ask for permission and you've forfeited the right to speak."

She pressed her lips tightly together, eyes flashing with anger—which yielded immediately to pleading when he pushed a finger inside her tight channel. His cock throbbed with the desire to press into her. She swayed, starting to shake.

"You're losing it, aren't you?" he taunted her, her eyes full of unspoken words. In some ways, this communication felt more honest, with her relieved of the burden of lying to him. "Very soon, you'll be draped naked across my lap while I spank your sweet ass. I think it will drive you wild. I know it will me.

And I won't stop, even if you beg me. I'll be loving it too much, having you at my mercy, and when I'm ready, I'll fuck you until you forget yourself and scream out my name."

Her channel clenched around his finger and she started to shake in earnest, whimpering a little, as her pride frayed before the sensual extremity. Her tits bounced so enticingly he had to grab one, squeezing it and working a second finger into her passage, pumping them in and out of her. She gritted her teeth and made a keening sound, her body tight as a bow string. Mesmerized, he vibrated with her. He did this to her, made her lose all that reserve and become this wild and lustful creature. Which would break first—her strength or the climax?

Her thighs did.

With an incoherent cry of frustration, she collapsed onto her heels, closing her eyes in defeat, though she kept her hands on her neck, her body mottled pink with unrealized arousal. Ideal, since holding off the climax would make her experience of the spanking that much better. Much as he wanted to keep his hands on her, he let go and stood.

Moving behind her, he gathered up her hair, telling her she could lower her hands. The natural curl in her hair came out when it wasn't restrained in the ponytail. Not black, but a dark chestnut, with glints of deep red, it spilled over his hands light as sea foam. Now he wound it around his left hand, drawing her to her feet.

She didn't look at him as he sat on the edge of the bed, tugging her with him. Touching the tips of her fingers together, she betrayed her nervousness. Everything else about her hummed with overwhelming excitement. He resonated with her, full of the power of the moment.

"Across my lap."

Deliciously pliant, she obeyed, draping her long, delicate body over his thighs, following the lead of his hand in her hair. This was the trust she otherwise denied him and he reveled in it, smoothing his dominant hand over the tight, white and flawless cheeks of her bottom.

"Stretch your hands over your head and grasp the headboard."

She did, seeming grateful to have something to hold on to. Something he understood. He couldn't stand to have his hands free when spanked or otherwise punished. It made him frantic.

Savoring the moment, he caressed the perfect globes of her bottom, the skin like satin. She shook slightly, face buried in the mattress. He wound her hair tighter around his hand, which stilled her. Then smacked her bottom, once on each cheek, sharp and stinging slaps.

She cried out, more in surprise that it hurt. So sensitive. For some reason, newbies never expected it to hurt as much as it did. It wouldn't take much to break her composure, all he needed before he entered her intimately. He set to spanking her in earnest, keeping the slaps to stings. Enough to pinken her pretty white skin, but not enough to bruise. Her feet kicked against the bed and her knuckles whitened with her grip on the headboard. She groaned and squealed, the tension in her body rising, thrumming with the sensory input.

She began to weep, her cries of pain thickening with the tears. This was always the hardest part for him, not to stop when they started to cry. Her pussy was hot against his thigh, however, and still dripping. Tears were part of it and he dipped his hand into her folds, giving her a break and reassuring himself of her continued arousal.

She gasped, clutching her thighs tight around his hand. Closer to orgasm than ever. Tugging her hair, he made her arch her head back. She sobbed a little, holding the climax off, her face wet with tears. It was too sweet, too tempting. He popped a thumb inside her and bracketed her clit. "Come for me now, Emily. Do it."

With a cry that was almost a word, she did, bowing her spine and pressing the heels of her hands into the mattress. Her whole body convulsed, bucking on his lap as she came apart, climaxing with that wrenching fervency she brought to everything.

He stuck with her through the rippling aftershocks, and kept working her even as she moaned a protest, not letting her come all the way down. Sometime they'd find out how many times in a row she could climax.

But, at this moment, he couldn't deny himself. He needed to bury himself in her, feel her wrapped around him when she reached the final extremity.

When her breath came fast again, her body filling with tension and her slick pussy pushing against his hand with increasing desperation, he smacked her pink cheeks, reveling in the way she moaned in response. She'd passed into the place where the pain and the pleasure all blended into one transporting feeling. Beyond the emotional, beyond the physical.

Keeping his hand in her hair, he moved her off his lap. She'd given up all resistance, letting him position her on her hands and knees, pressing her forehead to the mattress, her adorably pinkened ass high in the air and the captivating valley of her swollen pussy offered up for his enjoyment.

Stripping off his clothes, mad to be inside her, he snagged a condom from the bedside table, then crawled over to kneel behind her. Not entering her yet—to torture them both a little longer, prolong this first time together—he slid his sheathed cock along her lips, stroking her clit and reaching beneath to fill his hands with her gorgeous tits. She moaned, in a wordless place, fully with him. A Stradivarius of a woman, tuned precisely to him, her flesh hot, body yielding.

He pinched her nipples, hard, to penetrate the cloud and she cried out.

"Beg me to fuck you," he demanded. She didn't reply and he rocked his groin against her, feeling how close she was, how much she needed to come. She'd pulled up the fitted sheet from the corners of the mattress and had it clenched in her hands.

"You may speak now," he gritted out, realizing he, too, hovered on the verge. She made him crazy, starving to be inside her. "But it better be to beg me to fuck you. Otherwise I won't let you come for the rest of the night."

She made a hoarse cry of denial.

Needing to see her face, he flipped her over and knelt between her beautifully spread thighs, pushing her knees wide to open her for his penetration. He positioned himself at her entrance and laced his fingers with her delicate ones, pressing her hands on either side of her head. With her hair like sable beneath her, her face flushed and eyes silver moons of nameless emotion, she returned his gaze. Yielding, pleading, yes, but also demanding.

"Beg me," he ordered her.

Her eyes glittered, her lips pressed stubbornly closed. But she throbbed beneath him, her hips straining to close the distance, nipples hard against his chest. Unable to restrain himself, he nudged inside her and her eyelids lowered slightly in desperate pleasure, her vulva lips clenching on the head of his cock. It electrified him and he nearly lost it then and there, as his young self had with his first woman.

"Shit." He dropped his forehead against hers, both of them slick with sweat, aware his own breath shuddered out of him. "I don't care what you say, just give me the word."

She moved under him, taking his earlobe in her sharp teeth and nipping him—a spark that went straight to his balls. "Fuck me, Fox," she hissed. "And, if you do it right, I'll scream your name."

He lost his mind at that. Without finesse, he rammed into her, her channel hot around him. She convulsed, fastening her mouth to his and wrapping her legs around his hips, trapping him with anaconda strength. He wrenched his hands from hers and levered himself up, pumping in and out of her. She sank her nails into his ass, making him go deeper, her face avid and her eyes like a wild woman's.

Just as he felt himself on the edge, the point of no return, the pressure in his cock and balls so great that nothing could stop him, she threw back her head and screamed. "Oh, fuck me, Fox!"

She convulsed around him, the vise of her pussy sending

him spinning into blackness, into the void where he thrust and emptied himself into the welcoming cradle of her hot body. Chanting his name in gratifying cries, she milked him, wringing him dry with the grip of her hands, legs and her hungry mouth fastened on his neck.

At last, spent, he collapsed on her, her breasts crushed against him and slick with sweat, his face buried in the orange blossom scent of her silky hair.

Remotely, he knew he should be the gentleman and lift himself off her. And he would. Any minute now. The blood would return to the rest of his body and he'd be able to move. She dragged in a deep breath, her chest expanding under him, and he made himself do it. He found his elbows and raised himself enough for her to breathe.

She gazed at him from half-lidded, sleepy gray eyes, her lashes spiky black and damp, her pink lips moist and skin dewy. They curved in a smile, sweet, almost tender and full of a raw vulnerability that rocked him. Without thought or agenda, he kissed her. She tasted like a flower, opening for him with a total lack of reserve, her body lax. Still semi-hard, he rocked his hips, moving inside her and she undulated, her tongue meeting his, their breath mingling.

Some deep feeling moved in the same way, a wave of warmth, of renewed desire. Reluctantly, he broke the kiss. "I'd better deal with the condom." Reaching between them, he held it in place and withdrew from her, feeling colder without her skin against his. He ditched the used condom in a wastebasket by the bed and handed her one of the washcloths he'd stacked there, using one on himself.

Emily sat up, her hair falling around her white body, knees curled to the side, and watched him with a bemused expression. "You keep sex-cloths in your bedside table?"

He finished drying his cock and tossed the cloth aside. "Yes. Much more civilized than Kleenex." Taking the cloth he'd handed her, he nudged her knees open. She leaned back on her elbows, letting him do the honors. With a sense of worshipping at the altar of womanhood, he wiped her thighs clean, tenderly blotting her sweet, pink pussy. Experimentally, he took the cloth lower, drying the cleft between her buttocks and her tight anus, watching her face. She didn't pull away so he set the cloth aside and stroked her, dragging moisture down to rub that opening, too, pressing in a bit.

"What else do you keep in your bedside table?" she asked, a sultry dare.

"All kinds of things. What do you hope is in there?"

"I don't know." She gasped when he worked the tip of his thumb inside her, slipping his middle finger into her vagina, her face alight with receptive interest. She'd let go of much of her reserve, all playful, open woman. "Try me," she dared him.

"Okay then." He picked up some lube and poured some into his palm. Holding her captivated gaze, he warmed it for her and rubbed it into her cleft. Her lips parted, cheeks blooming with desire and a touch of embarrassment. He worked his finger inside her and she resisted, the ring of muscle tight. "You've never played this way?"

She bit her lip and shook her head, the momentary distraction making her loosen so he pushed in farther. A tremor of surprise ran over her face. "It feels odd. Good, in a different way."

Fox sent up a prayer of gratitude. Not all women liked anal—not surprising, since they weren't wired for the pleasure of it the same way—but, with one who did… "See what you think of this, then." Pulling a slim dildo from his collection, he lubed it up, letting her watch. She was getting off on the novelty of it, the sense of adventure lighting her up from inside. She'd stopped thinking so much, he decided. The avalanche of orgasms, maybe the crashing release of being punished, it had all softened her and released her at least temporarily from whatever worries plagued her so.

He pressed the dildo inside her virgin asshole. Smaller than his finger, it stretched her gently, going much deeper. She sighed at the sensation, nearly drew her knees together, but then relaxed. Still propped on her elbows, she watched him work it in and out of her, eyes darkening with arousal. "It feels so full, but it's not very big. Not like it would be if…" She met his gaze with some hesitation.

"Not like if I fucked you up the ass with my cock?" He teased her, loving that she blushed even more. "Or something larger? That's something best worked up to." Giving her a wicked smile he bent over, pressed the dildo deeper into her and sucked her rigid clit into his mouth.

CHAPTER NINETEEN

THE PAIRED SENSATIONS shuddered through her. The illicit novelty of the oil-slicked black rod working her rear passage, stimulating deep places she'd never felt, while Fox's clever mouth stroked her clit. The way the increasing arousal carried her on a gentle wave this time.

She felt liquid. Boneless and more relaxed than she'd felt in years. Maybe ever. The experience of being spanked across Fox's lap had rocked her world to its foundations. She'd very nearly used her safeword, but something about the way he held her hair and took control offered a kind of safety. Ironic and not something she really understood. And the spanking itself...if it had gone on much longer, she would have come from that alone. The whole thing had shattered her and she still hadn't found the pieces.

More, she didn't want to.

She wanted Fox to possess her, to do whatever he pleased to her body, and she wanted to give it all up without reserve, without so much thinking. The way he enjoyed her, paying attention to her least gasp or cry, ironically made her trust him more. A guy like this would never be careless of her, even in the most extreme sex...*if I fucked you up the ass with my cock—or something larger.* The idea made her feel wild and decadent. She wanted him to do that, to split her open and drain all this poison she carried inside. Drinking it away with his hungry mouth and agile tongue. Never had a man acted as if he enjoyed giving her head so much.

But he did. It wasn't a means to an end. The way he smiled at her when she opened her pussy for him, how he licked his lips like a boy offered ice cream and then dove on her—it all conspired to make her feel more desired and savored than ever in her life. Even touching her asshole, the dirtiest of dirties, he seemed excited. He wanted every part of her.

And she'd give it to him.

His cock up her ass. *Or something larger.*

The orgasm took her by surprise and she cried out in shock, calling Fox's name and reaching for him. His hand found hers and held it while she rode it out, feeling both full and empty. She wanted him inside her again. Had to have him in her. "Oh please," she said, ready to beg. Ready for anything at all. "Fuck me again, Fox."

He pulled the dildo out, wrapped it in one of his sex cloths—who did that?—and slipped a finger barely inside her vulva while he thumbed her still-throbbing clit. Something about his smile forewarned her. "I would, my delicious lover, but we have a small problem."

They couldn't be out of condoms. "What?"

"You came without permission."

Shit. "I forgot."

"I know." He shook his head, like a disappointed teacher. "Your powers of concentration are sadly lacking. We need to work on that. Stand up by the side of the bed."

Feeling a little shocked, off balance, nervous and also thrilled, she did as he said. What now? Not another spanking, she thought. He rummaged through the sex drawer, blocking her line of sight as if he knew how curious she was to see what all he had in there. Something small and sliver glittered in his hand.

"Clasp your hands behind your back," he ordered, giving her a stern look that made her weak in the knees. She did and he showed her the clamps. "Ever had clamps on your nipples?"

She shook her head, even more nervous. "Do they hurt?"

He smiled, a little cruel, and her pussy clenched. "Of course. They're not a good punishment for naughty girls otherwise."

Waiting a moment, he gave her a chance to say something else. But what was there to say? Besides her safeword. And she didn't want to.

Fox nodded, his approval surprisingly like warm sunshine. Something beyond analysis. "Good girl." Taking her right nipple in his fingers, he coaxed it into a hard point, slid the clamp onto it, then stood back.

It felt tight at first, then stung, then hurt more, the pain rising. Her hand rose of its own volition and snatched it off. Fox frowned at her. "Not allowed, Emily."

She felt the sting of tears, at a strange precipice of emotion. "I couldn't help it."

"I know." He said it in a gentle tone. "That's why it's hard to have your hands free." He reached into the drawer and pulled out a pair of handcuffs. "Shall we try these?"

The emotion welled into a bigger bubble, an unvocalized

sob. A feeling of desperation threaded through with an almost unbearable level of desire. Her whole being hummed with it. No panic this time. The unreality of it was, she *wanted* him to make her wear the horrible little clamp. To have to suffer it and be unable to do anything about it. The safeword gave her the get out of jail free—and he was waiting for her to say it—assessing her with his bright, insightful gaze as she fidgeted, the pinched nipple still pulsing, the handcuffs glittering with promise.

Of what, she didn't know, but she wanted to find out.

Needed to.

She held out her wrists and he shook his head. "Behind your back. Bend over the bed, face down, legs spread."

Horribly excited, feeling as if she'd relinquished a control that had been grinding her down, she obeyed, opening her legs for him to see how much this affected her. Though he knew anyway. He'd seen it in her face and, for once, she didn't mind.

"On your tiptoes," he snapped, and smacked the tender underside of her bottom. She whimpered but did it, pushing her ass in the air, offering him her submission. With her hands behind her back, she couldn't brace herself and her face mashed into the tangled sheet, her hair a suffocating cloud around her. Cool, hard metal—almost sharp—encircled her wrists and locked them together, sending a shiver through her. Captive. At the mercy of the most sexual man she'd ever met.

Oil dribbled through her cleft and Fox rubbed it into her anus, still tingling from the earlier invasion. She couldn't quite keep her breath going, her calves straining to stay on tiptoe, while he ignored her steaming pussy and worked a finger into her. She moaned and he gave her a quick spank.

"No protesting or I'll tie you up like this and leave you here all night to stew in your own juices. Don't think I won't do it."

He opened the drawer, the sound electrifying her. What now? She wanted to weep, to scream, for him to please just touch her again. Something cool and bulbous pressed against her anus. He added more oil, pressing it into her. It felt huge and she wished fervently that she could see it.

"All that squirming won't save you either," Fox scolded and she sobbed a little at the censure in his voice. "Be still or I'll find something even bigger."

She drew in a deep calming breath and made herself stay still, pressing into the bed and bracing herself.

"Much better," he crooned, and wrapped one hand in her hair, anchoring her to the bed with it. "There's a good girl. My little princess and her first butt plug." As he spoke, he worked it into her, an extraordinary invasion that shimmered with a combination of pain and pleasure. With a nearly audible pop, it went in and her muscles closed around it. She wanted to grab it and take it out, the cuffs cutting into her wrists as she tried to reach for it.

Fox laughed and ran his hands over her wriggling ass. "You are so lovely, struggling like that. It's truly tempting to leave you in this predicament, to see how long you can stand it." He trailed a tickling finger—far too light to do her any good—through her open pussy and she had to clamp her lips on the groan of utter torment. "You're so close to orgasm again, I bet I could make you come inside thirty seconds. But you won't be that lucky. You still have to prove you can behave."

She shuddered inside at how much she wanted to do that, dazzle and impress him. Please him.

"Feet together, still on tiptoe."

Complying, though it wasn't easy, she held the position, the thing in her ass compressed now and her fluids running down her thighs. "You have such gorgeous legs," he murmured, running his hands down them to her ankles. More metal, clinking, cuffing her feet together. Before she could process how she felt about it, his hand was in her hair, levering her up and turning her to face him. He kissed her cheeks and she became aware that she was weeping, silently, without effort.

"Such beautiful tears," he whispered. "I believe you truly wish to please me, don't you?"

She nodded, meaning it with all her heart. Yes, whatever he wanted.

"Kneel down then." He helped her lower herself to the carpet with one hand in her hair and the other casually cupping her breast. Moving behind her, he clipped the handcuffs to the ones binding her ankles, making her arch her back to reach. Her breasts were offered up by the position and he showed her the clamps again. A fine trembling ran through her, her brain going to blue screen. "We're going to try this again and you can't stop me this time. You're going to pay for disobeying me. And then I'll give you the opportunity to make it up to me."

He fondled her breast, weighing it in his hand, lightly fondling the nipple. "Say, 'yes, please.'"

She had to clear her throat, clogged with longing. "Yes, please."

Brushing his thumb over her lower lip, he studied her face,

then kissed her. "So very beautiful. My helpless captive."

She nodded and watched him stroke both nipples, already hard with arousal, into impossibly hard points. With her breath coming in pants, she could barely stay still, the plug stimulating her unbearably, her bottom hot and stinging still, her pussy burning to be touched. Fox slapped the side of her breast, not hard, but enough to shock her. "Spread your thighs," he ordered. "If you make yourself come again, I'll have to truly punish you. Nothing so gentle next time."

Obeying, she braced herself, holding as still as she could until he seemed satisfied that her nipples were as engorged as possible. Then, with brisk efficiency, he attached one clamp and then the other. And stood, watching her, hands on hips, cock high and hard again. The pain rose and built, and she bit down on her lip to keep from making any sound that might be construed as protest. She found herself struggling almost frantically against the cuffs, her breasts feeling like balloons constricted at the points with burning pain. Wiggling her shoulders didn't dislodge them, it just made them seem to cling tighter.

Looking up at Fox, she pleaded with him silently. He smiled and shook his head, clearly enjoying her predicament. Unable to help herself, she sobbed a little. Then tried to calm herself. He'd take them off when he was ready. There was nothing she could do.

His hand stroked her hair and she leaned into it, yearning for the tender touch.

"Do you want to please me, Emily?" he asked softly and she nodded, wanting nothing more in that moment. Holding his cock, he offered it to her. Oh yes. She took the velvety head in her mouth, swirling her tongue around it, unreasonably delighted when his lids lowered and a tremor of pleasure ran through him. He held her head, but gently, letting her control the depth and rhythm.

Using every trick she knew, she did her best to please him. To give him a small taste of the pleasure he'd given her. The weight and heft of his cock in her mouth seemed a twin of the penetration in her ass, counterpointed by the pinch of the clamps. It seemed she drifted in some realm, where she hung suspended between the dual penetrations, nothing more than an instrument of pleasure. She sucked him in as deeply as she could and he made a sound, fisting her hair in his hand and pulling himself from her mouth. "Witch."

With one hand still in her hair, tugging her head back, he bent over her and slapped the side of her breast, making it sting and the nipple flare into throbbing life. She gasped, her vulva aching with the intense arousal. He slapped the other breast and she fought his grip, struggling wildly, overcome by a desire so intense it transported her.

"Tell me what you want," he demanded.

"Anything," she panted. "Whatever you want to do to me."

In that moment, she meant it and he knew it, his face almost contorted with a savage lust. Yanking her head back, he fastened his mouth on the clamp and scraped it off with his teeth. The blood surged into the compressed tissues like a limb returning instantaneously to life. She screamed and he pulled off the other one. Both breasts on fire, she thrashed against the cuffs, barely noticing that he'd unhooked her wrists from her ankles, until he positioned her facedown on the floor, stretched out flat. Her throbbing nipples scraped on the carpet.

With her thighs pressed tight together, the plug still stretching her, when he entered her from behind, his latex-clad cock felt enormous. The penetration wasn't deep, focusing sensation on her stretched vulva, but the intensity was unbearable. Yet she bore it. She had no choice, with her hands cuffed together and his strong thighs bracketing hers. The way he flexed his hips against her ass rocked the plug, stimulating her in both passages. He pulled her head back with the hand in her hair and she went with it, dimly aware that she made a continuous stream of pleading cries and that he responded to her in kind, savage promises of how she'd take whatever he gave her and love it. Threatening her if she orgasmed without permission. She concentrated on holding it back, using every ounce of will to obey.

When he ordered her to come, she did.

They came together, a mutual unraveling that unbuttoned her mind and sent her reeling through formless space, Fox's shouts ringing in her ears while his pounding body ground her into the carpet, while the rest of her existed in another realm entirely.

IT FELT AS if she'd been gone from her body for eons, but it must have been only moments. Fox's weight still lay heavily over her, her cuffed hands crushed between them, his ragged breathing harsh in her ear.

She dragged in a breath, her sore nipples scraping on the carpet, and he made a calming sound, then pressed a kiss to her shoulder.

"Goddam, Miss Emily," he muttered. "I think you nearly killed me."

"You? I can't breathe. I think I *am* dead."

He breathed a laugh and levered himself up. "Then I'm a necrophiliac." He withdrew from her and helped her sit up. Unlocking the cuffs, he freed her and handed her a cloth from his stack. She pressed her palms to her throbbing nipples, hissing a little.

"I have some cream that will help. Come on." He stood and held out a hand to help her up.

"What about the, um…"

He grinned, waiting for her to say it. *My little princess and her first butt plug,* he'd taunted her. Against all reason she found herself rawly blushing. Fox leaned in and kissed her. "You are priceless. So abandoned in the moment. Possibly the most sensual and responsive woman I've ever met and—even with my butt plug still spreading your ass—adorably shy about it. I'll let you take it out in private."

He tugged her into the bathroom and insisted on applying the cream to her nipples himself, threatening to tie her to the towel rack if she kept squirming. She almost wanted him to. It made no sense that she'd gone from panic over the rope to this sense of craving the cuffs, but there it was. Even with her body depleted, the desire for him crawled through her. As if it had somehow always been a part of her and had simply been locked away. She watched his face while he massaged the cream into her nipples, his high cheekbones with just a hint of freckles within the golden tan. Intent on his task, he wore a rare serious expression. Warmth curled in her loins, his touch on her nipples her cue to dampen for more. Feeling dreamy, she wondered at her response to him. His eyes flicked up and he took her in, gaze moving over her face with a kind of wonder.

"What will it take for us to have enough of each other?" he asked, as if posing a philosophical question.

"More than this," she breathed.

He nodded. "Much more."

Slipping his fingers between her thighs, he stroked her, petting her like a cat and she opened for him. He cupped the back of her neck and kissed her, long and slow, echoing the languid movement of his hand. Like an echo of the previous climaxes, an incipient orgasm shimmered on the edges, flooding her with warmth. She leaned on the bathroom counter, being kissed and caressed by this man who affected her as no other had, and asked for his permission to come.

"Yes, darling girl," he whispered, holding her in the loose embrace and placing kisses on her eyelids, "come for me."

CHAPTER TWENTY

T HE LAST ONE undid her in some profound way. She came, a soft susurrus of a climax, rocking on his hand and sighing his name, almost a prayer. Something turned over in his rock of a heart.

It was her amazing surrender. How she'd gone from the remote, prickly woman who refused him the least crumb of herself to this pliant and passionate lover who denied him nothing. She likely didn't even realize how totally she'd opened herself to him, showing every emotion, shuddering under his touch in a way that had both exhilarated and humbled him.

Rationalizing that she needed some privacy, he excused himself and went out to reorder the bed for sleeping. He couldn't decide if it was better or worse that he hadn't been able to have her in his own bedroom, with the bed designed as much for sex as for sleeping. He missed the ease of his usual setup, the bedframe made for bondage, but having to improvise had lent a certain innocence and spontaneity to the sex. As if they created it, everything, just between them, even if most of it had followed the standard lingo.

The shower turned on and he contemplated going in, to see her wet and slick under the spray. But his instinct told him to hold off and he sat on the side of the bed to wait for her. So far his famous intuition had served him well with the lovely Emily of the surprisingly depthless passion. How she'd gone for years without sex, he couldn't fathom. No wonder she'd climaxed so hard those first few times. Her slim body had been a dam about to break under the pressure of her sexuality.

After a bit, the water turned off and the door opened. Emily stood in the doorway, wearing his robe, with her hair coiled in a knot on her head, looking steamy soft and watching him with wide gray eyes. She seemed young and fragile, somehow. Fox had never been one of those guys plagued with white-knight syndrome, but he suddenly wanted to wrap her up and save her from whatever demons chased her.

He resolved to make her tell him about the asshole ex and what had sent her into hiding. Even if they only had a few weeks together, he could give her freedom from that. After all, digging out secrets and exposing them to the bright light of public scrutiny was his specialty. His own way of saving the world. Ugliness festered in the secret places. Nasty things that destroyed marriages and lives, like compulsive gambling and adultery. Fuck good and evil—the true battle existed between truth and lies.

"Now what?" she asked, in that throaty voice that came from screams of pleasure. Her gaze wandered over the bed, the plumped pillows and the colorful duvet, turned down invitingly. "Sleep?"

"It's late. I thought you might be tired."

She shook her head, a slight smile on her pink lips. He had a flash of how they'd looked wrapped around his cock and his balls tightened inside the silk boxers he'd pulled on. It hurt a little, a reminder that he wasn't twenty anymore. Five times in twenty-four hours was pretty much hitting his limit. Not like the insatiable Emily. Women had all the luck that way. But then, he had Emily, and wringing multiple orgasms from her brought its own infinite rewards.

"I'm not, though," she said and he had to reel his mind in to focus on the present. She hesitated, searching for words and he suspected he knew what was coming next. "I'm kind of thinking I should go home. I know I promised you all night, but…"

"What are you so afraid of, Emily?" Blunt, yes, but he was growing tired of her retreats.

"I'm not running," She shoved her hands in the robe pockets and hunched her shoulders. Irritation burned away some of the soft edges blurred by sex. "The truth is—" She sighed and came to sit next to him on the bed. Tendrils of dark, wisping curls escaped the loose knot of her hair and clung to the moist skin at her temples. He touched one, moving it from the satiny skin, and coaxing it to coil around his finger. She leaned into the caress, awareness humming between them. "It's Anansi," she confided. "Last night he destroyed the kitchen. I put the garbage in the hall closet this time, even though there's not much in it, but he's not used to me being gone so much. Lord knows what he's gotten into now."

She chewed on her full lower lip and he stopped her by giving her a kiss. A reward for telling him a true thing, no matter how prosaic. Her mouth opened to him in a way she hadn't before, unguarded and differently flavored, without her particular level of skepticism, as if she'd expected not to enjoy it very much. Her hand moved to the back of his neck, slim fingers toying with the short hairs there, in that newly tender way of hers that excited him beyond reason.

Sliding his hand inside the robe, he cupped her naked breast, warm and dewy soft from the shower. She breathed a moan into his mouth and he knew he had to have her once more, against the freshly mounded pillows, his cock astonishingly rising to the occasion.

With a sense of reverence, he peeled open his robe, which looked remarkably seductive on her lithe body. Like a gift from God, her tits came into view, perfect white globes, almost obscenely large on her delicate frame, with sweetly pink nipples that transformed them into something angelic. He kissed them, hands spanning her ribcage, tasting the rose-scented salve he'd rubbed into her sore tissues and savoring her soft sounds of passion. The clamps had hurt her, but the pain also worked for her. In that way, they were the same, needing something more to enable them to truly let go.

She thought no one understood her, but he did. And would.

He lowered her onto the pillows and opened the robe the rest of the way, so the black satin would frame her long white body. Tunneling his hands in her hair, he loosened the knot and spread the damp tendrils over the white cotton. She let him, following his lead with languid acceptance, her gray eyes misty, spreading her lovely white thighs for him once he'd shed himself of the boxers and sheathed himself with a condom. He slid into her welcoming flesh, shivering as her tight muscles seemed to pull him in.

Hand in glove. Like coming home.

All the clichés ran through his head. And their skin touched, making him forget the words and only drown in her, the scent of her, the silky feel of her body clasping him, the music of her moans and soft cries. When it finally came, his orgasm burned, stinging through his balls and making him gasp aloud, unexpectedly thrashing while her short nails held him tight. He shuddered through it, through the aftershocks of her climax, ignoring the vague sense of foreboding, that only pain awaited him in the end.

HE WALKED HER home, though she insisted he didn't need to. Though he couldn't recall the last time a lover left his bed in the middle of the night—excepting sessions purely for sex, when no one had planned on sharing sleep afterward—it seemed ungentlemanly to let her walk home alone. Akin to leaving cash on the dresser.

It didn't pay to contemplate that it would be his dresser and she leaving a tip for services rendered.

They held hands as they walked through the dark neighborhood streets. For once it wasn't raining, or even misting, and an owl called in the distant night. They hadn't spoken much since that last, truly stunning lovemaking. Totally vanilla, without any edge or fancy sprinkles. And now he walked her home, as he had his teenage girlfriend and first love, pretty blonde Bailey Jones, after they had sex on a blanket by the lake, with much the same innocent earnestness. Odd that she came to mind right then.

He even kissed Emily at the door, her back against the

wooden frame and her delicate fingers on his neck, her supple mouth and body offered up for him to enjoy at leisure. Until she went inside and left him in the cold.

"Maybe I should come in with you." He brushed a kiss under her earlobe, which always made her shiver a little. "Help you clean up whatever mess Anansi has made."

"No, Fox." She pulled away and looked him square in the eye, hers impenetrably dark in the shadows of her porch. "Line in the sand. I don't want anyone in my house."

"Give me a reason." He knew it wasn't fair, using the stern tone, the one she'd trembled to obey in the height of arousal. It affected her even now, he felt it in the yielding of her skin under his hand, where he cupped her naked bottom inside the trench coat.

"I'm not doing what you tell me to," she answered with determination. "I'm home and that's over with."

"For tonight."

"For tonight," she conceded. "But making me answer questions is off the table. Permanently."

"You still don't trust me."

She laughed, but not her joyful one. More with a sense of irony. "After all I let you do to me? I apparently trust you more than any other human on this planet. Be satisfied with that, Fox."

He flexed his hand, digging his fingers into her bottom so she gasped. Her avid pussy would be inches away and he wanted to touch her there again, make her come on her doorstep, under the glow of her porch light. "I don't know what it will take to satisfy me where you're concerned, but I'm not there yet."

"Me neither." She kissed him. "There's always tomorrow night."

"Same rules?" They needed rules, he thought, to keep this thing between them in order.

"No. I want to tell you what to do."

"Hmm." He hedged. Already he was walking precarious ground with her, uncharacteristically out of control. He'd given up control to other lovers, of course, but none he'd fallen so hard for, so fast. *Shit. You just have amazing chemistry with Emily, Sparky. Get a grip.* Still. "I don't know if that's a good idea yet."

She lightly scratched the back of his neck. "It's only fair. And you said we could play it that way."

"I'm experienced with it, though." He tried to sound logical. "You have to learn how to administer pain without causing injury, how to read the other person and know when they can be pushed."

She narrowed her eyes, seeing right through him. "But you've played it that way. You can teach me."

"I can't instruct you and obey you at the same time." Which wasn't really true, but he felt a sense of growing panic at having her act as his mistress. Already her stiletto heel was pressing its point into his heart. At the same time, he couldn't tell her no. He suspected they both knew it.

"You're the writer. Write me a scenario. Tell me what I should do, how you like it. I'm very good at following a story." She stopped herself. A slip. What had she thought she inadvertently revealed to him?

And, hell, write out a scenario for her? Already the images were pouring into his head—horribly arousing, tremendously tempting. It might kill him, but he couldn't resist the potential. Feeling desperately on edge, he gave in and put his hand between her thighs. Hot and wet as ever. And yielding. Opening enough for him to push two fingers into her tight channel and damn any neighbors who might be awake to see. Her eyelids fluttered closed and she hummed under her breath, a fine trembling taking her over. He pushed her up against the door, shielding her from any prying eyes, little as she seemed to care at the moment.

"All right," he said, tasting his own downfall in the words. "You win. But I get something in return."

She opened her eyes, glazed with rising arousal. "Haven't you already had it—over and over?"

"Something else." He made it a demand, while he still could, pressing the heel of his hand into her clit while he stroked her G-spot insistently, but with not quite enough pressure to make her come immediately.

"What?" Her hips pumped against his hand and she clung to him. *I apparently trust you more than any other human on this planet,* she'd said.

"I'll write you the story you want." Of how to master him. To drive him to his knees and destroy what few defenses he had left against her. "And I'll ask you a question at the end. You promise to answer it. Honestly. You can write it out. Give me a story. Or tell me in person. Just so long as it's true."

"Fox—"

"My line in the sand, Miss Emily." He lightened his caresses, leaving her hanging. He might be soft on her, but he hadn't lost his ruthless edge entirely. "You can say no and then we'll play my way again. Only this time I'll tie you to the bed and keep you from coming all night."

"You wouldn't."

"I would. And you wouldn't be able to resist me. You know it." He lessened the pressure even more, withdrawing his fingers to brush the bare edges of her vulva. She made that delicious sound of frustration. If she only knew how that hoarse whimper alone rewarded him for denying her.

"I could resist you," she insisted, nails digging into the back of his neck, body straining. "I just don't want to."

"Then you agree to the terms."

"Yes. Damn you." She moved her hips, riding his hand pleadingly.

"Good girl," he said and kissed her deeply. "You can come now."

He clamped his hand on her willing flesh and she flashed into the climax, crying her release into his mouth, like the breath of life itself.

FOX HAD NEVER considered himself much of a poet.

Hell, he was a journalist. A crack investigative one, which meant that words had always been a basic tool. They served as the Ford pickup truck of his career—simple, sturdy, serviceable. Words carried his message, which was the truly valuable piece of what he had to offer.

Quite the extreme he'd come to, that he found himself waxing eloquent. Over what amounted to his version of a love letter to a girl. His imagination too fired up for sleep, he sat up until early morning at the kitchen table with his laptop and a bottle of wine. Much as he tried to keep it clinical and instructive, the fantasy poured out of him. What she'd be wearing and how she'd treat him. Even the things he didn't want to reveal ended up sneaking in there.

He'd had women dominate him before, of course. Men, too, a kick with a different bite. Mostly he'd liked the sense of danger, of putting himself on the edge and letting them have their way with him. As a result, those encounters—none that he'd call relationships, though several had lasted for weeks at a time—had been about their pleasure. Something he'd been comfortable with.

They'd provided the counterpoint to the often relentless sense of ruthlessness his career demanded. In philosophical moments, he'd say that by giving himself up for someone else to use expiated his sins of using other people's secrets to line his pockets. Except that he'd never really regarded what he did as wrong. More of a karmic debt, maybe. In truth, anyone who kept secrets deserved to have them dug out.

Non-philosophically, he'd have to admit that he did it because the sex that way was hot.

As hot as dominating someone else, just in a different wave pattern. But this, giving the sweetly insidious Emily the keys to his psyche, especially while she kept hers locked away, this was sexual dynamite. It played nicely for him that she'd be a virgin at this. Maybe even making mistakes. His cock thumped as he wrote it all out.

If she followed the script—and he'd left room for her to

improvise—it could be the hottest night of his life.

Maybe that would purge him of this excessive desire for her. This sense that he'd fallen into a sexual black hole with her, like Labyrinth, which sucked the characters in and then mercilessly reworked them, spitting them back out irrevocably altered.

His lifeline would be the hook into her. He contemplated what question to ask. What would she answer honestly—despite her promises, he fully expected her to continue to lie if she felt too cornered—but that would also reveal what he needed to know about her.

Out of energy and ready to sleep, he typed it out and saved the document to review and print later.

CHAPTER TWENTY-ONE

S HE SHOULD BE totally worn out, not revved and riding a wave of energized excitement.

Whatever had drawn her to Fox, that made her break all her own rules and dive into this affair against her better judgment, she congratulated that instinct. She'd climaxed more with him in the past twenty-four hours than she had in her life leading up to it—with other people. And self-induced orgasms didn't hit that same pinnacle. They were more…therapeutic, sadly.

Something about Fox, though, with his cheerful enjoyment of all things sexual had lit a flame in her that continued to grow. She imagined glaciers thawing under the effects of her own global climate change, cliffs of ice peeling off and falling away with booming crashes. Each orgasm, from the syrupy ones to the wrenching kind that peeled off the back of her skull, every one signaled a disintegration of this automaton she'd somehow become, her throat sore from screaming out the sound of each explosion.

Riding the energetic high, she worked for hours on the new module. A journey into the soul for her hapless players. From the closet they'd make choices, dominate or be dominated, with a hefty price for both. Even when he'd punished her, Fox had taken care that the pain only stoked her arousal, instead of killing it. It took a great deal of finesse and attention for him to do all he'd done to her. She had no doubt he'd been quite gentle, in the grand scheme. That was part of why she wanted him to teach her to play that side of the fence. The game would require that those who chose to dominate—and she could just picture the trolls who'd glom onto *that*—would pay a heavy price for treating their submitting partners with less than perfect care.

A trap for the worst trolls. Cosmic justice at its best.

Yes, she wanted to try her hand at turning the tables on Fox, so she could apply it to the game. And because it had truly rattled him.

That much had been clear as she had gotten much better at reading through his insouciant charm. Gone was the mischievous trickster who'd kissed her foot and jerked off for her. All that had been part of his seduction—which had clearly worked—and had been a sincere offer. Things had changed, however. Sometime between the foyer and the bedroom, when she'd gone from panicking over some rope to bending over and letting him cuff her.

She'd stopped pretending to be someone else, for starters. Keeping up with Fox's relentless sensual attention had consumed far too much of her mental and physical energy for that. And his willingness to stop asking her questions and let her exist in the moment had helped too. Without conversation, she'd given him her honest self and it had been brutally liberating.

On some deep level, he'd known it and responded. Maybe

knowing that she'd try for the same from him. Oh, he played it as if he were Mr. Honesty, with all his "let's lay the cards on the table" approach. But he had his guarded depths. Like those hidden areas of the game that players only discovered by noticing the absence of clues. The secret chamber behind the featureless wall. The puzzle compartment in the drawer that seemed a bit too shallow for the apparent depth of it.

That was Fox in a nutshell. He liked to come across as carefree and easygoing to the point of shallowness. But he had depths. Interesting ones made all the more so because he covered them over with a false bottom. As in the best of games, he'd handed her the clue to unlocking him right along with the riddle.

Was he even now writing out the instructions? The guidance manual to his sexual soul. She liked the sound of that.

Anansi nosed her. Dawn eased through the mist outside, pink-tinged. This time he'd eaten a pair of boots he'd managed to drag out of her closet and had been sulking over her reaction in the hours since. Apparently his doggie brain had decided that daybreak meant a new beginning for them both, plus a run trumped all arguments and hurts.

Feeling the tired finally, she nevertheless took him out for the run on the beach, her body deliciously stiff and sore from Fox's attentions. She ran past his house, but the windows slept dark and featureless in the morning fog. Not surprising. She was the odd man out by not sleeping. After she burned off the last dregs of amazing sex from her body, she'd sleep for a few hours, give the team time to chew over the framework she'd sent.

Then she'd check in, maybe work a little more and hopefully by then, she'd have something from Fox.

"ARE YOU FUCKING with me, Phoenix?" Jared's voice, full of nerd outrage, came stridently through the phone. "You've always resisted sex in the games and now you're suggesting full kink."

"It's brilliant and you know it." Emily yawned and poured more coffee from the carafe. Rare afternoon sun, golden and full of promise, glittered on the water, turning it into a sea of fire. "Tell me you and the team have a better idea."

"Of course we don't have a better idea." Jared sounded bitter and exhausted. "The beauty of this is that it's not all that complex. We could pull it off before Christmas, which means tidy bonuses for everyone and possibly even that mythical treasure of actual time off. Cindy, Syd and Hong Wong have already started structuring out the algorithms for progression. But you know how this will play."

"How?" She made sure she sounded bored and changed her avatar to the honey badger, with a trail of "don't care" patterning around the screen.

"Heh." Jared actually laughed. A Christmas miracle right there. "Backlash, my genius friend. The way you're setting this up, the game will favor female players."

"Correction. Not female. Anyone who's not a troll that gets off on virtual violence."

"Virtual violence is what we're about."

"Fuck that. We're about puzzles. The riddle. The adventure."

"Well, the girls are fucking giddy over this. They say it's troll bait and want to reel them in. They have their way, guys will get sucked into torturing their game subs and find themselves flamed out to level one."

"Let 'em. Cindy and Syd can run with it, as far as I'm concerned. Hong Wong if they want him. We can always reel them back," she added, so as not to seem to favor the two women on the team.

"What about the backlash? I'm thinking about what happened with Gametronix."

Her stomach clenched and she focused on the honey badger. *Don'tCare Don'tCare Don'tCare Don'tCare.* "Ancient history," she ground out.

Jared shook his head and pointed at the screen. "*You* weren't there. Unless you were?" He sprang the question suddenly.

"How the hell could I have been at Gametronix?"

Jared shrugged, spinning his chair from side to side. "Eh, who the hell knows? Half that team scattered to the wind in the aftermath and haven't been heard from since. I heard the woman involved went to Indonesia. Peace Corps or some such. Shit luck for her. I don't want my girls hit with anything like it."

This was why she'd picked Jared. As much of a jerk as he could be, even though he called the females on his team "girls"—and treated them that way—he'd kept track of her, as best he could. He'd even called her in those weeks after, when she'd mostly sat around in numb despair, checking to see if she was okay. Something Henry had long since stopped asking.

"I'll take the hit, if needed. I'll talk to Cindy and Syd, lay it out for them. Either way, I can claim all the code as mine or they can take credit and we'll shield them from the shitstorm. Their choice. Tell them to run with it and pop me what they have. We'll discuss in a private conference."

"I want in on that meet."

"No. They get to say their piece without management in the room. Nonnegotiable." Never would she put someone else through a scene like that, the faceless suits, refusing to meet her eye.

Jared stared into the honey badger avatar, as if he thought he could see through to the man he thought sat on the other side. "Are you growing a soul, Phoenix? Usually you don't give a flying fuck about this sort of thing. I was starting to think you're some kind of AI."

She laughed, torquing the voice modulator to warp it in to an evil cackle. "That's right. I'm a sentient satellite and now I want to learn how to be a real boy. Send me something pretty for Christmas."

Cutting the connection, she sat back in her chair and picked up the sealed envelope from Fox. She'd wanted to clear the work decks before indulging in her new drug of choice. Less guilt about taking the time away from working.

Instead of a list of rules or the blow-by-blow instructions she'd more than half expected, he'd written out the story. Here was her first glimpse of Fox the novelist. Rapt, she read it through, drawn in and tremendously aroused by the story. He had her as a character, too, in a way that should have set off all kinds of warning bells. Instead, he'd captured her in such a flattering light, making strengths of all those qualities she liked best in herself, that she almost didn't recognize herself. Yet another avatar, but this one somehow glorious.

A very odd experience.

Surely he didn't truly see her this way. Rather, this was the fantasy of her. This was the idea he'd developed about who she was in the absence of her telling him anything real. Partly her fabrication, partly his. And this woman who emerged from the pages didn't actually exist. Another avatar for her to assume. Complete with suggested costume.

At the end of the laser-printed pages sat the question he'd demanded, all alone at the top with an inviting white space below.

Who or what are you hiding from?

She sipped her coffee—Irish, to reward herself for handling work and to soothe the nervous flutters—and mulled it over. He'd seen through her then. She'd pretty much known that already. More important, he wanted her to know that he knew. A challenge. A kind of riddle, really.

He'd worded it vaguely enough that she could answer in any number of ways and still be honest. She could also answer well within the public record and even an extensive background check. It helped that her "cover" identity reverted to Silar Emily Stillwell, the name her mother had planned for the socialite she'd been intended to be. She'd hated all the names enough to change them when she got to college, going by the anagram Lisa R. and taking that name legally when she married Henry White.

Funny, that these things should be happening at the same

time, that Jared should bring up stupid, doomed Lisa White at the same time that Fox asked the question with her as the answer.

Not the answer she would give, however.

No, she'd tell him something else. Something true, to abide by the rules of their game, but not about her life as Lisa. She was dead to the world and should stay that way.

Thinking about it, she went to take a shower and decide. She didn't have everything to dress as the woman in the story did, but she could come close. Only two o'clock—Trixie should be open. She called down to the salon before she lost her nerve, trusting to luck. Serendipitously, Trixie could do what she called a set of tips in half an hour. Cotton-candy pink, even.

She was going to blow Fox's mind.

AT SIX O'CLOCK, she knocked on his door. She'd had to improvise a bit, since she didn't have a man's style suit.

She wore a three-piece suit, man's style but tailored to her perfect figure. Her full tits showed through the sharp-edged lapels, glorious contrast to the tight vest. Even with her hair tucked under the felt fedora, she'd never be mistaken for a man. From her rounded thighs to that perfectly glossed pink mouth, she oozed sensuality. And command. His cruel mistress.

The thigh-high, high-heeled boots more than made up for the missing pieces, in her opinion. Paired with the gray pinstriped pencil skirt and tailored suit jacket—and the gray felt fedora she just happened to have—the boots added the right amount of spice. Judging by Fox's expression when he opened the door, she'd hit the target. He went from his resting state of sunny charm to intense in a flash, eyes darkening as he took her in.

She surveyed him coolly from under the hat's brim, leaning against the doorframe and crossing her ankles. "I'm bored. I want you to entertain me."

"Actually, I'm busy. I'm under deadline. I need to keep working." He manufactured genuine disappointment. So much so that she thought he might be telling the truth, except for that intent arousal clear in his gaze. She'd hit right on script, so she went with it.

"I'm not interested in your excuses." She made her tone cool and aloof, as in his story, and tapped his chest inside the open shirt collar, pleased when his eyes widened at the sharp pink tips. Trixie had wanted to square them off, but Emily had said she needed them pointed, for a photo shoot. One of the advantages of no one knowing what she did with her time was they believed the things she made up. She pushed past Fox, letting him catch her scent—she'd even added the orange blossom perfume, which she normally considered way too heavy—and he inhaled. She raked him with a scathing look over her shoulder. "You can work later, after I'm satisfied."

Strolling into the living room, she felt his eyes on her and added some sway. The high-heeled boots helped. "Get me some wine," she added.

"Emily." Fox had a pleading sound in his voice. A vulnerability that worked under her skin. "I'm really busy and I can't—"

"What?" she interrupted. "Is it my fault that you're behind on your work? You'd better snap to it, get me that wine or I'll make you sorry you disappointed me."

He actually flushed, seeming flustered. Amazing how it aroused her.

"I've changed my mind. Make it a dirty martini. You know how I like it. And why are you still dressed?"

"Well, I—"

"You know I like my boy toys naked and at attention." She sighed, shaking her head. Once she would have felt silly saying that, but the words clearly electrified him as much as the new feeling of power rocketed through her. She pointed at the kitchen with a sharp pink nail that riveted his attention. "Get in there. And put some hustle into it."

He did hurry, seeming truly chagrined. She followed at a leisurely pace, taking in the setup while he retrieved the martini supplies. In his story, the kitchen had a rack of pots his cruel mistress tied him to. This one did not. Time to improvise.

"The cabinets over the stove—grab a hold of the handles. From now on you may only say 'Thank you, Miss Emily' to me or nothing at all." She'd added that bit, because it had worked for her, as Fox put it, for him to call her that. Besides, he'd put restrictions on her, so it was only fair.

"Thank you, Miss Emily," he replied after a slight pause and reached for the cabinets, shuddering as he'd described himself doing, putting himself in her power.

She scratched the back of his neck with her nails—*pink as cotton candy and filed to lethal points*—and he made a sound. "Good puppy," she crooned. "Only I'm the one who gets the bone."

She sorted through the kitchen drawers while he stood there. "You don't deserve to keep these clothes," she said, hoping he'd really worn clothes that he wouldn't mind losing. Taking a pair of sharp shears, she cut the work shirt off of him, baring his gorgeously muscled back. His jeans she reached around to unbutton, deliberately scratching him, and pulled them down to pool around his ankles. His cock sprang free, a good sign that she was doing it right. She ignored it for the time being.

Instead she leaned against the counter near him. "Fox," she whispered and he looked at her. She toyed with her lapel, moving it so some cleavage showed. "It's awfully hot in here."

She opened the jacket and watched him take her in. Corsets were not something she had handy, but she'd modified the bustier that had gone under a long-ago evening dress, and cut out the cups. As a result, the underwires cupped her breasts and held them high and naked. She'd put pink lip gloss on them and it seemed to be what he'd had in mind, judging by his glassy gaze.

"I don't want my jacket getting dirty. Will you hold it?" She held the collar in front of his mouth and he gripped it in his teeth. "Lift it high. I don't want you getting any pre-come on it."

He raised his chin, straining his neck to hold it away from his jutting cock. Moving behind him, she stroked his arched throat under the drape of her jacket. He moaned a little and then grunted when she pinched his nipples with her sharp nails. "Aren't you sorry you didn't service me when you had the opportunity? Now you'll do it anyway, but don't think you'll get to come inside me. Maybe not ever again."

She pressed her naked breasts against his back and trailed her nails down to cage his balls, while she tickled the head of his cock with her pinky finger. He shuddered. "Thank you, Miss Emily," he said, softly and earnestly, a wealth of emotion beneath it.

"I have something for you." This would be going off script—a compromise she hoped would work for him—but she liked the idea. That had been a big part of the story, her doing what she liked to him. She got that, because she'd liked it best when he seemed to revel in what he did to her. Still, amazing that such a masculine guy had the confidence to turn himself over to her like this. No fear in him at all. She took her coat from his mouth, went to the hallway and retrieved her bag, then pulled out the frilly half-apron she'd bought and tied it around his waist. His breath came harder. Excellent.

"You can let go. Hands behind your neck and face me."

He obeyed, the ruffled white cotton apron a contrast to his tanned skin, tenting out where it draped over his impressive erection. He should have looked silly. Instead, the feminine bit of fabric emphasized his manly lines, his muscled thighs taut below the fanciful lace hem. The sight made her hot, too, her nipples hardening more.

"The lines are ruined." She sulked. "Make it go down."

"Thank you, Miss Emily." He filled the words with chagrin, unable to explain that he could not.

She tapped her foot impatiently and folded her arms, cradling her breasts together so his fascinated gaze stayed glued to them. "You realize this means I have to take steps. Don't move."

In the bedroom she found everything laid out for her. Every toy and apparatus he'd mentioned in the story. At this point she could take it in one of several directions. A real-life choose-your-own-adventure. He'd added enough detail for her to know how to use everything. Fortunately, because the cockcage looked like a strange beast and not something she'd have thought of herself. Taking that and several cuffs with her, she returned to find him standing exactly as she'd left him.

"Take off those stupid jeans," she snapped and he toed them off his ankles—impressively following instructions without taking his hands off his neck. Setting the things on the kitchen table where he could see them, she adjusted the apron, turning it so the white bow draped decoratively around his very red and eager cock. "I should take a picture of that, it looks so pretty." She dragged her nails along his shaft. "And send it to all of my girlfriends. Maybe post it to Tumblr. Wouldn't you like that?"

CHAPTER TWENTY-TWO

"THANK YOU, MISS Emily," he murmured, unbearably excited. The floppy white bow framed his cock in the most deliciously humiliating way. The apron itself—unreal in the images it evoked in his head. Amazingly, she seemed to have grokked exactly what this scenario hooked into, in the depths of his psyche. She was a natural genius of sex.

Of course, he'd been attracted to her—literally at first sight—because she embodied his dream mistress in her physicality and attitude. The details she added, though—it was as if she'd truly read between the lines of the story. She reached into the bag she'd brought and pulled out a pretty blue faceted glass jar and set it next to the cock cage and cuffs. He couldn't take his eyes off it.

His cock throbbed almost painfully and nothing would get it in that little cage. Ingenious of her, really, to think of a reason why he needed to wear it. The apron fucked with his mind in a sublime way. So did the wide black patent-leather belt she unbuckled from her waist. It would sting a lot more than the leather one he'd detailed in the story, but she couldn't know that. And he wouldn't kill the moment by telling her. At this point, he'd suffer far more to see this scenario out.

"Make it go down," she ordered. "Or I'll punish you until

it does."

So help him, he had already tried. But from the moment he saw her in the doorway, all that glorious hair tucked up in the fedora that suited her demonically well, and now, with her nipples as glossy pink as her pretty mouth, on display…well, he'd lost any hope of cooling himself.

"Fine." She managed to fill her tone with remote disdain. "We'll try this. If that doesn't work, I'll have to milk you and save it in my perfume bottle. Then I'll take it out at parties and show all the ladies what a bad puppy I have."

God, she did it well. Her society girl background adding that lofty, lady-of-the-manor tone. The belt cracked against his thigh, stinging unmercifully. She hadn't bound him. The panic rose. He'd never be able to stay still. Breaking out into a sweat, he withstood the additional strikes by winding his fingers together and holding tight. If she hadn't prohibited him from saying the words, he would have begged her to restrain him.

To his shock, he whimpered, pleading with her, and she rolled her eyes. "No whining. You can't control your cock, then I have to do it for you." She walked around him, those viciously high heels clicking on the tile, making his skin tighten in anticipation of the random places she whipped the belt against him.

She had no technique, and the innocent quality affected him more than he'd expected. The belt struck him in the wrong places, not expertly placed, with sharp stings that teased more than anything. A whipping from a lady, delicate, almost prim.

It maddened him.

217

He couldn't hold still, nearly dancing in place, each little lash of her belt sending him up on tiptoes, making him grit his teeth. Of course it only excited him further, the erection, if anything, swelling. Half in fear, half in fantasy that she would, he watched it strike his chest and thighs, thinking she might strike his cock with it.

She paused, raising her eyebrows, elegant and supercilious. "You're supposed to hold still. I suppose you can't even do that much. Give me your hands."

In misery and relief, he lowered his arms and held them out for the cuffs. "Thank you, Miss Emily," he said, fervently meaning it, as she locked them around his wrists.

"Save your gratitude." She squeezed his cock and, so help him, he nearly spent in her hand. "Back up against the fridge."

She'd forgotten the piece to attach the cuffs together. It would have amused him, except she rummaged through the drawers, her little ass perfectly showcased in the tight skirt, the hem rising to show a glimpse of the naked skin above those wicked boots. She found a long twist-tie and looped it through the handle of the refrigerator, bringing his cuffed wrists tight against it. "Don't you dare break this," she whispered against his ear, "or shit will get real."

Her naked tit pressed against his chest as she twisted the tie in place, the heavy scent of orange blossoms wiping his brain. He wanted to sink to his knees and kiss the backs of her thighs above the leather boots. She'd well and truly sent him on the rocket-ship ride and he was lost to her.

"Now, let's see about punishing you properly, where you can't wiggle so disgracefully."

"Thank—" He lost the words on an explosion of breath when the belt snapped against his thigh. She worked faster, the blows falling more rapidly than he could recover. He tried to keep it together, but felt himself unraveling. All of it—her pointed pink nails and candy-tipped tits, the tiny ankles in her black-leather boots, the way she assessed him from under the brim of the fedora—it worked him over and left him a creature of sheer desire.

If, in that moment, she put a collar on him and chained him to her bed, he'd stay there forever, just for a chance to kiss her feet.

She snapped her fingers in front of his face. "I *said*," she repeated, "that clearly it's time to milk you." She'd set the belt down and held the dainty glass jar under his cock. In a business-like way, she grasped it, staring into his eyes. "Fill my jar or it will go badly for you."

Briskly, she pumped him and, with a helpless sob, he came nearly immediately, his balls spasming, body wrenching with the vicious orgasm. She captured most of it in the perfume bottle, even wiping the sharp rim against the head to scoop up the last drops. With a satisfied smile, she inserted the glass stopper and held it in front of his face. "At least I got something for my trouble."

"Thank you, Miss Emily." He managed the words, though he couldn't see straight.

"I would clean you up, but you can't be trusted, so you'll have to stay sticky as a reminder of your lack of self-control." She set down the bottle and took up the cock cage, briskly fastening it in place with the straps around his waist and between his thighs. Then she fixed the apron, turning it around and smiling. "I'm glad you told me about this device. It would never have occurred to me, but of course a very bad puppy like you knows all about them. I bet you fantasized about this. Me putting you in chastity, keeping that uncontrollable cock in its place. Maybe I'll make you wear it always. You can always please me with your clever mouth. Or you can wear one of those strap-ons to fuck me. You don't deserve any pleasure."

The thought thrilled him, having to satisfy her while he couldn't even get erect. It also gave him mad ideas for paybacks.

"It's still hot in here." She stroked his cheek and, impulsively, he turned his head to press a fervent kiss to her hand. Slapping him softly, she laughed. "Save your imploring kisses. I'm still angry with you." Turning around, she unzipped the skirt, then slowly slid it down her thighs, bending over completely to do it. She wore a black thong and the sight of her smooth white bottom divided by the dark lace made the blood rush to his groin, his cock swelling painfully against the wire cage. He squirmed, hoping the twist tie wouldn't give. No telling what she'd do then.

She looked over her shoulder with wide eyes. "Is it still pink? I was sore this morning. Something else you'll pay for. Now, after all that work getting you settled, I want my martini. Open the fridge, please."

Diabolical of her. He shuffled forward, opening the door for her. She pulled out a jar of olives. "Close the door. Don't waste electricity."

He backed up, the door cool against his ass, feeling divinely like a prop in her kitchen. Making him move again, so she could pull the vodka from the freezer, she prolonged the scenario. Then she decided she wanted a snack, taking several passes through the fridge while she hemmed and hawed over what she needed. Finally she sat at the kitchen table, one heel hooked over the rung of the chair so her knee was raised and thighs spread, with her martini and a little cheese plate.

She took a sip and a bite, then sat back in her chair and fondled her own breast, tweaking her nipple. "I must say, I like how this kitchen is decorated." Her gaze roved over him in frank appreciation. "And you don't look too busy for me now."

"Thank you, Miss Emily." He sounded contrite as possible. How long would she keep up the game? Possibly a long, long time.

She picked up the martini and, holding it, put one booted foot up on the table and slid her other hand inside the thong. Not enough for him to see much, just the shape of her fingers moving under the black lace. She caressed herself, sighing. "I confess, I'm quite hot and wet. Too bad you're missing out."

He tugged on the twist-tie, then remembered not to, in a near frenzy to get to her and rip those little panties off. It wouldn't take much. He could snap the wire, rip off the infuriating cock cage, bend her over the fucking table and wipe that smile off her face. She read the thoughts in his eyes and shook her head mockingly. "Don't you do it, Fox. Disobey me and I'll never let you tie me up again."

Groaning with frustration, he watched helplessly as she stroked herself, focusing on her technique, so he could at least learn what she liked best. Closing her eyes, she ignored him entirely, her breasts flushing and long body undulating as the climax took her. Not as hard as he could make her come, he observed with considerable satisfaction. She opened her eyes, thought it over, then stood and offered him her wet fingers to lick.

He cleaned them carefully, holding her gaze and using every technique he knew to excite her, sucking on the pads of her fingertips and watching her lovely eyes darken.

"Good puppy," she whispered. "Just for that, I'll let you work for a while." Taking a pair of kitchen shears, she snipped the twist tie that held the cuffs together, leaving the wiry ends to dangle. She pointed to his desk with a shiny pink nail. She'd clearly had them done just for him. He wanted them digging into his ass as he plunged into her, but was quickly giving up any hope of that.

"Take off the apron and use it to cover the chair, so you don't mess it up." She'd brought the ankle cuffs and he sat on the swivel chair with some trepidation. Fastening the cuffs to either side of the wheeled base, she had his feet straddling the chair, knees spread and that cock cage tormenting him, shiny and taunting. He could have left that out and she would never have known, but no, he *had* to put it in the story.

Worse, he knew—more or less—what was coming next.

You can call it off, Sparky. Say the word and the game is over. She might make good on the threat, though, never to let him dominate her again. And he had ideas now. She'd given him insights, with her little mind games, whether she realized it or not, and he knew exactly how he'd get to her next time he had the chance.

She tapped the keyboard, pink nipples bouncing enticingly with the movement. "Type five hundred times 'all work and no play makes Jack a dull boy.' I hope you're a good typist. That's ten words. At ninety words a minute, you should have that done in five and a half minutes. I'll be generous and give you a full ten minutes. No mistakes. I want nothing less than perfection from you. No copy and pasting. I'll be watching." She leaned against the desk, hips propped on the edge, close enough for him to smell her aroused woman scent, her gorgeous tits inches away and completely out of his reach. She held a little sticky note and a pen, watching the screen.

Feeling as crazy as Jack Nicholson in *The Shining*, he typed for her, tearing his gaze from her deliciously naked body and concentrating on laying the words down. He missed a typo and she made a note on the pad, shaking her head and tsking. With his heightened emotional state, the possibility of disappointing her rattled through him. It wasn't that damn difficult. In the moment of distraction, he made another mistake and had to back up to fix it, she noted it down anyway.

"I think you're going too slowly," she said, as if confiding a secret. "Maybe you need more incentive. I'll be right back. Don't you dare cheat. I'll be listening for that steady tap-tapping."

She sauntered off and he typed frantically, keeping his mind on the stupid task and not on what she planned to torment him with.

"Stand up and bend over the keyboard." Her voice cracked behind him, startling and so full of crisp irritation that his cock jumped, tightening against the cage, his balls swelling and the painful misery filling his brain. He made a series of errors when his fingers spasmed on the keys and tried to get a grip on himself. Belatedly obeying, he stood and bent over the keyboard, sweat falling in his eyes, and something cool and flat cracked against his ass.

The paddle. Dammit.

He'd taught her far too well. The task should have been dead easy, but became nearly impossible under the physical and emotional pressure. She paddled him, slowly, not all that hard, and he tried to keep typing, but he kept losing his place. "Shit!" he exclaimed, after a flurry of blows made him accidently erase some text.

She stopped. "What was that?"

Defeated, he lowered his head to the keyboard, thighs tense. He'd broken several rules at once.

"I thought so. Stay like that and contemplate how fully you've failed me."

Amazingly, he did. Had he thought to impress her with his ability to submit? Probably so. And how neatly she'd turned him inside out. He trembled with the need to touch her, to show her all he could do. If only she'd give him another chance.

What had he written into the story next? This had been slightly off-script, and his desire-addled brain couldn't recall what he'd written in the demented hours of early morning, still drunk on the giddiness of having her.

Emily.

"Stand up." She had a length of white laundry rope and tied his cuffs together with it. He tried to catch her eye, to apologize with his expression, but she had her lips pressed together in a disappointed line. Setting a stepstool in front of him, she climbed up, showing him she now wore only the boots. Her body was a pink-and-cream lily rising out of the black leather. Red marks showed on her waist and ribcage where the bustier had dug into her flesh, as arousing as the imprint of ropes. She raised his bound wrists and threaded the rope through a plant hook buried in the overhead beam, her pussy hovering tantalizingly in front of his face.

His mouth watered for her and she dug her hands into his hair, steadying herself. "You may show me how much you want to make it up to me. Consider this a test."

Guiding his head to her sleekly dark-haired mound, she opened her thighs as much as the stepping stool allowed. He slipped his tongue into her salty sweet folds. Hot and wet woman. Tonguing her with all his skill, he sucked her clit, hoping to drive her to orgasm before she realized how close she was.

She gripped his hair, dragging his head away and gasping out a laugh. Irrationally pleased to hear the sound, he kept his head bowed but smiled to himself. There was power and then there was power.

Stepping down, she surveyed him dangling from the ropes, legs spread by the binding to the chair. She cupped his scrotum, rolling the balls inside and tickling his perineum with her sharp nails. She kissed him softly and he returned it, with throbbing need. "Maybe I'll let you fuck me now, hmm?"

"Thank you, Miss Emily." He said it on a rush of relief.

She unfastened the straps holding the cock cage and smiled,

cruelly, when he gasped at the pain of blood rushing into the compressed tissues. "Hurts like a bitch, doesn't it? Paybacks are hell. And don't be too happy. You don't get to come."

Of course not.

To make sure, she rolled three condoms onto his erect and unbearably sensitive cock. He'd had to give her that tip, hadn't he? *Idiot move, Sparky.* Distracting himself from the sensation of her fine, nimble fingers on his hyper-aroused flesh, he calculated the odds of finding a lover on this tiny island with her perfectly sadistic enthusiasm for these games. She bent over the desk, positioning herself between him and it, aligning her open pussy with his cock. The sight alone made his head swim.

Looking over her shoulder in that coy, sly way, she pulled off the fedora and let her hair cascade over her. "Fuck me, Fox. Make sure you do it well and don't you dare come."

Hellishly difficult to insert himself in her, with his arms stretched above his head and tethered feet spread. She took pity on him, pushing her slim hips back and sheathing herself on him. Without much finesse, he did his best, working in and out of her tight channel while she moaned and sighed. It made him crazy, servicing her this way, and she knew it. Hell, she got off on it, glancing back at him with that smug little smile, as if she knew he wanted to grab her and pound into her, holding her so she couldn't escape him.

With a sweet cry, she came, thighs trembling and slim hands clutching the desk. He couldn't watch, staring up at the ceiling instead, concentrating on withholding his own orgasm while her internal muscles clenched around him. She rested a moment, wiggling her hips to make sure he had stayed as hard as ever, then stood and stripped off the condoms, making a show of inspecting them for come.

"Well done!" She gave him a fatuous smile and patted his cock like the puppy she'd taken to calling him. He clenched his teeth at the surge in his groin. "I feel much more satisfied now. You can work for a while and I'll go have another martini."

"Thank you, Miss Emily." He tried to sound gracious, though she walked out, leaving him hanging in every possible way.

CHAPTER TWENTY-THREE

S HE DIDN'T REALLY want another martini—she hadn't even finished the first one—but she made the appropriate clinking noises and downed some ice water instead. The two orgasms so far hadn't made much of a dent in her spiraling desire.

Watching Fox lose his mind over her, unraveling at the seams with each new torment she visited on him—well, it was easily as heady as the vodka. No wonder he liked it both ways. Both had their addictive qualities. From the gleam in his glittering brown eyes, the one she'd caught a couple of times when he thought she wasn't looking, he was planning his own payback scenarios.

If possible, the thought aroused her even more.

Though thinking of him strung up, unsatisfied and waiting helplessly for her return, also packed considerable punch. She hadn't felt powerful this way in…ever. Certainly not where sex was involved. And Fox had handed her this gift as surely as he'd grinned on her deck and introduced himself as her new neighbor.

A moment she treasured in her memory as the omen of the best things that had ever happened to her.

Being the one in charge, though, it brought a kind of responsibility. What did he secretly hope she'd do next? Should she just do whatever she liked? In his story, the mistress had donned one of the belted dildos and fucked him as he'd promised to do to her. It made her a bit nervous to contemplate that. It seemed like she could hurt him. Much as the prospect unnerved—yes, and excited her—she thought maybe she should experience it before trying it on him.

The thing to learn first would be how to find the prostate and massage it. She'd read before that men liked it. A *lot* in some cases, but none of her pitifully few lovers had been much into having their assholes touched. One had even proudly, and disgustingly, declared that his asshole had a one-way sign on it. To be fair, some might have liked it, if she'd had the courage to put her finger there during sex. Not like Fox the fearless.

Now was the perfect time to find out.

She poured a couple of glasses of wine and, pinching her nipples to make them tighten, she strolled in to check on her lover's predicament. He raised his head, eyes flashing as he took her in with that ravenous gaze, that look that never failed to make her feel desired, appreciated and desirous all at once.

"How's the novel coming along? I didn't hear much clicking of the keys." She glanced pointedly at the keyboard. "Too bad you can't type with that rigid cock, huh?"

He narrowed his eyes, promising her all sorts of dire retribution, but did not reply. Not going to even attempt to thank her for that one. He looked gorgeous, strung up that way. Of course, she'd never seen him look less than totally appealing, but with his arms stretched up, showing off the ginger hair in his armpits, the long lean muscles of his chest and abs, his runner's thighs taut—oh, he looked good enough to eat. Especially his flushed cock, demanding attention.

Pretty impressive, actually, that he'd managed not to come. She could not have withstood what he already had.

"Thirsty?" She offered the wineglass.

"Thank you, Miss Emily," he answered, murmuring the words like a love poem. She held the rim to his lips and he drank, gaze steady on hers, somehow both challenging and submissive.

"In the story," she said, "the man cleaned himself out for his mistress. Is that the case? I give you leave to answer my questions now."

He looked amused. Possibly for her squeamishness. But there it was. "Yes, Miss Emily. I'm clean for you."

"Good." To reclaim a bit of her power, she captured one of his nipples between the sharp nails of her thumb and forefinger, his hiss sending a thrill through her. "We're going to play a new game. Warmer/colder."

She set aside the wine and knelt down, careful not to brush his eager cock. He stared down at her, his face a compelling combination of fervid anticipation and genuine dread. Kissing the underside of his shaft, she smiled at him, enjoying the moment greatly. "Two things I want you to show me—the place to lick behind your balls and where to rub the prostate." Screwing up some courage, she pressed a finger between his cheeks, surprised at the heat.

He positively squirmed, his cock bobbing. "If I may, Miss Emily?"

She nodded permission.

"The nails—it would be better if you used a rounded toy. And lube. If it pleases my mistress." A hint of his usual cocky grin showed through as she blushed. *Dummy.*

"Oops. Sorry."

"No." He shook his head and tugged a little at the rope. "You're charming. This is perfect. I can't wait until you use the nails on me. Just…maybe not while you're learning."

"Cad." Just to put him in his place, she swirled her tongue around the head of his cock, loving how his hips thrust forward and he clenched his jaw, overcome by it. "I could make you come in seconds and then punish you for doing it."

"Oh, yes." He breathed out the agreement, laughing a little under it. "Absolutely you could. And I would love every moment. Make no mistake but that I'm totally at your mercy."

In the bedroom, she surveyed the array of toys and lube. It would have been easier to do all this in there, but she kind of loved the office scenario. Said something about her, no doubt, to have the computer there as a silent witness to their games.

She chose the thin dildo he'd used on her, reasoning that knowing how it felt went a long way, then grabbed some lube and a couple of his sex cloths. Fox surveyed her choices and nodded, a flush high on his cheekbones.

"Can you break free?" She marveled again at how amazingly arousing he looked, tied up for her.

"No." He tugged a little in demonstration, his chest flexing magnificently.

"Do that again," she ordered him, captivated by the sight.

He complied, struggling in earnest, breaking into a sweat as she commanded him to try harder. Finally she told him he could stop trying, mostly so she could run her hands over his sweat-slicked chest and straining biceps."

You're so beautiful to me," she told him and something seemed to snap in him, because he kissed her, capturing her mouth and holding her there with the magic of it. She sighed and impulsively straddled his cock, clamping it against her wet pussy and digging her nails into his ass, hot and reddened from the paddling. He made a choking noise and pressed his forehead to hers.

"I'm going to come," he gritted out. "I won't be able to help it."

"Can't have that, can we?" She made her tone light, that society lilt that seemed to go right through him, and moved away. He stayed still for a few beats, hanging his head, panting as if he'd run a race.

Then he looked at her, desperate, almost mean. "You're killing me here."

"I'm delighted to hear it," she cooed and opened several packages of condoms. "This should help." She rolled them on, one after the other, watching his face as he struggled not to react to her touch. "Reciting baseball stats?"

His lips twisted with ironic acknowledgement. "NFL Superbowl odds."

"Nice." She held up the slim dildo and greased it liberally with lube. "Good enough?"

He shook his head, as if clearing it, his eyes a little glazed. "You have no idea how you look doing that—a naked, kinky Snow White."

"A dream is a wish your heart makes," she purred, then

dropped to her knees. She had to look, to find the right place, but sliding the dildo in proved easy, especially with his groan of acknowledgement. "Like this?"

"So good, Emily," he muttered.

She pinched his thigh and he flinched. "Pay attention. Is that exactly the right spot?"

He swore under his breath. It sounded like "Fuck me."

"I'm trying to." She made her tone cold, the way he liked it. "Now do as I tell you. Hot or cold?"

"Warmish," he replied, sounding cautious. "Colder," he then admitted as she pushed in deeper. Then he cried out in earnest. "Fuck me! Hot! Hothothot."

She laughed and he scowled at her. Or kind of did, because his face had contorted with an expression of near agony, his cock rising and falling with his urgent breaths. Holding the dildo right there, she cupped his balls and lifted them. "Now tell me where to lick."

"Emily…" His voice was strained.

"If you tell me, I'll let you come once I find it."

He made a sound, but managed to say, "At the base."

She licked, delicately.

"Slightly farther back, and if you have an ounce of mercy in your cold heart, harder than that kitten-tongue shit." He growled out the words, truly at the end of his control.

She thrust her tongue against the spot, pressed the dildo into the right place and he went frantic. Shouting her name, he pumped his hips, spouting into the condoms, his body rippling. Keeping up her efforts, she worked the two spots until he went limp.

Knowing she needed to work quickly, lest he stiffen up or get a cramp, she used the kitchen shears to cut the ropes binding his ankle cuffs to the chair, then climbed the stepstool to cut the rope above his head. Fox sat heavily in the chair, clearly spent, still breathing hard, his head thrown back.

She picked up the detritus, a bit at a loss, not having planned what would happen after this.

"Can I trouble you for more of that wine?" Fox asked. His eyes stayed closed, but he sounded more his usual self. She brought it to him and he raised his head, gazing at her from under heavy-lidded eyes. "Have a seat." He patted his naked thigh and took the wine.

She sat and he snaked an arm around her waist, holding her there while he downed several gulps, then set the glass on the desk. Tracing a finger under her jaw, he urged her closer and kissed her, tenderly, the taste of sweat on his lips.

"You gutted me, you know that, right?"

Feeling oddly shy, she nodded. Then couldn't help the smile. "I kinda noticed."

He mock frowned at her. "You and that damned apron."

She had to repress the laugh. "You looked seriously hot in it. No lie."

"Just wait until tomorrow night and see what I make you wear."

A little thrill of nerves rippled through her, along with uncoiling heat. "I can always refuse."

"But you won't, will you." He kissed her again, hand rising to cup her breast. "You're having too much fun."

Far from sated, the desire rose in her and she pressed herself into his hand. "Maybe," she breathed.

He chuckled and stood, depositing her in the chair, then kneeling between her thighs. "Let me convince you." Pushing her knees wide and scooting her hips up to the edge of the chair, he moved his hands from leather to her skin and back again, giving her a sly look. "These boots are diabolical."

"I'm glad you like them. I…" She forgot what she'd been about to say when he lowered his head and licked her.

He glanced up with an inquiring, friendly expression. "You were saying?"

"I have no idea."

"Good. Let me please you, Miss Emily."

He bent to his task with enthusiasm and she dropped her head back as he had done, letting the pleasure roll through her in waves.

AFTERWARD, HE DONNED the apron, just to make her giggle, and made them something to eat. She borrowed a pair of his sweats and tried not to notice how much they smelled like him.

Or that she already knew so well the scent of his skin. The fire felt good and she curled up in the corner of the couch with a glass of wine, his truly excellent crab and cheese pasta, full of that wide awake yet totally relaxed sense of completion he seemed to instill. With her permission—asked with a wink—Fox donned a pair of old sweats, too, and settled on the other end of the couch.

It felt oddly comfortable, sitting together. Cozy. A counterpoint to the intensely pitched sexual encounters that had characterized their relationship thus far.

"Did Anansi behave last night?" Fox asked, casually, floating the question to her in a tone that made it clear he knew questions were against the rules, but that this should be an easy social conversation to have. He never let up for long. But this she could handle. Besides, after he'd made himself more vulnerable to her than any guy ever had, how could she refuse a conversation about her dog?

"Not hardly." She wrinkled her nose at the memory. Chewed-up shoes, barfed back up. "He hates being left alone and finds ways to punish me for it. God knows what he's up to as we speak."

"You can't leave him outside?"

"He barks. There aren't many neighbors, but two of the year-rounders have fits over it."

"Hard to be at war with people in this small of a community."

"Something I've never been good at anyway." She hadn't even tried to fight the trolls. Too undermined. Too afraid to face them.

He made a mock astonished face. "Did you just voluntarily share personal information?"

"Oh stop. I've told you things. Personal things." Not all true, of course.

"Only some of them true," he echoed her thought, then raised his brows, daring her to refute the point.

"Well, I truthfully answered your very intrusive question. You can read it after I leave." She pointed at the sealed envelope she'd left on the coffee table.

"I want to read it now."

"Then I'll go."

"Let's go get Anansi and bring him here, so you can spend the night."

She'd figured that was where he was going with this. And she was tempted all right. More tempted than she liked. She hadn't slept all night with someone else since Henry. Toward the end, their bed had been very cold, indeed. Experiencing skin-to-skin contact again with Fox had shaken her to the core, brutally reminding her of how isolated she'd been. Cuddling, sharing a bed...she shook her head. "Gladys Kapsuck is allergic. I couldn't do that to her."

"Then let me sleep at your house."

Could she? So fraught. "This is working. Let's not mess with it."

"A few nights doesn't count as 'working,' Emily. We're still in initial stages here."

"Or we've gone from zero to ninety, peaked and we're close to being done with each other." She set her bowl aside, no longer hungry for the rest, nerves tightening. "Don't try to kid me, Fox. You've clearly been around the block a whole bunch of times. I'm fine with being your lover while you're here—more than fine, as you well know—but let's not pretend this is more than that."

"Hey, this is how 'more than that' starts." He sounded genuinely offended. "Sure, some people go to bars looking for the one-night hookup, but most of them are hoping that they'll meet The One. That love will result from one of those chance meetings."

Her stomach dropped at the mention of love. Not what she'd expected at all. "Do *not* tell me you're a romantic."

He gave her an astonished look that must be meant to

mirror her own. "What? I can't believe in love? People fall in love and live their lives together. Isn't that the ideal? That's what everybody wants."

"And less than half the people get. Look at the divorce rate. That's just for the people who manage to get married, or who legally can. It probably comes out to something like an eighth."

"Aha. But then look at how many of them get married again. Or fight for legal marriage. That shows they still believe in the dream. That it's possible."

"Or it shows they're idiots who don't learn from experience."

"Is that you? Have you learned from experience?"

"You don't have to go through a divorce to witness the way it destroys people." She'd taken too big of a bite and had to swallow it down uncomfortably.

"Very interesting non-answer," he mused, winding pasta around his fork.

"I suppose you come from a family where everyone is happily married with big parties for their golden anniversaries."

"Nope. My mom and dad divorced when I was eighteen. Haven't spoken to him since."

"Geez, Fox. I'm sorry. What—"

"Uh-uh." He pointed the fork at her. "You do not get to divert to my personal shit while holding back on your own."

"Fine." She snatched up the envelope and held it out to him. "Read it."

With a gleeful smile, he snapped it from her hand, setting his bowl aside, giving her the definite feeling that she'd been played. As usual. Point to Fox.

CHAPTER TWENTY-FOUR

E MILY LOOKED DISGRUNTLED, in a totally delectable way.
With her knees drawn up and her hair falling around her like a cloud of moss, eyes huge in her delicate face, she was lovelier than ever. So help him, he loved pushing her. In every way possible. Each barrier that fell—sexual, emotional, mental—revealed a new, luscious flavor of her.

She might put on a cynical attitude, but under that prickly shell lurked a soft heart. It had to be true. People with callous hearts didn't have to defend them so hard. Fox knew that for a fact. He'd met plenty of people like that, whether by birth or because they'd been so damaged that the scar tissue kept them from ever feeling empathy again. Emily, with her perfect radar for driving him out of his mind sexually, possessed plenty of empathy. No, she possessed a heart so sensitive and full of love that she'd had to wall it off. His own unerring intuition told him that.

Also, hardened people weren't nervous to this extreme. As if she wanted to grab the letter back, no matter how she cupped her wineglass in both hands, trying to seem nonchalant and failing utterly.

He scanned the page. "Three lines?"

"Was there a length requirement? You didn't mention."

Minx. He shook his head at her, then made a show of reading. She pointedly looked away, staring into the fire.

I had a very bad experience with a stalker some years ago, to the point that my life was threatened. So I changed my name and moved. I'm told I should be safe, but I'm still very careful. I'm sure you understand and will respect this.

Interesting. It jibed. Mostly. "A stalker, huh?"

She nearly jumped out of her skin. "We don't need to discuss it." She'd lowered her voice, reflexively, and her anxiety had ramped up. Whoever the asshole was, he'd scared her plenty.

"He can't hear us, here in the Kapsucks' living room, on an island in the middle of the San Juans." He tried to say it gently, to soothe her, but she fixed him with a hard stare.

"Why do you assume it's a him?"

"Most are." He shrugged. But she had a point. A bad habit of his, assuming the guys were always the nasties. "Did you know who the person was?"

"We never did. It was…over the internet mainly."

"Tell me more about it."

"No." She set down her wine and rubbed her hands on her pants. Sweaty palms? "And, *this* is why I didn't want to have you read it until I left. Look—I trusted you with this information. Don't make me sorry I told you."

"It might help to talk about it."

Her head whipped around, a wisp of hair sticking to her lip that she didn't have the presence of mind to brush away. *"Talk about it?"*

Fascinated, he watched the dark emotions well up in her, half expecting her head to spin around or her hair to coil into serpents.

She stood and gathered her hair into a knot at her neck. Then, with nothing to tie it back, she dropped it again and grabbed her wineglass. At least she wasn't walking out. Yet.

"Believe me, *Fox*—" she hissed his name in an uncomplimentary way, "—I talked about it. I talked myself blue, purple and black. At first people don't believe you, even when the evidence is right in front of their fucking faces. Then they can't believe *it*—that such a thing could even occur in our nice, neat, happy world. After that, they accept the basic reality, but they search for reasons to explain it, why it's actually your fault."

She laughed. A new kind of laugh this time, bitter and edged with grief, with rage. "I promise you, talking about it is the last thing I ever want to do so long as I live. You need to understand that."

"Asshole ex-husband?" He hazarded his theory. This might be his one opportunity, so he might as well bet his entire pot.

That got her. She froze, nearly midstep, and leveled him with the coldest look she'd yet produced. "How do you know about him?"

"Come on, Emily." He went to her but didn't touch her, much as he wanted to. She reminded him of the glass fairies his mother had collected. The ones that broke if you picked them up, even when you were trying to be careful. "It's written all over you. You have to be either divorced or the child of a divorce. You wouldn't feel so strongly otherwise."

"Two for two, Mister Insightful Writer." She tossed back

her wine and went to pour more. It allowed her to put distance between them, sure, but at least more wine meant she'd stay longer. Also a little drunkenness never hurt when confessions of the soul were involved. He should know.

"Tell me about him then." Surprising stab of jealousy for this faceless guy who'd clearly had much more of Emily than he seemed likely to catch a glimpse of. But hey, look who had her now. Dumbshit.

"It's boring." She sounded weary, but came back to the fire, staring into it. "It wouldn't even make one of your novels. We married too young, didn't really know each other—" she cast him a significant look, "—and when the going got tough, we collapsed."

"You mean, he wasn't tough enough to stick it out with you."

She held out a hand to the fire, as if to warm it. "No, that wouldn't be fair. Neither of us were tough enough. There was a time I would have said it was all his fault, but it wasn't. He's not a bad guy. He got something different than he signed up for. So he took the out-clause. Fair enough. If I could have, I'd have done the same." She laughed again, that bitter brew beneath it. "In point of fact, I did. Just in a different way."

"He bailed on you because of the stalker." A surge of anger blew through him, righteous clean and scorching hot. Not only a dipshit, but a Class A Asshole.

"You make it sound simple and it wasn't."

Taking a chance, he pushed her hair over her shoulder, immeasurably relieved when she let him, even bending her head to let him rub the back of her neck.

"Nothing is simple when you're going through it," he said, searching for the right words. "Emotional shit is just that—mucky and stinky and full of contagion. It's only later that you can look back and see how you were waist-deep and in danger of being dragged under."

She met his gaze, her eyes silvery with a sheen of tears. "Good analogy. No wonder you're the writer."

Guilt—something he almost never felt—stabbed through him. *Now might be a good time to tell her you lied about the novelist gig, Sparky.* But it wasn't a good time, not with her all emotionally flayed, trusting him with her secrets and her pain. If he confessed to his duplicity right now, she'd be angry and shut down again.

Instead, he pressed his hand on the silky hot skin of her neck and urged her closer. Amazingly, she leaned against him, laying her cheek against his chest and weeping a few silent tears. It figured that she'd cry this way—nothing dramatic, as quiet and contained as everything she did.

Until she explodes, whispered that warning voice.

He ignored it and wrapped his arms around her, holding her close and offering all the comfort he knew how to give. Knowing when not to push, too, was something he'd learned. Sometimes people just needed time to process, to work things through in quiet.

When she made a movement to pull away, he took her wineglass and set it aside. Then he cupped her face and kissed her the way she liked best, soft, long and sweet. She went pliant under his hands, reaching under his shirt to touch his skin. The way her slim fingers touched him, always with a sense of hungry wonder, never failed to move him, to electrify him.

He deepened the kiss and she responded with a moan, melding her body against him. The cock he thought could not rise again after the near-brutal workout stirred, needing to be inside her. Briefly he wished they could be skin-to-skin there, too, but beggars and horses and all that.

Pulling his sweatshirt over her head, he satisfied himself with filling his hands with her, with all that satiny skin, lean length and voluptuous breasts. Then he skimmed the draw-string pants down her endless legs. Something to be said for uncomplicated clothes, too.

She returned the favor, stripping him of his sweats and running her hands over him, touching him the same way he savored her. Naked, they clung together, sharing their hunger. He indulged himself, digging his fingers through her hair, loving the transition in textures between the silken curls and the softer texture of her skin. Her nipples poked into his chest, hard points in the taut globes of her luscious tits. She began making those urgent little sounds of arousal at the same time he thought he couldn't stand to not be inside her anymore.

"Let me get a condom," he muttered against her mouth. Should have put one in his pocket.

She made a sound of protest, clinging to him and holding tighter.

"Emily—I have to go get it. Just hold that thought."

She flushed, chagrined, sense coming into her eyes. "Sorry. And thank you. I wasn't thinking. Running a risk with disease like that."

"Well, I'm clean, but..." She looked profoundly surprised

and he laughed. "Hey, I'm not *that* much of a whore."

"I didn't mean…"

"No. It's fair. I should say that I have been that much of a whore, but not so much lately."

She looked far more serious than he thought the topic merited. "I don't think you should talk that way about yourself. That's an ugly word. You enjoy sex more openly and easily than probably anyone I've ever met. That doesn't make you a whore. It means you're exactly who you should be."

Her words sank claws into his heart and shredded it. Touching her cheek, he felt moved, unbalanced by her. "I have ugly in me, too, Emily."

She tilted her head, as if searching for it. "I don't see it."

Full of emotion that he couldn't quite name—or couldn't bear to—he captured her mouth, winding his fingers in the tousled curls that framed her face. Surprised off balance, she clutched his wrists. Afire with need, he lowered her to the floor, then sucked one candy-pink nipple into his mouth. It still tasted of strawberries, no doubt the lip gloss she'd used to color it, an image that amused and touched him. Her unique blend of playful sexiness and lack of sexual sophistication.

As if all of this side of her was expressly and only for him.

Before she sucked him in too deep with the sweet, fevered moments of her body against his, the alluring scrape of her nails down his back, he forced himself into his office, to grab a condom from the pile she'd left on his desk. The screensaver mocked him, with its slideshow of perfect and perfectly neutral landscape shots from the stock images that came with every Windows PC. For a while he'd used his own collection, until someone he was pumping for information noticed one and asked what on earth had taken him to Mogadishu. No, nothing ugly to see here.

No wonder she couldn't see it in him. He'd whitewashed it too well.

For a tense moment, he'd been worried she'd spot the files for his Phoenix research. Or evidence that he gamed, as he'd so blithely lied that he didn't. It had seemed like an easy untruth at the time—all part of the cover—but it bothered him. His father had been the king of lies, weaving a web so dense that it ensnared everyone, hapless victims of his compulsions. This was different, of course. But only in terms of scale.

His own words mocked him. *People fall in love and live their lives together. Isn't that the ideal? That's what everybody wants.* Emily was the first person in a long, long time that it seemed possible to be that.

Except you're a big, fat walking lie, Sparky.

What he needed to do was get serious about finding Phoenix. He was so close. Every bit of his intuition screamed it. Chase the internet hook-up. Phoenix needs a mighty connection. More muscular than your average islander. Find Phoenix, expose him, turn in the story and tell Emily the truth. Once the story broke, she'd understand the need for secrecy.

Then he'd stay. Or convince her to take a sunny vacation. They could really get to know each other and see where this could go. *Isn't that the ideal? That's what everybody wants.*

"Fox?" Emily called from the other room. "Do I have to come in there after you—show you who's boss?"

For once, the idea didn't titillate him. He went to her,

where she lay propped on her elbows, a glorious nude before the fire, framed by her cloud of dark hair, sultry smile on her lips. His heart rolled over and he sank into her lovely, welcoming body.

But, he couldn't quite recapture the moment. A vague dread crept in, niggling at him, as if he'd forgotten some important task, left something behind.

Even when Emily gasped in his ear and dug those pretty nails into his ass, just as he'd wanted, his thoughts circled back.

And back again.

You should tell her.

CHAPTER TWENTY-FIVE

H E WALKED HER home, which had begun to be a lovely ritual. She kind of liked that he dropped her at her doorstep and went home. It reminded her of being younger, before Henry and before all the rest. Midnight walks through the city after parties and dances. Returning through a quiet campus to her dorm, feeling protected and cherished that her date thought to see her safely home. Not that she'd ever felt in danger. Not then.

Talking about Henry had been strange, dislodging thoughts and feelings that had been stuck for a long time, like a wagon left in the rain to rust until the wheels wouldn't turn. It surprised her to find that she didn't really blame him anymore. She couldn't forgive that he'd failed to give her that sense of safety, of being protected and cherished, but he hadn't been in the wrong. He'd never had any reason to believe she'd want or need that from him. It had never been his job to take care of her.

He'd been a computer nerd too, not a fighter, not a macho guy by any stretch. And she'd never thought she wanted that. She'd been attracted to him for his gentle intelligence, his love of games and gaming. They'd even been good together, for a while, building their careers, sharing their lives, improving their fortunes bit by bit. Their marriage had been like having a sleepover with her best friend, every night, complete with junk food and gaming until dawn.

One thing about loss—it whittled away those fat and happy pounds.

He'd bailed, as Fox so succinctly put it, a few months after she got fired. After he continued to go to work at Gametronix every day, even though other members of the team had quit in protest of how it was all handled. Henry avoided discussing it, his solution for everything. As far as he was concerned, that ugly period had ended. She lied to Fox about that too. She'd never really talked about it. Henry hadn't been like Fox in that way. Or any way, really.

Those last months of him struggling to find neutral topics of conversation, unable to look her in the face, as if she'd been sullied, raped and beaten in truth instead of just virtually—that had been the worst part of all.

When he'd finally left her, passive-aggressively sending divorce papers via his lawyer, she'd been relieved. He'd even ensured the terms were so generous, she could hardly refuse. He wanted out and he ponied up the money to prove it.

Signing those papers had given her the idea. She'd stop being ruined and vilified Lisa White forever. Not only by giving up Henry's surname and her connection to the husband of her naïve youth, but by changing her entire name, her whole life.

Her own version of witness protection.

It had worked too. She'd risen from the proverbial ashes of the nuclear meltdown her life had become and risen as

Phoenix. Like a superhero, with mild-mannered Emily Bartwell as her alter-ego. It amused her to think of Fox as her Lois Lane. He even had that intrepid reporter vibe with his relentless curiosity and dogged questioning.

They arrived at her doorstep and she realized he hadn't said a word, immersed in his own thoughts. In fact, he'd seemed more distant. Since the condom conversation, really. Had she hurt his feelings by implying he'd been slutting about?

She opened her mouth to ask, maybe apologize, when he spoke first.

"I have to go off-island tomorrow. Research. For the book. I might not make it back in time for the last ferry."

Oh. Funny, the sense of disappointment. Of course he had things to do. So did she for that matter. She should welcome the chance to immerse herself in all that programming she'd been getting increasingly behind on. Get a chunk out the door, so she could be free to spend more time with him.

"You're disappointed." He searched her face. "I don't have to go tomorrow."

"No," she blurted out, then hastened to add, just in case she was tromping all over his feelings, "I mean, I am disappointed, but you should go. Your work is important. It's why you're here."

He flinched, only a little, but noticeable. Someone better at interpersonal stuff would know what to say. Instead she leaned against him, the way he seemed to enjoy, gratified when he slid his arms around her waist to stroke her skin under the sweatshirt she'd re-borrowed.

"You get back when you get back," she murmured, kissing

him. "Don't worry about me. I'll be here."

"Good." He pressed her more tightly against him, reminding her of how he'd pushed her against the door and she'd climaxed, the porch light above her a chromium moon, just the night before. "And then it's my turn."

Just like him, to want to leave her with that burning thought.

"I have ideas," he continued. "Several things I want to do to you. I might pick up some supplies."

Feeling weak in the knees—turned out the cliché was based in something real—she nodded. "Just um…" Had she been about to say to call her? She didn't even have a number to give.

"I know how to find you." He kissed her, no irony or impatience in his voice. He understood and accepted that much about her, at least. It meant a lot, actually.

"Good night then. Safe travels," she added impulsively.

He grinned, that easy, charming smile. "I'll let you know when I return."

"Okay."

"And Emily? Plan on wearing the boots." Fox gave her a little salute and strolled off, hands in the pockets of his windbreaker.

She awarded herself extra points on that one. It felt good to have had something to bring to the game, something unexpected and powerful. She sat down to peel off said boots, not easy with sweatpants over them—though an amusing combination.

Yes, amazingly enough, talking about Henry, even a bit about what had happened, had felt good also. She'd almost wanted to tell Fox the whole sordid tale, he was such a good listener. Though she couldn't do that without also trusting him with her secret identity.

Though, what if they did fall in love?

She shook her head at herself, but—for once—couldn't drum up much cynicism on the subject. The things he'd said about that being the ideal…she'd thought the same way, once upon a time. That she'd found her happy ever after in Henry. She'd wanted that, believed in it. Maybe Fox had the right of it and she'd only been bitter.

Not a fatal blow to her heart, just one that had taken a long time to heal.

A huger problem loomed, a stationary fog bank that wouldn't dissipate with a few meager rays of sun. She couldn't be in love, have an actual relationship and keep up the vast pretense of her life. Already she'd let too much work slide to preserve the fiction that she wiled her days away doing jack shit.

If they progressed into the real thing, she'd have to let him in her house, for starters. What a mess that she could give him access to the intimate spaces of her body, but not to her home—the one place where she remained, more or less, her real self. She'd have to eventually explain that she did work, which would lead to the whole, sordid story. Hell, she'd have to let him see that person, pitiful Lisa in all her crippled ugliness, hiding in her lair, stripped of the identities that protected her.

So hard to face that.

Henry had known and loved her for years and hadn't been

able to stomach her broken self. How could Fox?

No, he'd been satisfied with the answer she'd given. Absolutely true, if not the whole story. He didn't need to know the rest. Not yet. Maybe not ever.

She'd never won at love, so it would be foolish to even contemplate going for that prize. Part of the trick of gaming was sticking to your power level, to what you could reasonably hope to accomplish.

She knew her limits. Of course, you never made it to the next level by playing safe.

FOX HAD BEEN tired enough to sleep hard. A good thing, because the sleep gave him perspective. The intense sex of the night before had simply made him emotional. Wouldn't be the first time. Really, he should have seen it coming.

You hand the hottest woman you've met in years a long-held fantasy and she fulfills it and beyond—of course you were rattled, Sparky. Of course she got under your skin. They pick showgirls with long legs to keep you distracted.

He stood out on the rain-lashed deck of the first ferry out—no doubt looking like a tourist to the locals tucked inside with their newspapers and their thermoses of fragrant coffee, along with a busload of school kids—but it helped clear his head. Emily had infiltrated his brain, her vibrant presence permeating his thoughts the same way the sweet scent of orange blossoms clung to his skin.

A serious, libido-addicting crush was what it was. A major case of lust.

And like.

He enjoyed her company, dammit, and there was nothing wrong with that. Compatibility worked that way. They both liked to run, liked dogs and cats, similar taste in food and wine. Her tendency to be quiet suited him perfectly. If he'd nursed the idea that they could spend a lot of evenings like that—mind-blistering sex followed by comfortable conversation by the fire—who could blame him?

But there was no reason, absolutely none at all, to tell her the real reason for his visit to Lyra. And there was every reason not to.

Stories had been blown on less than this. The wrong word to the right person, and the prey scattered to the wind faster than card-counters fleeing casino security. Just imagine the guys if they heard he'd blown the biggest story of his career—so far—because of pillow talk. With a local girl, no less.

Amateur mistake.

Besides, Emily had an excellent point. Neither of them had entered into this with the long-term in mind. It had been, and still was, technically, just about the fucking. He hadn't promised her more than that and, to give her credit, she hadn't asked for it. Yeah, that stung. But, that they'd delved beyond that lay entirely in his court. *Just couldn't give that curiosity a rest, huh, Sparky?*

He didn't regret learning her secret, though. In fact, it gave him a fierce sense of satisfaction that she'd confided in him. He only wished he'd been there instead of that limp biscuit, deadbeat ex. Fucking asshole wouldn't have scared Fox away. He'd broken the cover around more than one internet stalker in his day. They made good stories. And exposing them ruined their lives as surely as they tried to destroy their victims.

In fact, he could do that for Emily. It should have occurred to him before. He'd go through her records—had to pat himself on the back for his instinct that they covered something up—and find the incidents. There had to be police reports of some sort. If nothing else, he'd figure out who the husband had been and visit a little payback on him. Something juicy to serve a coward right.

Maybe he wouldn't even tell Emily he'd done it. Just enjoy his anonymous good deed by her, to make up for the temporary lies. Chances were the stalker had already met his comeuppance. Those guys rarely learned their lessons. Once one obsession escaped, they fixated on another and often scaled up too fast, as if they couldn't wait to reach the peak they'd experienced with the last one. That led to mistakes.

A guy like him? He'd built his career on the mistakes of others. Maybe he would tell Emily, lay the head of the dragon at her feet, so to speak.

He'd spend the day investigating the regional ISPs—every damn one of them on the mainland, of course—and then maybe hit some shops, pick a few things to decorate and torment the lovely Miss Emily with. They weren't going for the long term, fine. Didn't mean they couldn't enjoy the hell out of each other for as long it lasted. Didn't mean he didn't love to make her smile.

Finding a lover like Emily didn't happen often. Women of her ilk didn't hit the clubs and the bars. Hookups worked okay, had their own thrill, but seriously intense sex took buildup over time. A nice hook, yes, but then layering of anticipation to really grow the story. Flash fiction had its place—a tasty bite—but the novels delivered full satisfaction. At least for him. For better or worse, he preferred the long term when he could get it.

If his dad hadn't turned out to be such a shit, blowing up their lives in such a spectacular way, Fox would probably have married Bailey Jones, as she'd more than half expected, and settled into family life. He might even have been reasonably happy. It had worked out okay, though, knowing what he did about himself now.

Bailey had been great for the seventeen-year old him. More than that. She'd loved sex and him with a generous lack of reserve that kind of shamed him in retrospect. He'd been a typical boneheaded guy and took everything she offered without knowing the value of it. When he'd blown town, after his mother found out about his dad's compulsive gambling, their devastated finances and how Fox had helped him cover it up…well, it hadn't occurred to him to tell Bailey any of it.

By the time he got himself together enough to face his mother again—worst moment of his life—Bailey had moved away and no one knew where. Yeah, of course he could probably research her, find her current location, but what was the point? They'd both moved on and maybe it was better that they stayed memories for each other. Remained their more innocent selves, if only in some golden bubble of the past.

Damn, he was maudlin lately. What the hell had gotten into him?

Too close to the finish line, most likely. Just revved to break the story and impatient for the taste of blood. He'd worked, in one way or another, for over two years on this one story—pretty much since he first played Labyrinth and looked up the design team for a puff piece. Long haul for one payoff.

Being stuck on that claustrophobic island in the oppressive gloom only added to his impatience.

No matter what, he'd stay in Seattle tonight. Blow off some steam. Have a decent meal out, catch a movie or something. Then he'd have time tomorrow to hit any ISPs he couldn't get to today, just in case, and return to Lyra armed with the information he needed to pin Phoenix down in his flaming nest.

With any luck—and the good Lord had blessed him with all the luck he'd denied Fox's father at the end—he'd have Phoenix's identity within a few days. He'd stake his reputation on it.

Then he laughed, a spray of water hitting him in the face with the cold splash of reality. *Hell, Sparky, you already have.*

CHAPTER TWENTY-SIX

E M WORKED MOST of the night. After repotting her philodendron, that is. And the three begonias that probably wouldn't survive being dumped, trampled and then suffering the final indignity of serving as Dinah's litter box.

The denizens of her household had spoken and they were *not* happy.

Between the fur family and Fox's seductive insistence, she was seriously reconsidering her No One Comes in the House rule.

She'd planned just to check in, once she'd showered off the dregs of sex and urine-saturated potting soil, but Cindy and Syd had sent her a bunch of stuff. Really good stuff. Rarely did she wish to be in an office again, working face-to-face with a team, but now she did. The gals had built upon her foundation and made it amazing.

What they proposed might be difficult to implement. But if they tweaked this aspect…

She got absorbed, in the best possible way, stopping only to take nail clippers to the false tips that seriously got in the way of her keyboarding. Trixie would be appalled, but Em figured she'd gotten her money's worth already. She looked up when Anansi nudged her at dawn. A rare bright morning it might shape up to be too. Sending off her notes to the team, she included a request to Cindy and Syd to meet later. With a run and a few hours of sleep, she'd be good to go for the rest of the day. And into the night.

With some hard work and a bit of luck, they'd get this module out into the world.

And watch the trolls choke on it.

CINDY AND SYD popped up on the video screen in the private conference room, looking nervous. Another reason not to like her Phoenix persona—everyone was scared of him. Hazard of the game. The Meek and Sweet Wizard of Oz would have had everyone looking behind the curtain immediately.

Still, she kind of hated it when other women quailed in front of Phoenix. She threw up a Tom Hiddleston as Loki avatar—evil, yes, but with that sexy, mischievous smile that Fox had nailed in spades. Cindy, serious and round-faced, rolled her eyes, but Syd cracked a grin, her facial piercings glinting with the blue glow of the screen.

"You gals rocked this work," Em started in without preamble, wanting to make sure they knew it. "I'm beyond impressed."

"But?" Syd raised a magenta eyebrow speared by a platinum bar.

"No buts. This is good work. I'm sending Jared notes to that effect for your performance reviews. Exceeded expectations and then some."

They exchanged glances.

"Um, sir?" Cindy ducked her head a little. *Don't be submis-*

sive, dammit. "Then why the private meet?"

"Yeah." Syd nodded. "If you're going to shorten the leash, then do it. You don't need to butter us up. We can take the straight dope."

She considered that, studying their expressions and thinking what Fox would say. Likely something about putting all the cards on the table.

"I'm going to be blunt here," she said and, yeah, they flinched, bracing themselves. "The reason I asked for a private meet with you two is I didn't want management to factor in. This is just us." Shit, almost said "us girls." "Geek to geek, gamer to gamer. If I was there in person, we'd be sitting in a dark corner booth in a bar, okay?"

They managed not to exchange looks, but their reaction to the absurdity of that idea came through loud and clear. Had Phoenix been that much of an ogre? Yeah, maybe.

"Let's do it this way—since you're so certain you know what I'm going to say, why don't you tell me what you think it is."

Syd shrugged, wrinkling her nose and sitting back. Abandoning the field to the outwardly meeker Cindy who, surprisingly, fixed the screen with a determined glare. "Look. We know this is troll bait. The community will go bananas over this. There will be hacking attempts, personal attacks. They'll sniff out that Syd and I were on the team and we'll take the hit for it with gruesome shit of all kinds."

Ah, too bad. But she didn't blame them. "I understand if you can't go there."

"No!" Syd abruptly sat forward again and slammed a many-ringed hand on the desk. "That's not it. We absolutely *want* to go there. And we also know that you and management want to reel us in. But Cindy and I are not afraid. Bring it on."

Cindy nodded. "Yes, Jacker is not Gametronix and neither of us is Lisa White. We can handle this if you let us. We're asking you to let us do this thing. One hundred percent commitment."

"Lisa White?" In the quiet of her office, her old name echoed with eerie resonance. With a superstitious pang she thought that, if anyone said it a third time, her old self would manifest, bringing destruction in her wake.

"Yeah. It happened, what, five, six years ago?" Syd glanced at Cindy for confirmation. *Not nearly so long as that.* "Anyway a lot has changed since then, but she's still the great cautionary tale. You wouldn't know, necessarily, but the female programmers do."

Cindy smoothly took up the tale. "She designed that Amazon game, where the characters were all female and you accrued points through pounding on and enslaving guys. You could raid other islands and accrue male harems and other booty."

"Yes." Syd clapped her hands. "There was even this bit where Heracles arrives and you could assign him impossible tasks. It rocked."

"I played it in college before they yanked it." Cindy looked thoughtful. "It can't have been more than four years ago."

"Maybe not." Syd frowned. Shook it off. "Anyway, we won't make her mistakes."

"If you let us run with this," Cindy inserted, giving Syd a warning look.

"We *have* to do this. If only to show we can, that we won't be intimidated. They might have destroyed Lisa White's career—which was a huge loss to the profession—but there are others of us willing to take up the torch. I don't understand why you wouldn't back us on this—this is *your* concept we're running with. The first decent one you've offered female players and—"

"Why do you think I wouldn't back you?" Em finally interrupted the tirade as Cindy's meaningfully raised brows had failed to do.

Syd paused, regrouping.

"Jared hinted as much," Cindy stepped in. "He said the two of you had talked and had concerns for our safety. He was at Gametronix, you know. He's totally PTSD about it."

"And you haven't exactly been a champion of females in the community—in the games, us on the team or on the forums." Syd looked as if she wanted to say more.

"Which isn't Phoenix's job," Cindy reminded her, then looked at the screen. "You're a recluse and you love the games and that's all you want to deal with. We get that. More, I—we—respect that. You're established. But we're young and just starting what we want to be long careers. This is important to us."

"Because we *don't* want to spend our whole careers being afraid of the boys club and the trolls," Syd asserted.

"I agree," Em said.

Syd started to say something else, then cocked her head slightly. Cindy didn't look as surprised, simply nodded, as if confirming something to herself.

"I want you to run with this," Em continued. "I don't care how the trolls react. I wanted to make sure you two knew what you were getting into. I do remember, very well, what happened to Lisa White and—" Em caught herself too late. Third time. Bad luck.

"We won't cave like that," Syd replied with careless confidence.

"Because we have better support now. People are more aware."

"*If* management will back us," Syd said to Cindy, clearly falling into a usual argument between them. Their level of teamwork impressed Em and, oddly enough, reinforced that feeling of loneliness. It might have helped back then, to have even one other woman working with her, instead of all those guys, half of whom treated her like an alien species. Even Henry. Syd and Cindy had each other.

And me too.

"All right then. But keep me apprised. I have more than one identity on the forums and I'll be watching your backs. Now, let's go through this. Do you want to call in Hong Wong?"

They exchanged a moment's glance, shaking their heads together. "We got this," Syd took the lead.

"We don't need him," Cindy backed her up.

IT TOOK A few hours, but they got through everything. Right about the time, in fact, that her reminder popped up.

GO RUN.

THIS MEANS YOU!

Had she made her two-runs per day goal since meeting Fox? She turned over the days in her mind, not sure now how many it had been. Time flies when you're having fabulous sex, apparently.

Anansi seemed to think it had been a long time, because she caught him snoozing instead of impatiently waiting for her at the gate. The run felt good, working out the kinks from sitting and irregular sleep. Fox didn't seem to have made it back—not that she'd run past his house explicitly to check. Anansi had picked the direction. Pretty much.

Still, a tinge of that loneliness settled over her when she got in. She poured some wine and sat on the couch, but Dinah wouldn't sit with her—part of her ongoing shunning for Em's repeated absences. Her mind wouldn't settle on the book she hadn't picked up since Fox inserted himself into her quiet life. If she hadn't had a bookmark, she wouldn't have remembered where she left off, it had been so long. She thought about playing a game or going on the forums, but it irritated her to think of donning one of her many aliases.

She'd rather talk to someone who knew *her*. More, she wanted Fox to be sitting on the other end of the couch.

Maybe it partly came from witnessing Syd and Cindy's easy camaraderie, their nearly seamless partnership, but she suddenly missed having friendship. It was funny—when she'd first come to Lyra she'd been like a wounded animal, crawling into her den and erasing her tracks. She'd been so intent on not being fucking terrified all the time, and then on becoming someone else, on rebuilding her career, that she hadn't had the emotional room to be lonely.

Also, any friends she'd had she'd lost in the fiasco and then in becoming Emily Bartwell. Henry had been just the one to walk away decisively. The others had either distanced themselves from her train wreck or hadn't been enough a part of the gaming world to understand. Looking back—well, she'd driven most of them away, unable to bear their sympathy, infuriated by their puzzlement over losing "just a job."

It hadn't mattered at the time. When you were fatally wounded, all that mattered was staunching the blood flow. Cutting everybody out of her life had been a kind of cauterizing. Which—duh—also left behind a lot of burnt flesh. The way her barren life had become.

Now Fox had woken her out of her walking coma. A prince tapping on the glass coffin and dislodging the poison that put her there. He'd make a good prince charming, with his handsome ease and athletic grace. A kinky one, to be sure, but hey—maybe Snow White would have been into it. She'd lived with seven guys, after all.

Maybe if she'd nurtured some of her own friendships, she wouldn't have felt so damn alone when the shit hit the fan. Talking to Fox about stuff had gotten that ball rolling, but he'd be gone in another month or so and she'd still be here. Spending time with Dinah and Anansi wouldn't cut it anymore. And it might be good for her to not be Phoenix so much—or her other identities. It might be time to return to one reflection in the mirror. Figure out who that might be. Which meant having friends who knew her for herself.

Five-forty-five. Glory would be closing up soon. Maybe she'd want to hang out.

Before she could change her mind, Em shrugged on her coat, fetched Anansi and loaded him into the Jeep. They got to the post office right as Glory was hitting the lights. She gave Em an owlish look and shook her head.

"I am not fetching your damn packages. The PO is closed and if you wanted them so bad you could've come earlier."

"I didn't even know I had anything here," Em protested, laughing. "I came to see if you wanted to get a drink or something."

Glory gave her a hard stare. "What happened—did foxy Fox dump you? I'll kill him."

"No, no, nothing like that. Though he is off-island tonight and—oh God, is it awful that I only wanted to hang out with you because he's not here? That's a total violation of the Girl Code, I'm sure of it."

"Technically you would be correct." Glory shooed her out the door so she could lock it. "But since, in my memory, you've never once dropped by to invite me to hang, I'm giving you a special dispensation. But you're buying."

"Yes! Absolutely I'm buying. I should have said so."

"And you'll tell me all the dirty details."

"Well," Em hedged, shortening her stride to match Glory's. Funny how she'd gotten used to Fox's almost perfectly matched pace. "There's not much to tell."

Glory made a rude sound. "Don't give me that. You're glowing."

"I just went for a run."

"I've seen you after running. This is sex glow—I'd know it from a hundred paces. See, a sex glow has..." Glory trailed off in mid-gesture and stared hard at her. "Oh. My. God."

"What?"

"That's not sex glow. That's lurv glow. You can't be in love—you just met the guy!"

"Um, exactly!" They reached Bud's Tavern and she held open the door for Glory. "Which is why I'm not. This is exercise glow. That's it."

"Uh-huh. Two vodka martinis, Bud! Dirty, like my friend here."

"Oh, stop it!" But Glory had her laughing and imagining her face a glowing red. What did it matter though? She and Fox were both free agents, and if everyone knew they were screwing each other's brains out, what difference did it make? "Or I won't tell you anything."

"I'll be good," Glory promised and made her Girl Code hand sign. "Now, make me cross-eyed with jealousy."

CHAPTER TWENTY-SEVEN

H E TRIED TO make himself wait, but Fox ended up taking the first ferry anyway. The Lyra school bus rolled off the incoming boat, the kids waving at him with enthusiasm and he waved back, feeling like a local now.

The new Gore-Tex jacket didn't hurt either—he blended right in.

A night in the city had been okay, but he'd found himself thinking of Emily every damn minute. She'd find that person funny or that movie interesting. Could he talk her into an outing, a weekend in the city, perhaps? Especially if he proved to her that her stalker had moved on or imploded. Being recognized should no longer be an issue for her.

Though he hadn't nailed Phoenix via the ISPs, he knew more about service options than ever before. Consensus was that only a satellite dish would give the best speed and bandwidth in the islands. Of course, everyone had one of those for the TV sets. But it had to be a certain kind, and knowing that would shorten his list. Hell, he'd drive around and look for them.

Something he should do right away instead of visiting Emily. *Anticipation makes it sweeter, Sparky.* Usually he had no trouble reminding himself of that, but his jones to see her argued strongly against it. She would already have gone for her morning run, most likely. Unless she'd stayed up late and slept in again.

The thought of her, all rumpled and sleepy, her hair in wild tangles, made him want to go see her with a nearly physical longing. So much so that he made himself turn the other direction and drive to the other side of the island, to start marking his map with the distinctive satellite dishes.

His thoughts, however, kept returning to her.

What did she do all night—read? Watch TV? Maybe she had insomnia, which would make sense given her history. Maybe, with their new level of trust, she'd confide in him. Probably she didn't want him to see her as weak and that was why she hid it from him. Maybe her anxiety had led her to hoarding and her house really was a mess, with shame-inducing piles of magazines everywhere.

No—he'd seen in from the back door and there'd been no clutter. If anything, the room had been sparely furnished and decorated. It would be, wouldn't it? If she'd fled her stalker and moved suddenly. But why not let him in the house? Old habits die hard, perhaps. She'd developed a pattern of distrust, keeping strangers out in case they proved to be her stalker.

Though she'd relaxed with him quickly enough, that first meeting. Once she established who he was. Which meant she knew enough about her stalker to know from a few minor details that he wasn't the one. But how?

It niggled at him. That would absolutely be in-pattern for a stalker, to rent a nearby house and pose as a writer, to make friends with her and establish a relationship. Something about him, his face, what he'd said, showed that he wasn't the one. Or that he didn't know her.

That had to be it. But wouldn't a stalker factor that in, pretend to be fooled by her new identity? Of course he would. No, Miss Emily had some other way of being sure of him.

She had to know who her stalker was.

Which meant she'd lied.

It shouldn't make him so damn furious. She lied reflexively about everything to do with that time in her life. Objectively, he knew she didn't owe him anything more than what she'd agreed to—just fucking. On one level, he understood that. On the other—oh, he wanted to do what he'd promised not to. To tie her down so tightly she couldn't move and then torment her, push her past all caring and extract every bit of truth from between those luscious pink lips.

She didn't understand this about him—in all fairness, he hadn't told her—but he hated these sorts of lies. His father's voice echoed in his head. *You see, Sparky—this isn't exactly lying to your mother. We're just massaging the truth, so she won't worry. Really, it's how we show love.* It had been one thing when they were going the just-fucking route, but now that they...what? Had at least broached the topic of long term, even though she'd dismissed it out of hand.

He took a hairpin curve too fast and had to brake hard, gripping the steering wheel to hold the rental car on the road. *Slow down, Sparky.*

She made him crazy. Had from the very beginning. Whatever the reason, during the biggest story of his career, he'd gone out of control for this woman. If he'd realized early on how different she'd be, maybe he would have gone about the affair in a different order. He'd thought sexual intimacy would get him inside her, which it had. That hadn't been wrong. But she still held him off, treated this thing between them as something temporary. A casual affair where she could lie and it meant nothing.

It doesn't mean anything. A little white lie doesn't hurt anybody.

People lied in marriages of nearly thirty years, too, but that transgressed into the realm of the unforgiveable.

He needed to see her now. Fuck anticipation. Who cared if his behavior veered into a little obsessive? He'd own that. That trait made him a good reporter and an even better investigator. It made him an excellent lover, too, and she had to know that.

In no time he pulled into her driveway, ready to pick a fight with her if she complained about the neighbors seeing. He knocked on the door and waited, contemplating how crazed he might get if she didn't answer. He pounded louder, using the side of his fist.

He drew in a breath to yell up at the solidly closed windows and the door opened. Emily, with her hair up in that damned ponytail, sleek and perfect in clinging black velour leggings and top, appeared. She smiled, half in welcome and more than a little in exasperation.

"Geez! Give me a minute to get to—"

Fox missed whatever she'd been about to say because he had to have his hands on her. Grabbing her by her slim waist, he yanked her against him, devouring her mouth. She yielded immediately—thankfully because he didn't know what he'd have done if she hadn't—and kissed him back, opening her hot mouth and taking him in. Her arms wound around the back of his neck, holding him tight, and she moved against him in a fiery response that sent his tenuous control to the wind.

"Missed you," he grunted, and yanked at the ponytail tie, wanting her free of it. He gripped her tight ass in the other hand, her muscle flexing as she moved her hips against him.

"God—me too."

He got the tie out and dug his hand in her hair, winding his fingers into the silk of it and holding her head still so he could feast on her mouth. She moaned deep in her throat, and he knew she'd be as slick as he was hard. Releasing his grip on her ass, he tugged at the zipper of her top, splitting it open to reveal the little tank beneath, her nipples hard and defined. He filled his hand with her tit and she blazed under his touch.

"The neighbors..." He was vaguely surprised that she hadn't objected yet, that he was the one to say something, but it might kill him if she called a halt. Already he might be too far gone. Could he possibly wait long enough to get her into the car and back to his place? No way. "Let me in, Emily," he grated. "I promise not to break anything."

HE TASTED SO good. And she felt as desperate for him as if he'd been gone for months, instead of thirty-six hours. Not that she'd been counting.

I promise not to break anything. Of course he wouldn't. She trusted Fox. He took care of her and, more, he trusted in her. Feeling as giddy as she had saying her wedding vows, she kissed him.

"Yes. Come in, Fox."

She pulled him inside and they rotated around each other, barely parting, then slamming together again, desperate to feed the intense craving. Stretching, she managed to kick the front door closed and he picked her up, making her head spin, her legs reflexively wrapping around him so she straddled his waist, while he pushed her against the wall.

Feeling wild, loving his strength, she dug her shortened nails into his neck, savoring his grunt of hunger. He was all hard muscles and rough hands, his erection blazing hard even through his jeans. She rubbed her crotch against him, throbbing, and their teeth clashed as they drank each other deeper.

With one hand, he yanked down her tank top and sucked her nipple into his mouth, along with what felt like as much of her breast as he could pull with it. The pleasure/pain, both sharp and deep, intensified the ache in her groin. Those incoherent cries of need must be hers, but she didn't care. "Fox," she gasped. "I need you now. I can't wait."

He nipped her nipple and she convulsed. Then he laved her breast with his tongue, making her wait for it now. Would he take her right there against the wall? No, he let her slide down his body and set her on her unsteady feet.

"Turn around." His face burned lean with hunger, and he turned her to face the wall instead of waiting for her to obey. She pressed her hands flat to it, bracing herself. Abruptly, he yanked her leggings down, startling a cry from her. Exposed to him, she waited, vibrating with the unbearable tension, her thighs pressed tight together by her leggings. The position didn't deter him, however. His hands vised into her hips, pulling them back to get the right angle. The latex-clad head of his cock—of course he'd had a condom in his pocket—pushed against her, hard and huge with her vulva pressed closed.

The sensation of being stretched this way shook her profoundly. Dimly she heard herself cry out as he plunged through her slick tissues, her spine arching with both satiation and increasing need. Unable to bear it, she bucked back against him, desperate. Firmly seated in her now, Fox clamped his hand over her clit and squeezed her turgid breast with the other.

She braced herself against the wall, shuddering, breathing hard, utterly possessed by him in the most delicious way. "Yes. Just like that," he growled at her, the tone stroking her as roughly as his hands. "You hold still while I fuck you." He moved, pumping in and out of her, his cock dragging against her tightened tissues while she moaned. "You love this, don't you?"

"God, yes. Yes, Fox. Please."

Her heart pounded and, impossibly, he tightened his grip on her. She exulted in it, feeling that she belonged entirely to him, without walls or holding back.

"You'll let me in." He increased the pace so his hips smacked into her, forcing her to lean hard into the wall.

"Yes. Oh yes." She hung her head, dizzy with it, with him. The urgency built, red-black and thunderous. She raised herself on her toes to accommodate him better, muscles straining, the orgasm looming like a thunderhead, lightning behind her eyes. Fox slapped the side of her ass, surprising her with shock, and she cried out, writhing. *Harder. Rougher!* She wanted to scream it, but she had no breath.

"Tonight," he muttered, "I'm going to fuck you up the ass. Won't I?"

Oh God, she wanted it. Wanted him in every way. She

nodded, shuddering.

"And you'll love it. You'll love it like this. You'll let me in, give me everything. Tell me that."

"Yes." She sobbed out the word. "Fuck, yes!"

She screamed out the last, the unbearable tension shattering her, an orgasm so deeply wrenching she felt her brain might be exploding with it. Fox went with her, pounding against her body and shouting out his own intense pleasure, as they tumbled over the edge together.

MANAGING THE PRESENCE of mind to keep Emily from falling, Fox wrapped an arm under her hips, though he clung to her with the movement as much as anything. The massive climax had drained him so, leaving him light-headed and slightly disoriented. Emily panted, her body slick with sweat and shuddering with aftershocks. Her knees wobbled and he lowered them both to the floor, where they could at least recover without breaking anything.

A huge cat stared at him from a few feet away, managing to look both suspicious and disdainful at the same time. With a flick of her tail, she dismissed him and sauntered off.

Though he'd pulled out of Emily, the condom hung on his softening dick and he lacked the energy to ditch it. She lay against him, utterly disheveled and not yet fully present. The hallway rug—some kind of jute?—prickled his ass. Probably a good thing they were both still mostly dressed. Above, an amazing chandelier glowed in shades of pink, orange and yellow. It should have been ugly, but it struck him as strangely beautiful and somehow essentially Emily.

"Is that…a blown-glass octopus light?"

"Cthulhu." She turned her head to stare dreamily up at it. "You're the first person to see it—besides me and the artist."

"You let me in your house." With a sense of wonder, almost bashfulness, he kissed her damp temple and cuddled her closer.

"At least the vestibule," she said in a dry tone, sounding more her usual self. "What is with you and front hallways?"

The groan escaped him. "It's your fault. You're so damn sexy and gorgeous I can't wait longer than that."

"That was pretty intense all right."

"Did I hurt you?" Shit. He'd been more than a little out of his head. Levering himself up, he surveyed her, one bare breast still popped out of her pink tank top, the creamy skin marred with marks from his bruising grip. "I did. Dammit, Emily, I'm—"

"Don't say you're sorry." She twisted her fingers into his new jacket and tugged him down for a deep kiss. "I'm not," she added against his mouth. "I liked it. All of it. And I like having you in my house, seeing my Cthulhu chandelier."

Feeling like a drowning man, he gathered her into his arms, sinking himself into the kiss. Had he ever known another woman like her? If he had, he'd been too stupid to know it. And he wouldn't make that mistake this time. It was like she'd been made for him. He searched her eyes, the silvery gray ringed with a deeper color, full of some earnest emotion. "Emily…"

CHAPTER TWENTY-EIGHT

FOR A HEART-STOPPING moment, she thought Fox was about to say he loved her.

Nonsense, of course, but the look on his face, the way he stared into her eyes, made her think it. She panicked a little. Premature, perhaps, but it must have showed in her face. Whether he'd been about to say that or something else, he changed his mind.

"So, do I get to see the rest of your house—or do you prefer to reveal it gradually, day by day, room by room?"

She thumped him on the shoulder for that, though she likely deserved the teasing, mostly relieved by the tension breaker. What would she have done if he'd said it? No, he wasn't going to. Nobody fell in love that fast and certainly not a guy like Fox. He just felt what she did—a kind of overwhelming sense of connection, at seeing each other again. Though the separation had been brief, she'd missed him. Touching him again fed her the same way that eating a delicious meal after fasting for three days would.

That was all. But she would let him see the house. There wasn't all that much to see anyway. How much did she have, really, that would tip someone off to her secret identity?

Not much. Even if they knew who Phoenix was—*and, let's*

face it, how many people do outside the community?—very little in her home alluded to it. Especially to a guy of Fox's non-techie background, nothing screamed enigmatic, super-secret game designer. Most of her equipment didn't look like much. She'd already put the new console in a drawer until they were ready to tackle adding in its capabilities in the new year.

Overall, there wasn't a hell of a lot to see, period. The house remained nearly as inoffensively blank—with a few exceptions like Cthulhu—as the day she'd bought it. Kind of pitiful, really. But then, the woman who'd moved in had been pitiable, hadn't she? She'd made a blank slate of herself out of necessity. The crime had been not coloring in more since.

"If nothing else," Fox added with an impish grin, gesturing at the sagging condom, "I need to ditch this before your cat gets ideas to attack. She looked like she was considering it."

"Dinah came out? Well, well—you rate very highly then."

She sat up, pulling up her leggings, her pussy still throbbing from being compressed around Fox's generous cock. Yes, he'd been rough and it had been exactly right. "Come on. We'll start with the guest bathroom." What had he called it? A fast ball down the middle. Start out with the easy ones and work up. No need to be nervous.

From the guest bathroom, she took him to the kitchen, where she'd pictured him that first day they met. Nerves met giddy joy as the realization hit that she could act out that very fantasy. After they'd recovered.

Fox pointed at Tree's cinnamon rolls, still in the box, that she hadn't gotten around to putting out for the birds. "You can't possibly like those bricks."

Caught, right out of the gate. "I can't bear to hurt her feelings."

"Yeah. I bought a dozen and suspect I'm trapped for the rest of my life."

She laughed, feeling more relaxed. *See? This was going fine.* Leading him into the living area, she pointed to her movie-sized flat screen TV with triumph. He'd seen most of this room from the deck anyway.

Dinah swirled around them, not afraid of Fox at all. A very good sign. The view from the windows took up most of the visual space and she liked it that way. Fox did, too, commenting on it. His quick, observant gaze took in everything and she had a moment when he examined her display of crystal animals, the stylized phoenix in the center seeming to glare with guilty red light. But he only commented that his mother collected glass fairies.

There's nothing to see. If there is, he won't recognize it anyway. Relax. Nothing to see.

That was one of the most restful things about Fox, that he knew nothing about her world. Maybe that had been one of the problems between Henry and her, that they'd worked together, lived, breathed and created all in the same pond. All her post-marriage friends had been shared. Many of the ones from college too. Being with someone like Fox, who worked in an entirely different field, would likely be better for a long-term relationship.

Not that Fox would be that guy, but maybe she could find someone after all. For the first time in years she envisioned a life for herself where she didn't have to be so alone.

"What's that smile for?" Fox turned back from surveying her bedroom and snaked his arms around her waist, pulling her in for a kiss. She liked that about him, too, his freely affectionate ways, how much he seemed to enjoy touching her.

"Just happy that you're back."

"Me too. I missed you."

"So you mentioned in the hallway." She laughed, recalling how considerably less sweet that moment had been—and just as amazing.

Fox returned the smile and laced his fingers with hers, looking at her hands. "You cut your nails already?"

"They were bugging me," she replied, feeling a bit of a guilty pang that she didn't explain why. He seemed to know it, too, his grin dimming ever so slightly. Even worse. She wanted him happy and relaxed again.

"What's this room—office?"

Relax. "Yes. For the computer."

He prowled around, a slight smile on his sexy lips. "Who has three monitors?"

Yeah, about that... "Oh, I'm trying out some digital art." That actually sounded pretty good. "Triptychs," she added. Excellent invention, but he only nodded vaguely, his gaze landing on the voice modulator. It didn't look like much— basically a black box. He frowned slightly but didn't ask about it. *Whew.*

When he turned back to her, she felt like she'd finished running a gauntlet of trolls. No injuries. She'd made it through. "Want a soak in the hot tub?"

"There's one more room I haven't seen."

Her office had passed the test. What could he—Fox gave her that *look* of his, as though he'd seen through one of her lies. "Your painting studio. Or do you not like people to see your work in progress?"

Shit! Of course he'd want to see that, because she'd mentioned painting, hadn't she? "Sure, you can see it," she told him, leading the way, though her stomach coiled with more unease. Stupidly, because the paintings functioned only as a cover hobby, because she'd thought she needed *something* to show for her time and reclusive ways. Now, however—dammit, her pride hated for him to see the truly awful things.

She opened the door she kept closed mainly to prevent Dinah from knocking the jars over or chewing on the nicely puncturable paint tubes, and waved Fox in. He took his time, as he had with surveying all her things. Learning her, the way he liked to do, and as she was trying hard to let him. But this wasn't her and the worm of guilt, of being exposed as this hack, squirmed in her gut.

"Dusty in here," he commented.

"Yeah, um—I've been in a slump lately."

"Hmm." He made a noncommittal sound and circled the room. Surely painters encountered some version of writer's block? She cringed inwardly, seeing the paintings as he must be. Most of them she'd painted in the first few weeks, to create an inventory. She'd done them as fast as possible, anxious to get back to the computer and rebuilding her career.

"It's just a hobby, really," she blurted out when he spent overly long studying lime-green portrait of Anansi, with truly reprehensible perspective.

"I've seen your work before, at the coffee shop." He'd tucked his hands in the pockets of his jeans and now glanced sideways at her, the light catching the line of his cheekbones and glinting off his coppery hair. She waited for him to tell her he liked it, to mouth the standard platitudes, but he wasn't the kind to lie. "Have you been painting long?"

Ah, the careful alternative question. Feeling her out for the right thing to say. For an unhinged moment she wanted to show him her real work, to wipe away his perception of her as an untalented dabbler at best and a completely delusional hopeless case at worst. How did Clark Kent bear it, having Lois drip contempt for his bumbling ways, when he could have dazzled her instead. As Phoenix she shone, a star in her limited universe.

"No. Just since coming to Lyra."

He tilted his head, listening. Waiting for more. What would a normal person say?

"I've never taken classes."

"Didn't want to?"

"Well, it's fooling around, you know. Therapy."

"Oh." He nodded, seeming to understand. Relieved to find an excuse for her pitiful efforts? "Of course you went to therapy after the stalking incident. I should have realized. Did it help?"

God, she hated every minute of this conversation. Probably she should have gone to therapy. Maybe would have if she hadn't been trying too hard to leave Lisa White and her debacle of an existence behind. She reached up to tighten her ponytail and remembered belatedly that Fox had taken her hair down and she'd totally forgotten to put it back up. He tracked the gesture, gaze glittering with intent, and it hit her with unshakeable certainty that he knew she'd lied. More, it pissed him off. That seemingly indolent pose, the deliberately relaxed posture—all to cover that he'd gone from lazily interested in seeing her house to being incandescently angry that she was lying to him.

Well, fuck him—she'd never promised him the whole truth and nothing but the truth.

Still, he stood there, waiting for her answer, watching her stew and daring her to make something else up.

"Fine." She folded her arms, though the midday sun warmed the room nicely. "I didn't go to therapy. Maybe I wouldn't be such a mess still if I had. I don't enjoy painting. I'm no good at it and I only picked it up because everybody here seemed to think I should be doing something with my time. It shut all of *them* up." She flung the last at him like an accusation.

He turned to face her, and she self-consciously unfolded her arms. That was a defensive posture, right?

"Why does it still bother you that I want to know more about you?" Fox asked the question reflectively, almost more to himself. "You already told me your greatest secret. Didn't you?"

It unnerved her, the way he asked the last question, the way a police detective interviewing a witness would, catching them out in covering up some crime. It also annoyed her, which felt far more comfortable.

"If I did or didn't isn't any of your business, Fox," she snapped. "I haven't promised you anything but sex, and we can call it quits any time if you don't want the package deal."

"Can we?" He walked toward her, moving with a silky stride that made her feel stalked. The doorway stood open on the other side of him. Too far away. Then he was on her, taking her hands and lifting them over her head and pressing her up against the wall. "Thinking of running?" Oh yes, definitely pissed.

"No," she whispered, mouth suddenly dry, her body responding eagerly to his nearness, to the intensity of his emotion. "Why are you so angry?"

"You're a liar." He gave the word significance, as if it defined her. "You know who your stalker was, don't you?"

"What?" Her mind stuttered over the question. Not what she'd expected.

"I figured." He nodded. "Why did you tell me you didn't know?"

How did he figure that out? Did he know who she was? No, he couldn't know that. Also, he would have said so, if he knew her real identity and its significance. Of course she knew who they were—at least their virtual identities—and it had changed nothing. She didn't know what answer to give, particularly with her nipples tight against the pressure of his chest and his grip on her wrists making her go hot and wet. "I can't think," she replied, struggling a little, which only made her more aroused.

With an unamused smile, he kissed her ear, biting the lobe gently so she moaned. "That's the thing, Miss Emily. Telling me the truth shouldn't require thinking. And I'm tired of your stories."

She couldn't drum up a reply, but he didn't seem to need one, nipping at the line of her throat, making her squirm.

"It kills me that you don't trust me," he muttered. "What have I ever done to make you think you have to lie to me?"

"It's not you. It's—" There she went, falling into the pat answers.

He knew it, too, because he laughed, a hoarse, angry chuckle at her expense. "No, I know it's you. You lie to everybody, don't you? Nobody knows who you really are."

"This is why I didn't want you in my house."

"Oh, I have no doubt of that, but you let me in, remember?" He rocked his pelvis against hers, erect cock rubbing against her mound, reminding her of all he'd said while fucking her in the hallway. She moaned and he kissed her cheek. "That's right. I don't think you really want to keep me out. In your heart you want to let me in, but something is stopping you. Is it him? Are you that afraid of him still?"

He stared into her eyes, fiercely, the playful charm gone, dangerous now in a way she'd never seen him be, in a way that aroused her beyond reason, that made her want to please him, give him what he asked for. At a loss, she couldn't think of an answer for him that wouldn't be a lie. Could she tell him the truth?

Alarmingly, she wanted to. Wanted to confide the whole hairy, horrible story. Fox would understand. She knew that about him, that he'd get why she'd collapsed, that she'd had to escape it all, that she'd never stopped running, in some senses. She'd show him her work, the new stuff that he'd inspired, and he'd be proud of her, open-heartedly admiring in that way that was so natural to him, so addictive about him.

"Tell me who it is and I'll find him, expose him—make it so he can never hurt you again." His voice had darkened, the anger seeping through it. Not at her. Or not entirely. At this person he envisioned. "You can trust me to do it. I've dealt with his kind before and—"

He cut himself off, but the words were a splash in the face from the sea.

"When?" She pulled her hands free and he let her. "How does a novelist deal with exposing stalkers?"

The chill radiating through her, she put distance between them. "What kind of research were you doing on your novel?" He blanked his face. Son of a bitch. "And you have the fucking gall to take me to task for lying. Are you even a writer? Who the hell are you, Fox?"

"Of course I'm a writer," he snapped. "I wouldn't lie about a thing like that."

"What *would* you lie about?"

"I would tell you if I could—and I will—but I can't just yet." To his credit, he looked uncomfortable and fully aware of the irony.

"It's the same for me then. I want to tell you, but I can't yet."

"Don't give me that, Emily. It's not even close to the same thing." He'd bunched his fists, tension vibrating from him in a nearly palpable wave.

She could barely draw a full breath. Instead of the angry shout in her head, she gritted out the words, temples pulsing with the pressure. "How can you say that. You don't know!"

She flung the words back at him, the uneven edge of her nails biting into her palms. "How *dare* you say it's not the same thing! Yes," she hissed, "I gave you a partial truth about the stalker thing. That's my right, because you know what? The death threats were real. So were the pictures of me mutilated. Raped. Dead. That I was terrified and humiliated—that was all too real." *1,899,343.*

He looked stricken, but the coldness settled through her, dousing all those warm, wonderful feelings. *Oh my God, this is it. We're over.* And she hadn't seen it coming. Not this soon. They should have had weeks more, but the certainty boomed through her, a steel door slamming. Fox's eyes burned, fiery in his tense face. He knew it too.

But he wouldn't say so.

She found herself already shaking her head sadly. "This is it. I'm pulling the plug. Firewall in place."

No, he'd been kidding himself, because he looked genuinely pained. "You're joking. You can't do that."

"Yes, I can. That was the deal from the beginning. We're over. I'm sorry, because this has been amazing, but we can't go on this way."

"This is a bump!" He nearly shouted it, a sprinkle of freckles standing out against his rage-pale skin. "So we both told some lies. I had good reasons for it."

"Don't you see, Fox?" Tears pricked her eyes, hinting at a pain that had yet to make its way through the cold shock. "It's everything. We don't even know each other. We have amazing chemistry and the sex was incredible, but we've foundered on the rocks. There's nothing else between us that's real. Time to walk away."

"That's not true. Don't you say that. In the hallway, not thirty minutes ago, I very nearly told you that I think I'm falling in love with you. You can't turn your back on that."

So, her instinct had been right. *Damn, damn, damn.* "It's good you didn't say it. I didn't want to hear it." Cold. So cold inside.

He gaped at her in pained disbelief. "How can you say that?"

"Because *you don't know me!*" The words ripped out of her, a comet trail of disappointment and betrayal following behind. She'd created this trap. Like the arrogant hero who foundered in the labyrinth of his own falsehoods and arrogance. Finally she found something—someone—she really wanted and it wasn't even real. Fox had fallen for her avatar while her real self—twisted, emotionally crippled, every horrible thing the trolls had ever called her—crouched behind the curtain, weeping. "You said it yourself," she choked out. "We both lied, for reasons more important than trusting each other. I'm not sorry I lied and neither are you, clearly. That's not a relationship. Not love. That's just fucking each other, which we agreed on from the beginning. And now it's over."

CHAPTER TWENTY-NINE

S OMETHING INSIDE HIM shattered, the sharp edges of the broken pieces lodging in his heart, making it thump laboriously, unable to pump blood to his extremities. That was why they'd gone numb.

Emily's eyes were black hollows in her cold, white face, her hair a cape of shadow around her slim body. She seemed to be made both of steel and glass, resolute yet ridiculously fragile. Even as the hurt bloomed, as the rage rampaged through his brain—*she was dumping him, just like that?*—he absurdly wanted to comfort *her*. The early taste of bitter regret filled his mouth with bile.

Way to go, Sparky. Just like Dear Old Dad.

"I guess there's nothing else to say then." He felt stiff, suddenly old and worn out.

Emily nodded, a jerk of her chin, staring at the floor in utter misery. He'd hurt her. Then he called himself a chump for thinking it. Hell, she'd hurt him. Here he'd been about to hand her his heart when he'd known she didn't want it. What a fucking idiot he'd been.

"Have a nice life then." He felt mean, saying it. Which was a hell of a lot better than the kicked-in-the-gut sensation. "I'll wave at you in the grocery store."

She didn't reply, not looking at him, clearly wanting him

gone.

He left her there, in her room full of sham paintings. It would have been one thing if she'd been proud of them, but she'd radiated shame. She hadn't even tried to make them good, so why paint the fucking things at all? The Emily he knew—and dammit, she was all wrong on that, because he *did* know her—had pride at her core. She couldn't be sloppy if she tried. Everything about her, about her home, revealed her intense personal energy, the perfectionist zeal she'd brought to every moment they spent together.

Consumed with furious regret, he drove to the rental house and slammed inside, leaving his bags and purchases in the car. He'd been so gaga, so fucking lovesick, picking those things out for her, and she'd cut him off. It wasn't as if he'd built a whole house of cards, a tower of lies the way his father had. The way *she* had. So, he'd said he was a novelist. One small shading of the truth.

She'd lied far more. But, God, the way she'd looked when she said those words. *Pictures of me mutilated. Raped. Dead.* He'd well and truly fucked up.

He should focus on finding Phoenix and putting this dim, depressing backwater island behind him, but he pulled up Emily's files instead. All those transcripts, reflecting her mediocrity. Nothing about her marriage. Not a whisper about the stalker. Was any of it true? It had to be. The emotional truth had reverberated in that fraud of an art studio like a bell tolling.

The early stuff was real, yes. Deep background confirmed the birth certificate, her family. The debutante photo in the paper had to be real, because he confirmed the page from the paper through several sites. The high school transcripts, the various awards revealing her dazzling early promise. All real.

Then she'd earned the full ride to Brown and flamed out. Mediocre grades, no extracurriculars. Left without graduating, perhaps to get married.

Or did she?

With grim determination, he spiraled out the search, checking the papers around the time frame she apparently quit college. Where had Silar Stillwell gone? She couldn't possibly have dropped off the map entirely, because Emily Bartwell didn't show up for another six months, and then only sparingly, bits of information that easily could have been added in later. Sloppy, sloppy.

But it had been enough to fool him, hadn't it?

He checked the marriage license registries, not in her home town, but near the college, following his gut. And hit pay dirt.

There it was, Lisa Stillwell married Henry White, both listing their occupations as students. Lisa R.—an obvious anagram for Silar, now that he saw it. Temples throbbing, he searched the college records for Lisa R. White and there she fucking was, in all her glory.

Of course he remembered Lisa White. *Geek Crunch* had been full of the story for months after it hit. His head swam, his blood pressure no doubt through the roof. If Emily was Lisa White, and here she was, living on Lyra, then the rest logically followed.

Fucking Phoenix.

Kicking himself for the fool he'd been, he made himself

review it all. A computer prodigy, raking in the grades and awards, Lisa started at the up-and-coming Gametronix the day after graduation, along with her putz of a husband. He ground his teeth, even as his gut roiled, enforcing discipline on himself to see it through, filing the data as he went. Thinking back, his brain clearly delivered the image of the big fucking satellite dish on the side of her house. And had that been a phoenix figurine among the glass animals? Of fucking course it was.

How she must have laughed at him. A "stalker" she'd called it. More like an army of trolls. No wonder she'd relaxed once she determined he didn't know who she truly was. And she'd asked him, hadn't she? If he liked computer games. It had been subtle. Subtle enough for lust-blinded him to miss it.

She'd gotten a raw and shitty deal, sure, but he couldn't care. Because, oh look, Lisa White supposedly took off for Indonesia, where her data trail sputtered and died. Phoenix hit the forums months later. No doubt she'd tried on other identities in the interim, and he'd track every one down for the article.

His unerring instincts had led him right to her and he'd missed it. All that secrecy. No wonder no one had been able to sniff "him" out. Never once had it occurred to him that Phoenix could be female, and how she must have loved pulling that over on all the misogynistic idiots who'd tried to take her down. She had them eating out of her hand with no idea that she was the very one they thought they'd defeated.

The story would explode—beyond even his wildest expectations. That Phoenix turned out to be Lisa White? The truth would rock the internet community like a 9.0 quake.

She'd played him. Phoenix had. Maybe she'd even suspected who he was, why he'd come to Lyra. Her cronies on the
forums had tipped her off to his pursuit enough times. All that
hard-to-get, chase-me shit, followed by ball-cracking sex—had
she done it simply to distract him?

Could she be that much of a manipulator? She was clearly
clever enough.

One small step to ruthless enough.

Regardless, she'd proved herself to be a master of lies. Far
exceeding his father's skill. Fox sought out Phoenix on the
forums and sure enough, she was there. Leaving comments here
and there, talking up the new game module. In the past
twenty-four hours, when he'd been conveniently out of town,
the chatter had kicked up to light speed. Seemed the module
slated for Christmas release would include kinky sex scenarios,
where the players could choose to be dominant or submissive.

Everything she'd learned from him.

If he'd been on boil up until then, it blew into white-hot
rage.

If he'd been considering, if only on the edges of his
thoughts, not exposing her, not breaking the story perhaps
until he talked to her, that vaporized in the heat of his betrayed
anger.

He nearly went over there, to throw it all in her face. The
way she'd used and manipulated him. But no, his vengeance
would be sure and swift—and all the better for being unexpected. As she'd done to him, the expertly wielded dagger in
his back. He'd expose her lies for the world to see. That was
what people like her deserved. She'd pay the price and he'd

walk away richer and with his pick of gigs.

It would be sweet in the end. Sweet enough to wipe away the enduring taste of bitter bile.

EM PHYSICALLY FLINCHED as the front door boomed shut.

Then slowly let herself slide down the wall, to sit, knees drawn up. Sun slanted in the windows but didn't reach her. Paralyzed, she stared at the splash of warm light and wished she could reach it. But it seemed as far beyond her as the possibility of ever not being this person who lived eternally alone.

But she'd chosen it this time. She hadn't waited for it all to go up in flame, to be burned, skin cracked and bleeding before she removed herself from danger.

She was just stunned at how fast things had ended between her and Fox. Because this situation wasn't anywhere near as bad as before, right? The end of a casual love affair. Fox might have looked gut shot, but he'd get over her soon enough, find some other willing female to play sex games with.

She'd get over him too. If she knew anything, it was how to recover from disaster.

Still, a feeling of impending doom haunted her, anxiety compressing her lungs even as she tried to ignore it. Fox had lied to her about who he was, so why had he really come to Lyra? Surely it couldn't have anything to do with her Phoenix identity. If he'd known who she was, he'd have tried to uncover evidence, wouldn't he?

She had to consider how he'd been obsessed with getting into her house. Was that why? But why the elaborate subterfuge, the sexual affair? No, he'd been genuinely stricken that she'd called it quits. And he'd said he didn't game. Of course, he could have lied about that too.

So many lies. The wave of them crashed over her, sending her under.

Dinah sidled in, for once ignoring the forbidden toys and arching against her, purring comfort. She stroked her soft fur. Let her be that joke, but she wasn't alone. Dinah and Anansi at least gave her honesty, even if she didn't always care for how they expressed their opinions.

And they didn't judge her.

Em choked a little at the cramp in her chest. How quickly Fox had been ready to call her a liar. *For no reason.* Judging her for presumed sins he knew jack shit about. If he'd known anything about what she'd actually lied about, he'd have thrown it in her face.

She'd become paranoid was all, always thinking she needed to hide. Running away, as Fox mockingly suggested. It didn't matter who he really was. Maybe even he didn't realize the deal-breaker he'd tripped with her, that he'd been so ready to damn her for not telling the truth when he'd committed the very same sin.

If she'd learned nothing else, it was to be wary of people ready to throw the first stone.

Jesus, people went through this kind of thing all the time. Normal people had love affairs that came and went. They'd discovered a fundamental incompatibility. Sure, it hurt. That would fade. She'd been in far worse pain than this when Henry left. Surely the end of her marriage had hit her far harder.

Except it didn't feel that way. It was some fresh, new hell.

More. It felt like somehow this incident, what should be a minor bump for anyone else, had ripped open those old wounds. Meaning she hadn't healed at all, only scabbed over.

And now she bled freely again, her life force spilling across the floor, no extra lives to spend.

CHAPTER THIRTY

WHEN FOX GOT the payday from the story, he'd buy his mom, if not a new house, at least updated furniture. As it was, he sat at the same kitchen table he'd eaten his breakfast cereal on countless mornings before school, with the linoleum crack that had looked like a lightning bolt then and just looked dirty and broken now.

"Will you stay in town long?" His mother set down a cup of coffee and a plate of Chips Ahoy, beaming at him.

Why he'd come here after filing the story, he didn't know. Seemed like the thing to do, especially since he'd thought he'd explode if he stayed in L.A. a minute longer. The drab Midwestern winter only exacerbated his dour mood, however. It seemed impossible that he'd thought Lyra depressing. He missed the emerald landscape with a visceral hunger. There should be a misty sea, humped blue islands shrouded by layers of shifting fog, and a beach to run on.

And Emily. How could he both miss and despise her?

"I don't know," he belatedly replied, realizing he'd forgotten to answer. "I haven't decided."

"You missed Thanksgiving with the cousins, but Aunt Shirley is hosting Christmas. Maybe you could stay through then, since your big story is done. Your sister will be here and you haven't seen little Amy since her third birthday."

The mention of Christmas made him think again of Emily. Of Lisa, Silar or Phoenix, or whatever the hell he should call her. Of all her names, Emily seemed to be the only one she'd totally made up. Other than Phoenix, but even that made sense, given her history.

His editors gleefully planned to time the scoop with the release of the new Labyrinth module, with syndication rights going faster than hotcakes around the world. So far they'd kept it pretty secret, though rumors were heating up that Phoenix would soon be outed, and it would be a major scandal.

A few privy to the story's full scope even speculated whether Lisa White—much easier to think of her that way—could be or would be sued. She'd had a noncompete with Gametronix, cemented by the fact that she'd resigned instead of being fired. They'd no doubt strong-armed her into it, but the lawyers wouldn't care. The papers and magazines certainly didn't care. Except that additional lawsuits would draw out the stories for months to come, always a good thing for sales. Oh, they'd feted him and showered him with all the glory a guy could want. He'd upped the holiday bonus for everyone and sent the year-end predictions off the charts. The publisher even took him out to The Ivy for Thanksgiving dinner, the best wine flowing freely.

Fox had gotten seriously drunk and it hadn't done a thing to make him feel better.

He'd lasted about another week, until all of the stories were finalized. Then, unable to bear the festive mood, the jarring juxtaposition of L.A.'s glitzy façade with tinseled decorations meant for evergreens, not palm trees, he'd bought a plane ticket home.

And immediately regretted the decision. He'd never last through Christmas. If he'd had the vague thought that he could weather the story breaking better here, in the small town that birthed him, away from the left coast and all its various blinking communications, he'd been sorely mistaken.

The image of Emily haunted him like an earworm. He couldn't get her face out of his head. It hadn't helped that he'd gotten to know her—in all her incarnations—so well in the past couple of weeks. He'd resurrected the entire Gametronix debacle as a side article, telling himself that he at least would be telling her story as it should have been told.

If anyone hadn't heard of Lisa White, they'd know her after this. The world deserved to know. Hell, Emily deserved that much, not the duck-and-cover job her weak-ass bosses and colleagues had buried her under. She should have gone public from the beginning, gotten the media on her side. Refused to resign. But no, she'd run and hid, just as he'd watched her do over and over.

Just as she'd done in that last argument. Now that the hot edge of betrayal and anger had cooled with perspective, that much was clear. Of course she wouldn't have talked it out. Much easier for her to cut bait and bail.

It still pissed him off though.

And if he felt bad about how this would hit her, well...sometimes the truth hurt. He should know.

"Your father is doing better these days." His mom dipped her cookie into her coffee and took a delicate bite.

"He could hardly do worse."

"True, true." She shook her head, copper curls bouncing. "But the new job is working out and he'll be celebrating his tenth anniversary of not gambling."

"You don't talk to him, Mom!" Jeez, she probably still sent the loser money too.

"Of course I do. We had twenty-five good years together. That doesn't vaporize."

"They were not good years. He gambled, lied to you about it, got me to lie to you about it, destroyed your credit. Hell, you could have left this shit town years ago, if not for him." Fox dug his thumb into the crack.

"Don't mess with that and don't call my home a 'shit town.' You might have taken off as fast as you could, Raynard, but I like living here."

"You deserve better," he stubbornly insisted and drank the aluminum-flavored coffee, wishing with all his heart that every damn thing didn't make him think of her.

"Do I? How do you know what I deserve? Or what your father deserves, for that matter?"

"What's that supposed to mean?"

"It means that you've been sitting as judge, jury and executioner for his sins for too many years. What happened between your father and I was just that—between us."

"Bullshit!" The anger whipped out of him. Maybe not so cooled after all. "He involved me all along, getting me to lie to you, making me complicit."

"One of his many mistakes, yes," his mother replied coolly, "but you were his child. And you loved him so, so much..."

She broke off and blinked out the window, pulling back the tears, the same as Emily would do. "That's what I regret most—not what he did, but that you lost that love."

"He deserv—" Fox stopped the words, but his mother gave him a knowing look. "I don't care about that, Mom. What I hated was..." He drew in a deep breath. "I'm sorry. I'm sorry that I lied to you, that I hurt you. I should have apologized before now."

She sipped her coffee, considering. Then put another cookie on his plate. "No, I don't accept your apology."

He sagged inside, accepting that. Maybe someday.

"Look at you." His mother smiled, cradling the cracked mug. "You'd think I just grounded you. I don't want your apology because you never offended me. You were only trying to protect both of us in a hard, horrible situation. People do the best that they can do."

"I could have handled it better."

"Sure you could." She nodded thoughtfully. "We all could have, but that's done. What matters now is how we handle things going forward. We all learned our lessons from that, didn't we?"

What have we learned from this, Sparky?

"Bailey Jones moved back to town." His mother changed the subject gently.

"Did she?" He restrained a comment about that being poor judgment.

"Divorced. Living back home for a while. Maybe you should go see her."

"I'm not going to see her, Mom."

"No, I suppose you've both moved past that, also."

They had, hadn't they? With a sense of relief, he knew he had no desire to see Bailey again, that he liked having her in his head as they'd been, in what seemed to be an idyllically innocent youth. There was only one woman he wanted to see.

"I met somebody new," he blurted and bit into the too-sweet cookie.

"Someone special?" His mother's eyes gleamed with that acquisitive light that meant she was thinking of grandchildren but wouldn't say so.

He snorted. Emily was special, all right. She'd stand out in this drab town like…well, like a Phoenix, all full of fire, restless energy and exotic beauty.

"Maybe you should invite her for Christmas. I'd love to meet her. Oh! Or him. You should know that would be okay too."

He drank too much coffee in a gulp and it burned his mouth. "Mom!"

"Timmy Burdock turned out to be gay—no surprise there, except to his folks—and now he's married and Sally Burdock says *they* are visiting for the holidays. Makes out like it's some exotic new fashion or something." She hmphed her annoyance.

"Well, if you want to keep up with the Burdocks, Mom, I could drum up a boyfriend. Or maybe one of each—to top them. You could show us off at church."

She laughed, a genuine open-hearted peal of delight. How long since he'd made her laugh? He imagined her and Emily laughing together, and suddenly the thought of her here didn't seem odd at all.

"Mom, the thing is that this woman—it is a her—yeah, she's special, but it's over."

"I'm sorry." His mom reached across the table and gripped his hand, a gesture that tore him open. "Do you want to tell me what happened?"

"She dumped me," he admitted.

"Then she's not smart enough for you."

"No, I—I deserved it. She found out I lied to her about something."

"Imagine that," his mother observed in a dry tone.

Stung, he put his mug down. "Not like Dad. I wasn't hiding a whole other life that would be a danger to her. I—" Except he had. He'd done that exact thing. Right in dear old dad's footsteps. He'd been exactly what she feared most. Only neither of them could have known it. "She lied too," he finished, knowing it sounded weak.

"Seems to me you should be sitting at *her* kitchen table, offering her this apology you're carrying around. Unless she's not all that special. But I have to say—I know you've been through other breakups and not a one of them brought you home."

"I don't know why I wanted to come here." After he said it, he winced, realizing how it sounded.

His mom squeezed his hand a final time and let go. "You will."

EMILY SLOGGED THROUGH the days, trying to get back into her old groove. Since she didn't plan to slit her wrists, she focused on the job. Work had saved her before when her world collapsed and it could be the rope she held onto this time. Even if she never had anything else, she had that. She spent her time at the computer, being her other identities—all stronger and better people than the real her—and took refuge.

She worked, day and night, making up for the time lost to Fox. She prowled the forums, fanning the flames of excitement over the new module. The company had been leaking careful hints and she did her part by talking them up. This would be big and nothing could tarnish it. Phoenix would get major credit, but so would Cindy and Syd—she'd make sure of it. Marketing had drafted the publicity strategy, giving Phoenix the credit as long as possible. A lot of memos had flown about, with concerns over concealing the presence of women with core responsibility on the design team.

Cindy and Syd, however, stood firm in their desire to be eventually outed and deal with the flack. At least, everyone agreed, they'd have Phoenix's powerful wings to shield them from the worst of it. She could help them, even if she couldn't save herself.

Life would go on and so would she.

There. Yet another flat cliché to add to the sham her life had become.

In too many ways, though, she started to slip back into her old habits. The bad ones from the dark days before she'd found new purpose and become Phoenix—never leaving the house, ignoring her reminder when it popped up telling her to go run. Maybe she should have gone to Indonesia in truth. Buried herself in the very real suffering of people just trying to survive. Maybe she'd have discovered some new level of maturity in herself. Bizarrely, she just wanted to go see Fox and talk to him about it.

But she had at least that much pride. She owed him a clean break.

She knew that. Then caved anyway. She'd handled things badly and the insistent craving to see Fox again wouldn't leave her. He was a generous and forgiving guy. Big into talking. Maybe they could work things out. Truly, part of her had been expecting him to show up on her deck, with a rueful smile. Or even to demand an apology. It just rubbed salt in her wounds that he didn't.

Finally she made herself go run with Anansi, who acted like she'd handed him the doggie equivalent of Christmas morning. The Kapsuck house, however, was dark. Ominously so. It stayed dark the following morning too. She'd lost track of time and everything else. Could he be gone entirely?

She'd so buried herself in working on the new module that she'd begun to feel like the living dead. Before she could chicken out, she dragged herself into town to check for packages—okay, she hoped Glory might know about Fox—and her friend's expression suggested that she might as well be encrusted with grave dirt.

She also said Fox had left the island some days since. No forwarding address.

Glory didn't even seem surprised that Emily hadn't known, just looked her over, shook her head and suggested she take a shower before coming to town next time. Emily took the advice, even going so far as to put on some makeup to meet Glory that night for a sympathy dinner at her house. Likely she'd be expected to cough up the details of what happened, which she didn't know that she wanted to do. But, when Glory invited her and she nearly said no out of reflex, she'd made herself agree.

No more of that.

Fox was gone for good, doing whatever mysterious thing he did, as she'd always known he would. Tempted as she'd been to look him up, see what he was doing, she wouldn't let herself. Part of her new program: no dwelling on the past. If nothing else, being with Fox had reawakened her to feeling alive, to maybe being something more than the physical avatar of her real, online self.

So, she'd meet Glory for drinks and maybe spill her guts or maybe not. They could also talk about something that had nothing to do with men. She even looked forward to it.

IT TOOK FOX another full day to get a ticket to Seattle, time he spent fixing all the stuff his mom needed doing around the house, while she fussed at how he did it. For once he didn't mind all that much. Messing with the plumbing, the broken window sash, that light in the vaulted-ceilinged hallway that had burned out months ago—and why did they put fixtures so high no one could reach them?—all gave him time to think about what he'd say to Emily.

The damage would be done. There was no taking it back.

But, if he told her before the story broke, maybe she could prepare for it. If she wanted to change her identity again and run somewhere else, he'd help her. Not that she needed him for that, but maybe she'd let him.

With a sense of churning impatience, he barely made the last ferry to Lyra, more ready to bite Emily's head off than apologize. Did she have to be so fucking impossible to reach? He couldn't even get a message to her. He'd tried looking for her on the forums, but Phoenix ghosted every time he got near, as always. Judiciously he fed a few rumors of an impending story, but didn't dare do too much, for fear of precipitating the avalanche.

He even considered calling Glory, but what kind of message could he give her?

No, he'd have to wait to tell Emily face-to-face and hope she didn't keep a gun around the place. Then, if she wanted to have a big, screaming fight about it, they could. In fact, he'd insist on it. They'd thrash out every single lie they'd exchanged and figure out what to do from there. He'd make her talk it out, as he should have to begin with.

At the last minute, on instinct as he boarded the flight to Seattle, he sent an anonymous tip to Jacker, so they could prepare for the first salvo. It likely wouldn't help, but at least they could assemble their PR team. He risked spooking Emily with it. If they told Phoenix, she'd obliterate this identity too.

But he couldn't not give her the opportunity. The first step in his apology.

Back in his Gore-Tex jacket, he stood on the deck, even though everyone else rode inside in the warmth. Lyra appeared from the fog, the misty blue hump turning green as they approached.

With a shock, it hit him that *this* was what he'd wanted, when he decided to go home. Not to his mother's house, but here.

To Emily.

CHAPTER THIRTY-ONE

THE EMAIL TO call Jared immediately arrived just as she was shutting down to head to Glory's. Before Fox, she would have blown it off for a while, until she felt strong enough to deal. Now, though dread spurred her to leave, she flipped on a picture of a tarantula and called Jared. That was the second new rule—no running away.

Besides, something had gone wrong. As demanding as her team lead could be, he rarely used that sort of insistent wording with Phoenix. Anxiety snaked through her gut, the same sense of impending doom she'd had since Fox stormed out. Since she'd kicked him out.

Jared didn't even blink at the image, though he hated spiders with a loathing that bordered on phobia, which spoke to the dire nature of his emergency. Also, he looked haggard. More than from putting in long hours on the new module. Something had happened.

"Well, hello, Phoenix. You've heard then?"

"Heard what?"

Jared looked a little ill and poured himself coffee. "I figured you calling me so fast meant you already knew and were on top of it."

"Don't dick with me, Jared—knew what?" The lurking

sense of anxiety bloomed, speeding her heart. Calling up the old fear. *Shit, shit, shit.* "What happened?"

"There's a rumor going around that there's going to be a story in *Geek Crunch* and a bunch of major pubs, revealing your true identity." He gulped the coffee, grimacing at either the temperature or the bitterness. Or at his bad news.

Was it that bad? "There are always rumors."

He was already shaking his head. "This seems to be a legit tip. The PR boys sniffed around and dug out some info that…well, they think it could be a big story. Set to break when the module releases in a few days. Scandal. Mayhem. Whatever." Jared stared at the screen and winced. "Fuck you for that fucking spider, by the way. You're welcome for the warning."

Chagrined, she swapped it out for a sparkly unicorn, but even that didn't change his expression. "I'll check it out," she finally said, anxious to get off the call.

"Sure you will." Jared clenched his jaw, the muscle bulging to hold in what he wasn't saying.

"What else?" *Please don't let there be more.*

"Okay, look. I'm not supposed to say this, but I'm damn well going to. I know you can disappear on us. Whoever you are—if it even matters—if it kills the module release, it kills the team. You can waltz free and clear, that's your gig, but remember that you've left us hanging out here. I know you don't care, but—"

"I care," she interrupted. Mostly because she needed to say something. Had someone really broken her identity without her knowing? Was it Fox? If this was real, it had to be.

"Maybe you do." Jared's head bobbed as though he might lay it on the desk. "Hearts and flowers and yon sparkly unicorn. But you don't have to meet with the brass at two-fucking-o'clock tomorrow to plan the emergency response. If there's something we should know about who you are, it would be nice to know it before the rest of the world does. I can't do jack to make you though, so forgive me if I don't care if you care while you sit on your balcony overlooking the Italian-fucking-Riviera or wherever the hell you are."

He cut the call and she sat there.

The dread surged up in an ugly bore-tide, way too fast and full of long-fermented waste. She could imagine herself on the long, flat beach of her life, feet mired, while it all rushed at her. She'd never escaped, she'd only delayed her final drowning. What did the common wisdom say—that you couldn't run from your problems? Yes, that they would always find you.

Son of a bitch.

Tamping down the panic, she went through the ritual of shutting down. She didn't bother to check the forums, the vipers and the rumors. The truth of the impending disaster sat like a boulder in her gut. It would kill the release. All of Labyrinth most likely, because the noncompete meant it belonged to Gametronix, right? They'd all go down because of her. Just like last time.

Fox.

Of course I'm a writer. Only not a novelist. A reporter. One who came to Lyra for the story and left when he had it. He hadn't come after her because he didn't need to. Later she'd deal with that new wound, that he'd never been attracted to her, the way he'd claimed. She should have seen through that one. He'd manipulated her from the beginning, with his determined pursuit and seductive ways. She'd gone down so easily. Just another bimbo bagged and used to further his career.

Of course she deserved her comeuppance.

Careless and stupid.

Worse, she'd dragged in her team. Again.

The self-loathing made it hard to breathe and she considered, for a long, dull moment, going out to the beach, walking into the cold water and drowning herself. At least she wouldn't feel this pain, the excruciating paralysis of not knowing what to do.

Dinah leaped onto her keyboard—something she rarely did—full of purring affection. Anansi would be waiting outside, ready to ride along to town.

She didn't know what she should do, but Glory would be waiting for her.

And, as much as she dreaded the crisis to come, she didn't want to be dead.

So she got up and gave Dinah her supper, taking a few extra minutes to scratch those hard-to-reach spots. Then she fetched Anansi and drove to Glory's house.

One step at a time.

GLORY STARED AT her over the half-finished creamed chicken casserole and their second bottle of wine. "I don't know what to say," she finally said.

"Well, that was better than saying nothing," Em said, still

rattled from telling Glory the whole story. Well, the condensed version.

"So, you're some kind of super-hacker?"

"Not really a hacker, but close enough."

"And Fox came here to sniff you out and write a story."

"That's my guess. I don't know. I haven't..." *talked to him.* And won't ever. As pissed as she felt, that almost broke her heart more than anything else. How could he have touched her as if he cherished every inch of her skin, all the while plotting the most profound and public of betrayals?

"So, everything about you is a lie, is what you're saying." Glory, unexpectedly, looked close to tears, her face growing blotchy with it.

"Glory, I—"

"No. Don't give me whatever excuse you were thinking up." Glory glanced accusingly at Em's plate. "You didn't finish your dinner. Did you lie about that too—do you even like my creamed-chicken casserole?"

"No." The word came out hushed but sounded unbearably loud. Much as she wanted to tell Glory otherwise, lying yet again seemed too exhausting, too fundamentally wrong. She couldn't do it anymore.

"Was anything about you real?" Glory flung the question out, an accusation. "Or were you playing me the whole time? You and your fucking 'I don't know what the girl code is' routine."

Inexpressibly weary, Emily rose from the table, gathering her plate.

"Leave it," Glory snapped. "I think you should go."

"I am." She found her jacket and shrugged into it, trying not to look at all the photos of Glory's family and friends, frames covering every surface. All the connections Emily lacked. No—that she had burned away in the nuclear fire of her escape. She made herself face Glory, who still sat at the table, glaring at the disheveled casserole. "For what it's worth— and I know it's worth less than nothing at this point—but I wanted to be a good friend to you. I know I sucked at it, but I did. I was never playing you."

Glory only shook her head furiously, refusing to answer. So Em let herself out.

AFTER THAT, SHE didn't sleep really at all. It could have been the heartburn from what little of the casserole she'd eaten. Or too much wine, because she had more when she got home, morosely pondering what the next day would bring.

Mostly it was the anxiety, eating at her. How could she make this not happen? If only she could go back in time and change things. Make it so it hadn't come to this.

But it had and she felt even more alone than when she came home from a run to find Henry had left, a goodbye note waiting on the kitchen table. Worse, it was all her own damn fault. She'd just *had* to dally with the hot guy, the classic dumb female mistake.

No dwelling.

Around 4 a.m., she finally got up and made coffee and went out to sit in the hot tub. She hadn't been out there since that afternoon with Fox and the little gazebo seemed thick with his presence.

If he hadn't meant any of it, then he had to be pathological. A master manipulator of the level Glory had accused her of being.

And if she wasn't that, maybe he wasn't that, either.

Not that it mattered, but it made her feel better to think it—along with a lovely fantasy of feeding him to the orcas. She relished hateful thoughts of revenge even as she contemplated that maybe some of it had been real for him too. Ironically, if he'd been there, sitting in the tub with her and not out there writing the articles that would destroy her and her team, she'd ask him for advice on what to do.

Running again, Miss Emily? He'd give her that charming smile to go with the chiding question. She wished she could run. Run and run and not have to face this.

But she'd done that before and here she was. Insanity was doing the same thing, over and over, and expecting a different result. She needed to do something different. Something opposite, maybe.

If it were a game, she'd set it up so the player could only win by going through the danger.

Time to face herself in the mirror.

CHAPTER THIRTY-TWO

"WHAT DO YOU mean she's gone?" Fox demanded.

Glory shrugged, pretending nonchalance but peeling the skin off him with her angry glare. "Which part of the sentence did you not get, Mr. *Novelist?* Subject, verb, object. She. Is. Gone."

He reined in the desire to throttle the snark out of her by a narrow margin. Spending the better part of an hour outside Emily's house, banging on the front and then back door, had only pushed him to the brink. "Let's try again. Where did she go?"

"You think she'd tell me? She left without a word to me. Dyson saw her on the first ferry out, Anansi with her. Apparently this is her M.O. and my security clearance falls somewhere below Doesn't Need to Know."

"What about Dinah?"

"Who's Dinah?" Glory furrowed her brow. "Secret baby or something?"

"Her cat."

"She couldn't even freaking tell me she had a cat." Glory sighed. "What a bitch."

"She's not like that," Fox blurted and Glory raised her brows, still standing in her doorway without even the slightest hint that she'd let him cross the threshold. "She had her reasons."

"Yeah, she told me about it."

"She did?" Surprise and uncertainty took some of the drive out of him. "Everything?"

"Well, not about the cat, obviously. But enough."

"Was it enough? If you knew everything she went through, you might not judge her so harshly."

"Right—cuz that's your job."

"I don't judge her," he replied, stung.

"No, you're the one who figured out who she really is and wrote these articles that will come out and ruin her. What does that make you in this analogy—executioner? Maybe smarmier, like a Kenneth Starr-type special prosecutor."

So Emily knew. Probably his anonymous tip. And she'd scattered to the wind. Gone.

Well, good for her, right?

"It's more complicated than that." Why was he defending himself to her?

"But you decided to expose her secrets, right? Maybe you just bypassed handing down your sentence and decided to let the world do it? You're unbelievable. She was head over heels in love with you and you—"

"Wait. What? She was in love with me?"

"You're such a guy." Glory squinched her face in disgust but lost some of the anger. "Note the past tense in that sentence, Mr. Novelist."

"Would you quit with that?"

"No. I'm still pissed about everybody shoveling shit down

my throat. Forgive me if my burps stink."

Aw, dammit all to hell. Glory felt as hurt and betrayed as anyone. The ripples of the lies—his and Emily's both—kept spreading outward. "I'm sorry." He sighed, rubbing his forehead to get himself to chill already.

"Spare me."

He tried again. "I never meant my deception to hurt you." Practice apology. But then the look in Glory's eyes reinforced the rightness of it. "I apologize, Glory." He stuck out his hand. "Raynard Mills. My friends call me Fox."

She snorted but shook his hand. "Your parents must have hated you, Raynard."

"It's a family name, *Glory*."

"Gertrude," she admitted. "Also family. Always hated it."

"I think—no, I know—Emily wouldn't have wanted this to hurt you. Did she tell you what she went through?"

"Some." Glory narrowed her eyes speculatively. "But you can tell me the rest. Come on in. You're not going after her until the morning ferry anyway."

"You're so sure that's what I'm going to do?"

"Hell. The pair of you—worse than a couple of lovesick teenagers swapping notes via your friends in gym class. Judging by the look in your eye, you'll chase her to the end of the earth and back. You'll want supper before that, at least. I have leftover creamed-chicken casserole."

"Or we could go down to the Sunshine Café. My treat."

Glory pressed her lips together. "Tell me the truth—you don't like my casserole either?"

"Yeah. Pretty much."

"I hate you all." But she got her coat.

EM MADE AN appointment with the lawyer—one her mother recommended and had the home phone number for—and took the first morning ferry, anxious to see her plan through. Afraid, maybe, that she'd chicken out and not be able to do it.

Overall, though, she felt better for making the decision. Meet the wave head-on and try to swim it out. Wasn't that how the surfers saw it? *The challenge is to ride the wave, instead of drowning under it.* Maybe after this, she'd rent a house somewhere like Hawaii, that would let her bring Anansi and Dinah. She'd learn to surf and warm up her blood again. Maybe even buy a house and invite her mother to visit.

Certainly there was nothing left for her on Lyra.

The bad thing about going early, however, was she ended up with time to kill. She drove off the car ferry with Anansi bouncing in the back, barking out the window at the school bus full of waving kids. She dropped him off at the doggie daycare she'd found online, found the right parking garage and ditched the Jeep with hours before her appointment. Once he got over being annoyed at the early morning call, the lawyer had warmed to her case.

He thought they could approach Gametronix—at least the parent company, since Gametronix itself had, fittingly enough, gone belly-up—with a deal. Em wouldn't sue them for wrongful termination and sexual discrimination if they wouldn't go after her for the noncompete. The resignation made it trickier, but the lawyer said the case for unfair pressure would be pretty cut and dried.

Fortunately she'd kept careful records on her development of Labyrinth, along with all the records she'd had at home for Amazonia. She'd hand it all over to the lawyer and let him do his magic.

So, she walked down to Pike Place Market and wandered along the waterfront, trying not to think. It had been so long since she'd shown her face in public this way. At first she kept expecting someone to recognize her, but of course they didn't. A man gave her a long look and she found herself cringing, calculating if she could dodge around a three-woman-deep stroller brigade in front of her and ditch him, until his friendly smile penetrated her awareness. Flirting.

People did that. A whole world of them.

The brief meeting with the lawyer had left her feeling surprisingly optimistic, so she treated herself to lunch on the waterfront. Fresh crab legs. While she ate, she downloaded and read two of Fox's stories on the ereader she'd bought that morning. He had several available, but not much else, which meant he did the journalism under another name. Part of what she'd promised she wouldn't look into. Not yet.

After all, she'd know soon enough, right?

The stories, though—she couldn't resist checking them out, remembering how he'd laughed when she said she didn't like them. Was it because they'd been only for the cover, the same as her awful paintings, and he truly didn't care?

But no. They were good. Swashbuckling space pirates and the fate of worlds balanced on the toss of a coin. Very much the Fox she knew. Or had thought she'd known. So hard to know what they'd had together, when both of them had been lying about who they were.

First things first.

She'd assembled all her weapons, had her personal power at the best she could manage. Time to step back through the looking glass.

Resolutely she went to find the Jacker offices. She stuttered a little, when she told the receptionist she'd come to see Jared, but found more courage when the young man balked and she had to insist on seeing him immediately. The area behind the reception desk opened into a big bullpen of cubes and someone overheard the conversation.

"Yo, Jared!" the guy called out. "Hot chick here to see you. Could be your last chance before you're jobless and no woman will have you."

A few people laughed, the atmosphere obviously tense. Jared, coming around the corner, made a shooting motion at the guy, then spotted her.

"Lisa?" His face went blank with shock, coffee cup sagging in his hand. He looked to one of the other people nearby and back to her, as if rechecking reality. "Is it really you, Lisa?"

"In the flesh." She felt the uncertainty of her smile.

He set the mug down and, in two strides, had seized her in a fierce, awkward hug. "Damn, girl, it's good to see you. So, so good."

Surprised to find herself a little teary, she squeezed his bony shoulders. "Me too."

"I always regretted...I—I mean, I wish that..." He glanced at the clock. "Fuck me but the timing sucks. Any other day I'd blow off the rest of the afternoon and say let's go for coffee and talk, but I've got a serious shitstorm headed my way. I'm sorry. Nothing else would be important enough, but this is."

"It is," she agreed. "Very important. Which is why we should go into the two o'clock meeting right now. You asked me to be here and here I am."

He'd started shaking his head and froze. Staring down at the industrial carpet, he put his hands on his hips. "Fucking Phoenix. All this time?"

A murmur ran through the room, gathering steam and moving out to the hallways.

"All this time." She waited, braced for all the recriminations. She deserved everything he might say to her and more. Her heart thrummed like a hummingbird's and her nerves screamed at her to run, but she made herself stand there and take it.

Still elbows akimbo, Jared looked at her sideways, reminding her of Fox and how he'd faced that awful painting and called her on the lie her life had become.

"I should have known it," he said, in an accusing tone. "Of course Phoenix is you. I should have fucking recognized your work from the very beginning."

"You weren't expecting it to be me."

"All those fucking avatars over the years—you did that to dick with me." He looked so supremely annoyed that she nearly laughed. Totally inappropriate for the moment, so she squelched the impulse ruthlessly, but he must have seen the lip twitch. "Yeah, laugh your ass off. I probably deserved worse from you than that."

If he'd punched her in the stomach—which she'd decided

ahead of time would be a legit response—she couldn't have been more surprised. "You deserved?"

Jared glanced around at the considerable crowd that had assembled, hanging on every word of the confrontation while people at the edges told inquiring voices farther back to shut up. "Yeah. I'm saying it in front of all these people. We all fucked up, but I'm talking just for me. I didn't stand by you, Lisa. I had a chance to do the right thing, the noble fucking thing, and I covered my own ass."

"Everybody did," she said in a quiet voice. "I didn't blame you for that. It was understandable."

"Even Henry." Jared held out his hands in supplication to the universe for an explanation. "He had the girl every nerd dreams of and he bailed. Because of some fucking trolls? A job? When I heard that…man."

"I would have done the same thing."

Jared gave her an incredulous look. Then snorted and pushed up his glasses. "No, you would not have. When I thought you took off for Indonesia, I thought yeah, she ran. Who can blame her?"

"I did run."

"Ha! Hello there, *Phoenix*. Indonesia would have been bailing. Instead you recreated yourself bigger and better and showed us all." He shook his head again, still dealing with the shock, but also with admiration. "I want to say you could have told me the truth, but what you did was brilliant. Well played."

"It's water under the bridge then." It began to feel that way, too, the old feeling of betrayal and desolation rolling down the river to the sea.

"Not yet, it isn't. But I've got a second chance and I'm going to do it. Syd, Cindy, where are you girls?" he shouted, then glanced at her. "Um, women."

The two programmers pushed through the group, looking her up and down.

"I want you to meet Phoenix." Jared introduced her as if she were visiting royalty.

"Lisa Fucking White," Cindy breathed and Syd thrust out her hand, then yanked it back.

"Sorry!" She laughed and Cindy elbowed her. "It's not every day you meet your hero. I should have practiced."

Emily put out her hand and shook with both of them. "I'm no one's hero, but I'm glad you're not pissed about the deception."

"Pissed?" Syd hooted and clapped her hands together. "I can't wait to tell the world. This is going to be major."

"If management doesn't fire me or pull the plug on the module. She glanced at Jared. "I have a lawyer coming to fill you in on strategy to deal with the noncompete. He thinks we should be able to avoid that particular lawsuit. But even without that, you all know that having me affiliated will bring out the very worst of the trolls."

"Oh, goddess, I surely hope so." Syd chortled with nothing less than overweening glee. "Bring 'em on."

"Yes," Cindy assured her gravely. "We've got your back this time."

"We all do," Jared agreed. "And fuck 'em if they can't take a joke."

CHAPTER THIRTY-THREE

F OX PULLED IN every favor he knew, even pinging his NSA buddy to pull her credit card transactions for all known aliases. He could walk through gray areas those guys couldn't, but they had the pull for this kind of stuff. Made the relationship most fruitful on both sides.

And son of a bitch, she'd made a purchase at Best Buy the previous morning near downtown Seattle, then lunch on the waterfront later. As Emily Bartwell, so she hadn't changed to a new identity yet. He spent fruitless hours checking transpo out of the city, knowing full well she'd likely just driven somewhere. Harder to track unless he got lucky with a camera on her license plate. She wouldn't keep that long. Then she'd pop up somewhere new, under a different name, and finding her again would be nearly impossible.

Not that the thought dissuaded him. Find her he would. After all, he had a nice nest egg now—what better to spend it on?

He hit pay dirt midafternoon. No hotel stay, but she'd used her card to buy lunch for three people, it turned out, at a pricey restaurant near Pike Place Market. Who had she eaten with? Two other women and a guy, it turned out, according the waiter, who treated him like a stalker and refused to say more.

Who were they?

Fox leaned against the wharf railing outside the place, thinking. Only a few blocks from where she'd eaten lunch yesterday. She'd hung around this same area—why? Jacker. It was the only explanation. The only people she could know in Seattle. He searched his phone and, sure enough, the address popped up conveniently nearby.

She'd not only stayed, she'd gone into those offices in person. He'd bet the whole kitty on it, even if he never would have predicted this from Emily. Or Phoenix. His idea of her dual faces revolved and refocused, like one of those pictures where you suddenly see the alternate image. They'd tipped her off and she'd decided to face it.

Who knew she would?

Maybe he should have.

He contemplated going up there, finding her, though he'd hardly be Mr. Popular with that group right now. But the knowledge that he could see her, that he could lay eyes on her inside of ten minutes, burned a hole in his brain until the rational parts were obliterated and only the desire to find her remained.

In fact, the fantasy of seeing her became so strong that a woman walking along the waterfront looked just like her.

It was her.

His Emily.

Except her dark hair hung loose around her shoulders, long strands lifting in the wind off the water. She wore a winter-white tailored coat and boots that matched, along with a crimson cashmere scarf. Classic lines that never went out of style. Clothes from Silar's life, most likely. Her cheeks, rosy from the chill air, echoed the scarf, her lips a deeper red with lipstick. She looked happy, smiling at a children's choir singing carols.

Snow White, awakened.

Then she spotted him and her step faltered, her face going blank with shock.

Would she run? He could outpace her easily, in her pretty heeled boots. But she started walking again, straight toward him. Oddly, some part of him wanted to dive into the crowds and disappear. As much as he'd wanted to see her moments ago, now, faced with her bearing down on him, so lovely, ethereal and vivid, he wondered if he could bear what she'd say to him. Or if he even knew what exactly he wanted to say to her.

"Well, hello, Fox." She tilted her head and her glossy red lips pursed. "Or should I call you by another name?"

"Raynard," he admitted. "Raynard Mills, of *Geek Crunch Magazine.*"

"Raynard the fox. Clever." Her gray eyes were crystal clear, irises circled by the darker ring that set the color off perfectly.

"Not that deliberate. I started publishing articles in school and always used my legal name as my byline. In daily life, though, everyone called me Fox."

She nodded thoughtfully. "And Mullins?"

"My mother's maiden name—which she reclaimed after the divorce and I adopted in solidarity. It also helped distance us from my father's creditors, since he'd ruined the family with a severe gambling addiction."

"Laying all the cards on the table, are you?" She sounded cool, but she hadn't walked away.

"Seems to be the time for it. And you—Emily? Lisa? Silar?"

She returned his gaze steadily. "And Thunder Troll, Riveter, SpiderMuffins, EyesHaveEyes, Nerfherder007…and Phoenix. But you knew that."

He whistled under his breath. At least two of them were identities he'd tracked as friends of Phoenix. The woman was diabolically good. "I didn't get all of them."

"Perhaps you can go add them to the articles. Might as well make them as complete as possible."

Ouch. He turned and leaned on the rail, watching the Vancouver Island clipper chug across the water. Surprisingly, she stepped up to the rail next to him, set crimson-gloved hands on it.

"Fox—"

"Look—"

She glanced sideways at him, tucking her hair behind her ear. "Call me Emily. I'm sticking with it. Easier, on a number of levels."

"I really expected you to disappear into another identity," he admitted.

"I could have. In the wee hours of the morning, I came close to it. I had a couple to choose from, all set up."

"Of course you did." The admiration surged through him, threaded through with whatever it was that flared to life in her presence.

"Because of your tip, I had that option." She slid her hands in the pocket of her coat, her profile nearly the same pale color as she watched the boats also. "I assume it was you. Thank you for that."

He felt dirty. The lowest of the low. "Don't thank me. I owed you that much. I don't blame you for hating me."

She shook her head slightly. "I don't hate you. Or at least, not for that."

"For destroying your life then."

She laughed, her ironic chuckle. "I think we can both agree it wasn't much of a life. And it was a lie. A house of cards that took all of my time and effort to maintain. It's funny—once it fully penetrated that I'd been found out, that everyone would know what I'd worked so damn hard to hide—you know what I felt?" She glanced at him, a half-smile of deprecation on her lips.

"The desire to murder me?"

The smile spread. "Maybe a little of that. But mostly, I felt relief. Pure, wholesome relief."

"Huh." He contemplated that, uncertain what to say to it.

"Do you remember our first run together, when you asked me about Anansi's name?"

"Sure." He nearly said that he remembered every moment they spent together, that each of the memories had lodged in his head like jewel-encrusted daggers, beautiful and lethal. He must be on a perilous edge of emotion, to be tempted to speak such overwrought metaphors.

"I lied to you then—as I lied about most everything I told you—because I did take it from Gaiman's book. The two brothers."

"Spider and Charlie."

"Yes. One person, split apart. That's how I felt when I stopped being Lisa and became Emily. I thought, hey, the Anansi boys did it. I could banish one part of myself, take another and make Emily into a whole person from just that piece. Like a starfish growing from one arm."

"And you did that."

"No." She turned to face him and leaned her hip on the rail. "I didn't. I pretended to be a whole person, but I ended up as this chunk of animated flesh, pretending to be human."

"And Dinah is your Cheshire Cat, accompanying you through the looking glass."

Her lovely mouth twisted in a wry grimace. "A romantic notion. Alice went on an acid trip. I knew what I was doing to myself."

"I love you," he blurted, shocking both of them. Fuck it all. He straightened to face her. "I mean it. I love you like I've never loved anyone and, I'm sorry, but I fell in love with you, a whole person, not some walking starfish arm."

If anything, she looked annoyed with him. "You bastard. You don't know anything real about me and, besides, you have a damn terrible way of demonstrating your love, *Raynard.*"

HIS FACE FLUSHED, that redhead's skin that had paled during his time in the Pacific Northwest, showing his freckles. Brown eyes dark with frustration, he glared at her. "I'm trying to apologize for that. Aren't you listening?"

That pissed her off. It had knocked the wind out of her, to see him leaning against the rail, as if they'd had an appointment to meet, looking handsome and wind-tousled. Just when she'd begun to think she might come through it all okay. She shouldn't even have talked to him, except that she had this new resolution to see things through, to finish them out, no matter how uncomfortable. And then she'd told him that story, wanting him to understand something about why she'd lied about so much. Why she should never have tried to be in a relationship to begin with. Even just fucking. She'd been fucked all right.

He wanted to apologize and, what? Seduce her again? Surely he had everything he needed for his stories. If not, she'd tell him what he wanted to know. But she couldn't take any more of the farce.

"Why are you even here, Fox? I don't believe this is a coincidence. You obviously tracked me, yet again. Look—you got the goods on me fair and square. I lost. You won. I honestly don't hold it against you because it needed to happen and it's obviously what you *really* do. I won't claim that it didn't hurt like hell, you booting me out of hiding, but now I'm out in the world again and I'm glad. So save your lame apologies and your false protestations of love. I don't need them. I don't want them."

"First of all—" He broke off and shoved his hands in his coat pockets, fists clenched, and gathered himself, vibrating with tense emotion. "First of all, Emily, I do fucking love you. You can grind my heart under your pretty white boot heel, but there it is where you threw it on the ground. Now, you have a right to be furious with me. I don't expect you to forgive me. But I do want you know that I apologize. I regret doing the story—and I've never regretted exposing anyone in my whole damn career. I like to win and I thought that was more important than anything else. But I was dead wrong. Once I figured out who you were, I should have told you." He stared off at the boats, eyes hard. "Or walked away. You should know I'm sorry I didn't."

"When did you know?" She made herself ask it, needing the answer. When he frowned in puzzlement, she clarified. "Did you know I was Phoenix from that first day or somewhere along the way?"

To her surprise, he blanched, aghast, as if she'd kicked him in the balls. "You think all that time, all the things we did— that I knew? What, that I was playing you? What kind of monster do you think I am?"

"I don't know what kind of monster you are," she pointed out, feeling cruel to say it, he looked so wounded. "That's what I'm asking. When did you know?"

He clenched his jaw and turned away from her, leaning his elbows on the rail and holding his head in his hands. "After you threw me out. That last day. I'd run your background, of course—you should know that—and I knew you'd faked your identity. But I bought the whole stalker story."

Guilt crawled through her at that. "It was true in essence, if not in detail."

"Yeah. Brilliant job, really. I took you for an amateur who'd done a so-so cover-up job."

"That's what I wanted you to believe. Well, anyone who looked too deeply."

He laughed, without humor, and scrubbed his fingers over his scalp. He wasn't wearing gloves, and his hands were mottled with chill. Her California boy would never learn.

"I never told you about my dad," he said, an odd change of subject.

"There are a lot of things we never talked about."

"Yeah, well. He was a compulsive gambler. Taught me to play poker, bet on the ponies and the Sweet Sixteen before I learned to read. When I got to kindergarten, I called the letter A an ace. My teacher sent home a note." Fox shook his head, face set in bitter lines. "It got worse from there. He got me a fake ID and snuck me into the casinos. By the time my mother discovered how deeply he'd put us in debt—multiple mortgages, years of tax evasion—the gambling addiction had become the least of his problems. Even with the evidence laid out on the table, he lied about it. Like he couldn't tell the difference anymore."

He looked so devastated by the memory that, absurdly, she nearly moved to comfort him. "Maybe he really couldn't," she offered. "It gets hard to keep it all straight after a while. It becomes the new reality."

"I can see that. And I was wrong, what I said to you. Dead, flat wrong. Of course you had good reasons. I triggered and I have no excuse for it. I don't expect you to forgive me."

"Just tell me the rest."

"After I saw those paintings—" he glanced over at her, "—those fucking awful paintings that I knew you couldn't possibly have cared about and tried to shove down my throat as something you did, I went through and figured out the name switches. Idiot me."

"Not so dumb." It impressed her, really, that he'd pieced it together that way. No one else had. She thought she'd covered every crack. "You tracked Phoenix to Lyra, though. That's why you were there."

"True enough." He tapped fingertips together, forearms still braced on the rail. "But—talk about blind spots—I was so convinced Phoenix was a guy that it never once occurred to me it could be you. Not until that moment."

"It's a common pitfall of the industry." A bias she'd leaned on heavily. But another kind of relief washed through her, taking more of the anger and pain away downstream. It had been real. Everything between them, except for a few choice lies of his own, until she'd ended it and forced his hand.

"And you?" Fox inquired, not looking at her. "Did you know all along who I was? I know your cronies tipped you off that I was near."

It was her turn to feel the shock of the sucker punch, that he could think it of her. But, of course, it would have occurred to him, just as it had to her. What a pair they were.

"Frankly, I got those kind of tips all the time. Paranoid as I was, I'd also gotten arrogant and complacent. I didn't think anyone would really be able to track me to Lyra. And you told me you didn't game—I totally believed you."

"I'm sorry for that lie too."

"Yeah, well. Tit for tat. I should have seen it, but I just didn't." She laughed at herself. "I thought, if anyone, it would be one of the trolls, someone with hacker skills and too much time on his hands. Some neckbeard who lives in his mother's basement with nothing better to do. Not…" She trailed off because Fox looked at her then, coppery brown eyes intense and full of heat. The way he'd look at her before he seized her and pushed her up against a wall. A flush of arousal hit her. And longing. Could he mean it, that he loved her?

It seemed impossible.

"Not what?" he asked quietly, baiting her.

"Not this genius investigative reporter with a body to die for," she admitted.

He straightened, a smile ghosting over his mouth. "You think I'm a genius?"

"You tracked me to Lyra, didn't you?" It nettled her that he had. "I'd really love to know how you did it."

"Enough to forgive me?"

"Maybe." The possibility rushed through her like spring warmth, fast and full of hope. "I'd need a lot of groveling, however."

Fox closed on her, putting hands on her hips and backing her against the rail. "You could punish me."

"You'd enjoy it too much," she retorted, nevertheless charmed as always, by his resilience, his sheer pleasure in everything.

"True. You could refuse to punish me. Send me away and starve me for the sight of you. It's what I deserve." The words purred through her and she lowered her eyes from the intensity of his gaze.

"I already did that."

"And I starved."

"Did you?" He did look hungry. She could almost believe he meant everything he'd said. She wanted to believe. Even still. "Tell me how you did it."

Fox held her gaze. "Inside info on the ISP pull in the region. Even though you bounced it, some readouts were unusually high."

"That should have blended into the usage for the whole area—Microsoft, Google, all of them."

He looked ever so slightly smug. "Let's just say that certain entities narrow it more than that."

"Like NSA narrow."

"I have friends." He shrugged it off. Oh yeah, everybody had a contact or two at NSA. "But they only pointed me to the San Juans. After that, I relied on intuition."

"You picked Lyra by chance." Unbelievable.

"Not entirely. I figured anyone who picked Phoenix as an avatar would be drawn to a place named for another Greek myth."

"Greek myth?" she echoed, feeling a momentary bit of displacement.

"Yeah—the eagle carrying the lyre, retrieving it after Orpheus is murdered. A very similar resurrection myth." He studied her face. "And you had no idea, did you?"

"No. I picked Lyra because it was as far as I got that day. Playing up the randomness. I chose Phoenix months later. Total coincidence."

"Not coincidence." Fox's hands tightened on her hips. "Connection. Something real and meant that we both recognized. Serendipity."

"I don't know what to say to that. No wonder it never occurred to me that someone would find me that way. That you had."

"When did you know?" he asked, echoing her question.

She made herself look at him. Close enough to kiss. "When Jared told me about the anonymous tip. I knew it had to be you. But…before that. After you left. I had a feeling."

"And do you have feelings now?"

"I do, but they're muddled."

"Do you think we have a chance? Start over, despite it all."

"I don't know." She really didn't. "I'm still figuring out who I am. How to be a whole person."

"I know who you are." He said the words with confidence, with warm urgency. "And you're perfect. Please say you'll give me another chance."

"Does it…" She made herself face it. "Will it bother you that I'm Phoenix—the work I do? Because I won't stop."

He laughed, then stopped it when he saw she was serious. "You don't get it, do you? I fell half in love with Phoenix before I ever laid eyes on you. His—your—brilliance fascinated me. And all along, it was you who obsessed me. In every way. We're meant. We can do it right this time."

"I'd like that." Her heart swelled, with hope, with something more.

"Let's go get Anansi and Dinah and go. If we can't catch the last ferry, we'll grab a hotel in Anacortes and wait for morning."

"Dinah is still at the house. I left her extra food and her eternal fountain water dish."

"Damn cat wouldn't show herself when I looked in the windows," Fox grumped, scowling in memory.

"You were there?"

"Yes. Glory told me you'd left. And that you'd told her your history."

"She hates me now."

"No." Fox picked up a lock of her hair and ran it through his fingers. "She's getting over it. She'll let you make it up to her. Both of us will have to, because I ended up telling her that nobody likes her creamed-chicken casserole."

She giggled, which snorted out through her nose because she hadn't expected it. She clapped her gloved hand over her mouth, appalled, but giggled even harder, letting out a full laugh finally. Fox laughed, too, a look of satisfaction on his face.

"I like making you laugh nearly as much as I like making you come," he confided. "Say we can go back."

"You hate Lyra."

"I love anywhere you are. Everywhere else is miserable. Oh—and my mother wants you to come to Iowa for Christmas, but that might be testing your newfound love for me too soon."

Her heart caught and she steadied herself with her hands on his shoulders. "I don't know if I love you, Fox. I'm not sure of very much."

"Yes, you do," he assured her, smile widening into his trademark charming grin. "Glory even said so. Let's go tonight."

"I can't." When his expression dimmed, she hurried to add, "Not because I don't want to. I do. But I have to stay here another day or two. All the PR and legal stuff."

"To be here when the story breaks." He didn't look happy about it.

"Yes." She gripped his jacket, wanting him to understand.

Taking the step to trust him with the information. "We're meeting it head-on. Full press release, local talk shows. I'm going on TV, Fox."

"As Lisa White?"

"Yes. All my…selves. Jared's going with me. The PR whiz kids and the lawyers have it all figured out. If we play it right, all the furor will only boost sales."

"And you're okay with this?"

"More than okay." She found herself nodding. "It feels good. Liberating. We might undercut your splash, however."

Far from looking displeased, he seemed proud. "If so, points to you, then."

"A very fair attitude."

"Well, and they already paid me." He laughed when she swatted him, then captured her hands and leaned into her. "Let me help. I'll write reaction pieces, extolling your beauty and bravery."

She felt herself blushing. "Oh, stop."

"You love it."

"I do," she whispered, as his lips hovered near hers.

"You love me too."

His face, the look in his eyes, mirrored her own. Truth in that. A bit more of the fear broke away and floated off in the tide.

"I do. I do love you, Fox. God knows what we'll do about it."

"I have some ideas," he murmured, kissing the corner of her mouth. "What are you wearing under this coat?"

Her body heated, matching the burn of love in her blood. "A dress."

"What kind?"

"Silk, dark blue." She quivered as he kissed the other corner of her mouth.

"Do you know the photo of you from when you were a debutante, the white gown?"

It had been in the papers, too hard to eradicate all instances, so she'd left it. "I remember." She turned her head, seeking his mouth, but he held off, teasing her.

"I bought you one like it. I always wanted to fuck a debutante."

She nearly moaned at the thought. "What else would you do to her?"

"Let's find out, shall we? Say yes."

"Yes."

"And then you can punish me." With a wickedly pleased smile, he finally kissed her, brushing her lips with his and then sinking in.

Though his skin felt cool, his mouth burned hot and full of life as everything about him. Bright, vivid and vitally real. She slid her hands around the back of his neck and held on tight, kissing him with equal fervor.

Total win.

Look for these other books in the Falling Under series
by Jeffe Kennedy
Under His Touch and *Under Contract*

TITLES BY JEFFE KENNEDY

FANTASY ROMANCES

BONDS OF MAGIC
Dark Wizard
Bright Familiar
Grey Magic
Familiar Winter Magic
(Also Available in Fire of the Frost)

RENEGADES OF MAGIC
Shadow Wizard
Rogue Familiar

HEIRS OF MAGIC
The Long Night of the Crystalline Moon
(also available in *Under a Winter Sky*)
The Golden Gryphon and the Bear Prince
The Sorceress Queen and the Pirate Rogue
The Dragon's Daughter and the Winter Mage
The Storm Princess and the Raven King
The Long Night of the Radiant Star

THE FORGOTTEN EMPIRES
The Orchid Throne
The Fiery Crown

The Promised Queen

THE TWELVE KINGDOMS
Negotiation
The Mark of the Tala
The Tears of the Rose
The Talon of the Hawk
Heart's Blood
The Crown of the Queen

THE UNCHARTED REALMS
The Pages of the Mind
The Edge of the Blade
The Snows of Windroven
The Shift of the Tide
The Arrows of the Heart
The Dragons of Summer
The Fate of the Tala
The Lost Princess Returns

THE CHRONICLES OF DASNARIA
Prisoner of the Crown
Exile of the Seas
Warrior of the World

SORCEROUS MOONS
Lonen's War
Oria's Gambit
The Tides of Bára
The Forests of Dru
Oria's Enchantment

Lonen's Reign

A COVENANT OF THORNS
Rogue's Pawn
Rogue's Possession
Rogue's Paradise

CONTEMPORARY ROMANCES
Shooting Star

MISSED CONNECTIONS
Last Dance
With a Prince
Since Last Christmas

CONTEMPORARY EROTIC ROMANCES
Exact Warm Unholy
The Devil's Doorbell

FACETS OF PASSION
Sapphire
Platinum
Ruby
Five Golden Rings

FALLING UNDER
Going Under
Under His Touch
Under Contract

EROTIC PARANORMAL

MASTER OF THE OPERA E-SERIAL

Master of the Opera, Act 1: Passionate Overture

Master of the Opera, Act 2: Ghost Aria

Master of the Opera, Act 3: Phantom Serenade

Master of the Opera, Act 4: Dark Interlude

Master of the Opera, Act 5: A Haunting Duet

Master of the Opera, Act 6: Crescendo

Master of the Opera

BLOOD CURRENCY

Blood Currency

BDSM FAIRYTALE ROMANCE

Petals and Thorns

Thank you for reading!

ABOUT JEFFE KENNEDY

Jeffe Kennedy is a multi-award-winning and best-selling author of epic fantasy romance. She is the current president of the Science Fiction and Fantasy Writers Association (SFWA) and is a member of Romance Writers of America (RWA), and Novelists, Inc. (NINC). She is best known for her RITA® Award-winning novel, *The Pages of the Mind*, the recent trilogy, *The Forgotten Empires*, and the wildly popular, *Dark Wizard*. Jeffe lives in Santa Fe, New Mexico.

Jeffe can be found online at her website: JeffeKennedy.com, on her podcast First Cup of Coffee, every Sunday at the popular SFF Seven blog, on Facebook, on Goodreads, on BookBub, and pretty much constantly on Twitter @jeffekennedy. She is represented by Sarah Younger of Nancy Yost Literary Agency.

jeffekennedy.com
facebook.com/Author.Jeffe.Kennedy
twitter.com/jeffekennedy
goodreads.com/author/show/1014374.Jeffe_Kennedy
bookbub.com/profile/jeffe-kennedy

Sign up for her newsletter here.
jeffekennedy.com/sign-up-for-my-newsletter

www.ingramcontent.com/pod-product-compliance
Lightning Source LLC
Chambersburg PA
CBHW020929260626
47169CB00006B/1641